A SPELL TO WAKE THE DEAD

ALSO BY NICOLE LESPERANCE

The Wide Starlight
The Depths
The Nightmare Thief
The Dream Spies

A SPELL TO WAKE THE DEAD

NICOLE LESPERANCE

G. P. PUTNAM'S SONS

G. P. PUTNAM'S SONS
An imprint of Penguin Random House LLC
1745 Broadway, New York, New York 10019

First published in the United States of America by G. P. Putnam's Sons,
an imprint of Penguin Random House LLC, 2025

Copyright © 2025 by Nicole Lesperance

Penguin Random House values and supports copyright. Copyright fuels creativity, encourages diverse voices, promotes free speech, and creates a vibrant culture. Thank you for buying an authorized edition of this book and for complying with copyright laws by not reproducing, scanning, or distributing any part of it in any form without permission. You are supporting writers and allowing Penguin Random House to continue to publish books for every reader. Please note that no part of this book may be used or reproduced in any manner for the purpose of training artificial intelligence technologies or systems.

G. P. Putnam's Sons is a registered trademark of Penguin Random House LLC.
The Penguin colophon is a registered trademark of Penguin Books Limited.

Visit us online at PenguinRandomHouse.com.

Library of Congress Cataloging-in-Publication Data is available.

ISBN 9780593856338

1 3 5 7 9 10 8 6 4 2

Manufactured in the United States of America

BVG

Design by Rebecca Aidlin
Text set in Arno Pro

This book is a work of fiction. Any references to historical events, real people, or real places are used fictitiously. Other names, characters, places, and events are products of the author's imagination, and any resemblance to actual events or places or persons, living or dead, is entirely coincidental.

The publisher does not have any control over and does not assume any responsibility for author or third-party websites or their content.

The authorized representative in the EU for product safety and compliance is Penguin Random House Ireland, Morrison Chambers, 32 Nassau Street, Dublin D02 YH68, Ireland, https://eu-contact.penguin.ie.

For Isla

A SPELL TO WAKE THE DEAD

CHAPTER 1

It's nine fifteen on a Saturday night, and I'm sitting in my car in the high school parking lot, waiting for Nora. A nearby streetlight keeps flickering off and on, off and on, and I'm trying to ignore the weird sense of foreboding it's giving me. Stifling a yawn, I hunch down inside my coat. It's been six days since we turned the clocks back, and I should be used to the time change by now, but I'm still not. It feels like midnight.

Every November when we shift everything back by an hour, I feel like I've entered a shadier version of my own life. Night sweeps in early, gulping up time and replacing sunlight with shadows. Places I used to go in the day have suddenly become nighttime destinations. Late afternoon means headlights and bone-deep cold and a strange, unexpected sense of loneliness. It feels like I've traveled somewhere new, but everything is the same except for the light. Or lack thereof. Sometimes I wonder if people become shadier versions of themselves too.

Outside, a bus pulls up and kids stream out, lugging trumpet cases and bass drums and flags, all heading across the lot to the band room. Wind buffets my car as I hum along with the cello concerto playing over my speakers. I should be home practicing my own cello right now, but Nora insisted that we go out. She wants to try a new spell at the beach, and it has to be done under the full moon, which is tonight.

A few minutes later, the band room door swings open and she comes out squinting, a dark wool cap pulled low over her black-and-crimson hair. She's dressed all in black, as usual: a vintage, fake-fur coat layered over a long lace skirt, tights, and a pair of chunky platform boots. Elliot and I like to tease Nora that she's the only goth in the color guard, and she says we need to stop being so closed-minded about color guard.

I flash my headlights and she swerves in my direction, a smile lighting up her round-cheeked face.

"Sorry we got back so late," she says, flopping down on the passenger seat.

"That's okay; I was late too," I say. "How did you guys do?"

"The band got second place," she says. "And we won best color guard."

"Of course you did," I say, but she just sighs.

"That was our last competition before championships," she says. "It's breaking my brain that this is my last fall season ever."

"I can't believe how many things we're doing for the last time already," I say.

Next year, we'll both be at college, and everything will be different. I'm trying not to dwell on it, but dwelling on things is basically my superpower.

"Can I?" Nora points to the stereo, and when I nod, she plugs the aux cable into her phone. "Elliot messaged me earlier, and I told him we'd pick him up at the pottery shop. You don't mind, right?"

My pulse skitters. "No, that's fine."

Nora settles on a song and turns up the volume. "This one's for you, baby," she says as the droning guitars and dreamy vocals of Mazzy Star's "So Tonight That I Might See" float out of the speakers.

"Thanks," I deadpan.

People are always asking me if my name, Mazzy, is short for something else, and it's embarrassing to have to tell them my parents named me after a nineties band. But this music was such a huge part of my childhood, and if I'm being honest, I don't hate it. Nora thinks it's cool in a retro way, and I think it sounds like cozy Sunday afternoons when I was little.

"Elliot's been acting weird lately," Nora says as we pull out of the parking lot. "Have you noticed that?"

"Not really," I lie.

"Something's definitely off with him," she says. "In a very subtle way."

"Are you sure you still want to do this spell?" I say, to change the subject.

She groans. "Yes, I'm sure. Will you please stop worrying about it?"

Worrying about things is another one of my superpowers.

The parking lot of Beech Tree Pottery is dark and empty and surrounded by leafless woods. A tall figure leans against the building, one foot propped back on the brick and the glow of a phone faintly illuminating his face. He's wearing a long, charcoal-colored coat that makes him look like a character from a Charles Dickens novel. As we slow beside the curb, he glances up and his eyes snap straight to mine. Something soft and warm thrums deep in my belly.

Elliot's been part of our trio since he moved here in seventh grade. He fell in love with Nora the second he laid eyes on her, but by that point Nora was pretty sure she only liked girls. He said it was fine, and that was just the normal balance of the three of us. But then, a few weeks ago, at Evie Greenwood's party, Elliot and I stayed up all night talking, and ever since then, it feels like there are magnets between me and him. Like I'm conscious of every single movement of his body whenever we're in the same room. I hate it, and I can't make it stop. It doesn't help that he's shot up about three inches in the past year and grown out his brown hair so that it just barely brushes his jaw.

As he climbs into the back seat of my car, I fiddle with the defroster, just to give myself something to do.

"Hey," he says, and our eyes catch again in the mirror. My face goes hot. Nora is busy doing something on her phone, and I suddenly can't think of anything normal to say.

"How come you were working so late?" I hope it doesn't sound like I've memorized every minute of his schedule—even if I have.

"I was teaching a workshop," he says, and I swear his voice has gotten an octave lower in the past year too. It's deep and resonant, like the C string of my cello. "Intro to Wheel Throwing. Only two people showed up, and one of them brought a three-year-old."

I laugh as I shift into drive. "Did you let the kid use the wheel?"

"God, no," says Elliot. "I sat him at a table, gave him a big hunk of clay, and told him to make whatever he wanted. But his mom and her friend ended up being even messier than him. There was clay on the *ceiling* after they left. It took me forever to clean up."

"Sounds like way too much work for just two customers," I say.

"Yeah," he says. "Pamela's thinking about cutting everybody's hours and possibly closing for the winter."

4

"That sucks," says Nora. "Will you get another job?"

Elliot shrugs. "I'll probably pick up some shifts at the grocery store. They said I can come back anytime."

The roads are strangely empty tonight. It's one of those times where you wonder if everybody else knows something you don't and is staying inside. Like there's a tornado coming or a meteor is about to crash into Earth. Or like everyone has suddenly and inexplicably disappeared off the face of the planet, all except for the three of us.

"Okay, so we need four moon snail shells, a sand dollar, a candle, and a rock with living barnacles on it." Nora holds up her phone to show Elliot the video. "I have everything, except the rock."

"What's it for?" He leans forward into the space between the front seats, and I swear I can feel the electrons zapping around the edges of him.

"It's a spell to uncover hidden things, conducted in the shadows of the full moon," Nora says.

"She found it online," I say, and Nora huffs in mock annoyance.

"Mazzy doesn't think I should do spells from the internet," she says.

"Why not?" asks Elliot.

"You know I don't have a problem with the internet." I flick on my blinker, even though there's nobody to see it. "It's anonymous people who worry me. That account only had one video, and it was that spell. And they didn't show their face or talk about where the spell came from or how it worked. How do you know they're not lying about what it does?"

"Even if they showed their face, how would you know they're not lying?" says Elliot, who is happy to come along on all of our witchy excursions but is skeptical about everything.

"Thank you." Nora beams at him, which makes my eyelid twitch. "Plus, not everybody has the luxury of being open about their practice."

"I know, I know," I say. "But it still feels like a slightly bad idea."

This is one of our never-ending disagreements. I like to do things by the book (as in, literal spell books) and Nora believes the best magic comes from intuition, from vibes, from random strangers on the internet. Regardless, it's weird to do this particular kind of spell under a full moon. Usually, you look for hidden things under a dark moon. The whole thing makes me vaguely nervous. But then again, Nora's always warning me not to confuse my anxiety with my intuition, and she's not always wrong about that.

"There's literally nothing to worry about," says Nora. "It's just going to be a general revealing of things in our lives that are unclear, obscured, or murky. We're looking for clarity. Transparency."

"So, like, you might find a random sock that's been missing for a year, or you might discover that you're actually adopted and your birth family lives in Detroit?" asks Elliot.

Nora laughs. "Something like that."

That's another thing that worries me, although she and I have already had this argument too. It's better to be clear about what you want from a spell. If you leave it too vague, anything could happen. Nora says that isn't necessarily bad, but I disagree.

As we follow the winding curves of Route 6A, the rambling Victorian houses give way to smaller cottages, and the sleeping woods between them get denser. A streetlight winks out just as we pass under it, and I shiver.

"Did you check the tides?" I ask Nora.

"Yep." She holds up her phone. "Low tide is at nine fifty-three. We need to do the spell exactly at the moment when the ocean changes direction and starts coming back in."

"You'll never find that sock if you miss the tide," says Elliot.

"Will you shut up about the stupid sock?" Nora flails her arm back through the seat gap and tries to hit him but misses. Again, my eyelid twitches.

We pass empty restaurants and dark shops, a liquor store with one car in its parking lot, and then turn down the road that leads to Mayflower Beach. The moon is slowly rising, glinting over the top of a tall tree ahead. Away from the main road, the light is different—silver instead of gold—and even with the windows closed, I can smell the ocean, briny and cold.

Turning again, we wind through a neighborhood of empty cottages, then pull up beside a little wooded lot that will soon get turned into another summer home. Most beaches are closed after sunset, and the police patrol the parking lots, kicking out the stargazers, the lovers kissing in their cars, the high school kids with their vapes and cans. But if you know where to park and where to hide, you can sometimes get away with coming here at night.

The moon has cleared the trees now, and everything is soft and silvery as we head down the road. The tide is all the way out, hundreds of yards offshore, so there's no sound of waves, but the wind is gusting in across the bay, damp and frigid. I button my thrifted velvet coat all the way to my chin, wishing I'd brought a hat. Nora strides ahead, a black tote bag with a pentacle on it flapping off her shoulder.

It's just Elliot and me now, in our own little space as we walk down the sandy road. I still don't know if the magnetism between us is something I'm imagining, so I say nothing, and neither does he. But there's no time to dwell on it because Nora breaks into a run, and then we're running too, across the empty parking lot and down the path of deep sand that cuts through the dunes.

Tonight, this bare, black-and-white beach could almost be the surface of the moon. Sandbars stretch in all directions, with shallow tide pools gleaming between them like mirrors. Elliot stops to pull his hair back in a ponytail, and I struggle not to stare at the cut-stone lines of his cheekbones, the sharp angle of his jaw. He's been described as beautiful by more than one girl at our school, and even though I always agreed with them on a purely objective level, it's hitting me in a different way lately.

But how am I feeling this way about *Elliot*, of all people? This is the boy who threw up on the bus after the eighth-grade field trip to Six Flags. The kid who had to go home early from school once because he couldn't stop crying about his pet turtle dying. The person who's been infatuated with my best friend for years.

"Come on!" Nora leaps across a channel of silver water. "The tide's turning in four minutes!"

We follow her farther out onto the windswept flats, where she crouches and pulls something out of a tide pool. Then she heads for the center of a sandbar and drags a circle in the damp sand with the heel of her boot.

"Here," she says, handing me a fist-size rock crusted with barnacles. "Careful, it's sharp."

"I guess we're doing this," I mutter as I set the rock in the center of the circle. Nora lays out four moon snail shells in a diamond shape, draws a sigil in the sand with her finger, and then places a dried sand dollar on top of it. The white disc looks like the full moon's twin lying in the sand.

Nora rummages in her bag and pulls out a white candle in a mason jar. I still don't love the idea of this spell, but as she and I work together, setting up our makeshift altar in the sand, I start to feel the gentle, calming hum inside my body that always comes with spell work. In the gusting wind, Nora struggles to light the candle, but eventually the flame takes, and she sets the jar down in a shallow hole to shield it.

Elliot sits on a boulder outside the circle, and Nora and I begin. Together, we speak our sacred words to begin the ritual. We've been writing and honing these verses for years, borrowing pieces from spells and lore I've read and adding various elements that Nora has intuited on her own.

Nora and I have been practicing witchcraft for years, but the results have only ever been modest at best. I've got a notebook full of our spells and sigils and incantations, along with notes on whether they've been successful (protection charms, herb oils for banishing nightmares, a cord-cutting ritual after the first girl I ever had a serious crush on broke my heart) and unsuccessful (a glamour to hide acne, a spell to ace tests we didn't study for, a numerology prediction to help my dad win the lottery).

Some of the spells have been inconclusive. In tenth grade, Nora cast a love spell—despite my warning her that it was a terrible idea—on Chloe Martins, and then Chloe invited her out for coffee the next day. They broke up after a few months, and I suspect Chloe already liked Nora long before she started messing with rose quartz and strands of people's hair. Lots of people fall in love with Nora without the need for witchcraft. Most of the time, that doesn't bother me.

"Focus," she whispers, and I drag my concentration back to our ritual, to the circle on the sandbar, the sand dollar twin of the moon. As Nora speaks the words of her newfound spell, I let my eyes go blurry, let it all flood through me. The wind burning my cheeks and pulling tears from my eyes. The salt scent of the ocean. The gentle hush of the waves, the constant drag of the tide. And the moon, high overhead, illuminating some things with its beaming silver light and shrouding others in shadows. It's impossible not to feel the magic building.

The wind gusts again, and the candle winks out. Nora sits back on her heels with a grunt.

"Do you want to start again?" I ask.

"No," she says. "I think that's a sign that it's over."

"Already?" I say. "That felt really short." It might be my anxiety, not my intuition, but something about this whole ritual is just . . . off.

"Not everything needs to take a long time to work, you know." Nora's tone is slightly sour as she starts gathering up the shells.

I glance over at Elliot, who shrugs.

"Looked fine to me?" he says, but of course he'd say that, because spells all look the same to him. Nora's the one who planned the ritual and collected the ingredients, so who am I to question her? But everything about this has been strange, and now it's unfinished, and I don't know how she's okay with that. She drops the mason jar lid, and when I hand it to her, she won't meet my eye.

"I'm going to put this back in the ocean," she says, picking up the barnacle-covered rock.

"You could just put it in the tide pool where you found it," I say, but already she's hurrying off.

Elliot stands and stretches out his lanky frame. "What's wrong with her?"

10

"I don't know," I say. "That was weird."

He starts to speak, then pauses. He's so close I can feel the electricity of him again. In the silvery moonlight, he looks like a silent film star, shadowed and striking with his gray eyes fixed on me.

He clears his throat. "Can I ask you something?"

"Sure." My pulse is thundering. The wind roars, whipping my coat, throwing my long, black hair around my face, shoving me toward him.

"Is it—" Elliot stops short, his eyes cutting to something over my shoulder.

Down at the ocean's edge, Nora screams.

CHAPTER 2

We race toward her, our boots pounding the wet sand. There's another tide pool between us and the ocean, and Elliot charges through while I find a shallower place to cross. Nora is still screaming, and in the moonlight, I can see her backing away from a large object on the ground.

Elliot reaches her first, bends low to look at whatever that thing is, and then staggers backward. He wraps his arms around her, pulling her away from it, and I still can't understand what's happening, can't make out what the thing is. Maybe a dead seal or dolphin, washed up by the tide? But we've seen those before, and they wouldn't make Nora scream like that.

And then I'm closing in and I see it, and my brain starts to understand. Dark hair splayed out like seaweed on the sand. A long, gray dress tangled around thin legs. Skin so pale, it's almost glowing.

I crash to a stop beside them, hands clasped over my mouth. "Oh God, oh God," I keep muttering against my frozen fingers.

"I th-thought it was a dead animal," Nora stammers. "Then I got closer and I thought it was a person sleeping. Like, maybe kids were drinking out here and somebody wandered off and passed out. Or maybe they ODed."

It wouldn't be the first time somebody overdosed around here. It happened to a girl from our school last year. She'd just graduated, and her friends were too messed up to call an ambulance to save her.

Through the wet fabric of her dress, the dead woman's ribs stand out like the rungs of a ladder. I can't tear my eyes away from her.

Nora's teeth are audibly chattering. "I c-came over to try and wake her up before the tide came in. And when I touched her shoulder, she . . . she rolled over. And . . . oh God, she was so cold." She buries her face in Elliot's chest and he hugs her tighter, and underneath the shock and horror, for a tiny, selfish moment, I wish that was me.

The tide is slithering closer, tiny waves licking at the ends of the dead woman's hair. It's impossible to tell how old she is—or was. Her eyelids, just barely cracked open, reveal a glimpse of white inside. Her cheeks are sunken holes. But what keeps drawing my gaze is her mouth. It hangs open, revealing torn gums. Sour nausea floods my own mouth.

"Where are her teeth?" I say.

"Where are her fucking hands?" says Elliot.

I peer at the lace sleeve that's draped across her stomach, and my throat closes up. He's right. There's no hand under there. I can't see her other arm—it's tucked under her back at an unsettling angle. This woman didn't just overdose or pass out. Somebody killed her and took pieces of her. Eyes watering, I swallow hard.

"It seemed she was going to sit up, right before she rolled over." Nora sobs. "I still keep thinking she's going to wake up and say something."

"God, I hope not." I take a big step back and pull out my phone. "We need to call the police before the tide pulls her out."

Maybe we should drag the body closer to the shore, but I can't bring myself to touch it. Plus, every cop show I've ever watched has told me that'd be tampering with evidence. It takes me three tries to type 911 into my phone, and as I hold it up to my ear, the wind roars harder, blotting out all other sound. The dead woman's flimsy sleeve flutters over the place where her hand should be.

"Hello?" I yell, only faintly able to hear the person on the other end of the line. "I'm on Mayflower Beach, and there's a dead body here."

~ ~ ~

Twenty minutes later we're standing in the dry sand by the dunes, wrapped in crunchy silver blankets and blinded every few seconds by industrial-strength flashlights. I'm numb, with the wind swarming all around me. Nora is on the phone with her mom, who's in the middle of her night shift at the nursing home.

"No, it's fine. I'm fine." A stray beam of light hits her face, making the tears on her cheeks shimmer, but her voice is steady. "Don't leave work. I'm with Mazzy, and her mom's on her way."

"Do you want to sleep at my house?" I ask.

She repeats the invitation into her phone, and then nods and gulps. "Okay. Yeah. No, really, I'm fine."

I put my arm around her shoulders. She's shaking. We're both shaking. Elliot and his dad are over by the path through the dunes, talking to a police officer. He hasn't made eye contact with either one of us since we came back from the water's edge, and I can't blame him—he's probably in shock—but I wish he'd come over here. It feels wrong for us all not to be together right now.

A figure in a flapping bathrobe comes stumble-running down the path, and then my mother's arms wrap tight around me and Nora. She was baking earlier this afternoon, and the warm, cinnamon scent in her hair and clothes washes over me and, suddenly, finally, I'm sobbing. We stand there for a long while, all clinging to each other, until I can breathe again.

"Where's Henry?" I ask, wondering if she left my four-year-old brother in the car, because my dad's working until at least eleven tonight.

"He's at home, asleep," she says. "Jan from next door is keeping an eye on him."

Way out on the sandbar, a floodlight illuminates the body, which is now lying on a stretcher, zipped inside a body bag. The water in the tide pools is getting deeper by the minute.

"Can I take the girls home?" my mom asks one of the many police officers hovering around.

He relays the question into a walkie-talkie, then nods. "The witness statements are all set. We'll call you if we have any further questions."

I don't know what I expected, but it feels wrong to just walk away from this monstrous event. There should be more—we should all go down to the station to figure everything out now. But the officer just turns his back and stares out at the sandbar. Nobody knows what to do or say. This isn't the kind of thing that regularly happens on Cape Cod, especially not at this time of year when the summer chaos has faded away.

We catch up with Elliot and his dad by the parking lot, and our parents exchange useless words like *awful* and *tragedy* and *traumatic*. Nora, Elliot, and I just stand there, waiting for them to come to some kind of closure, and then we all head silently to their cars, which are parked next to each other.

It's funny, somehow, them parking so easily here. If this had happened on a sunny July day, they'd never have made it into the packed lot. I can't stop imagining that handless, toothless body floating up to this beach, jam-packed with people in midsummer. One of its long, slack legs brushing up against a little kid swimming. Suddenly, my stomach heaves and I have to stop walking because I'm about to throw up on the gravel.

"Come on, hon. I'll drive you to your car." My mom holds the passenger door of her car open. Nora is already inside, and Elliot's dad is backing out of his space. Elliot's devastated face appears in the window as they pull away, and his mouth opens like he's going to say something, but then they're gone.

The wind gusts again, knocking me sideways, and inside the frigid blast of air, I almost think I hear a woman's voice singing.

CHAPTER 3

A Christmas movie plays on the TV, even though it's only November, and Nora and I are both scrolling on our phones. My mom keeps bustling back and forth between the kitchen and the living room, asking how we're doing every time she brings us a new drink or snack. They're starting to pile up on the coffee table: mugs and glasses and popcorn and chips and M&Ms and a plate of fresh-baked pumpkin bread that turns my stomach every time I look at it.

"Do you want to change the movie?" she asks, draping a crocheted blanket over Nora's legs and then pressing her hand to my forehead, like I might have caught a fever from tonight's trauma.

Nora and I exchange a glance. She shrugs.

"We're fine," I say. There's no movie we'll actually watch, but it's nice to have something droning in the background.

"Okay." She looks at the empty spot on the couch next to me, then at the clock. "Henry's going to wake up in a few hours. Do you need me to stay up with you?"

"I think we're good," I say. "Are you working tomorrow?"

"Not until ten," she says, "and I can call in if you need me to stay home."

My mom manages a gift shop in Hyannis, so there's no such thing as a real weekend for her. Or for my dad either, who is snoring in his recliner in the corner. He works as a line cook at one of the biggest restaurants in town, and it was eleven thirty by the time he finished his double shift and got a ride home. When we told him what happened, he blew out all of his breath and said, "Well, fuck." He stayed with us for moral support, but as soon as my mom turned on the TV, his eyes started drooping shut. I'm not mad about it. His snoring is less stressful than my mom's constant hovering and questioning.

"Okay, well . . ." She checks the popcorn bowl, which is still as full as ever, then picks up two empty mugs. "You know where to find me if you need anything. Good night, girls."

"Night," I mumble, swiping to the next video, but even the tiniest, fluffiest kittens aren't calming my anxiety like they usually do. The sloths aren't helping, and not even the red pandas, lifting up their stubby arms to intimidate potential attackers and looking like teddy bears who want a hug.

"The problem is," Nora says, "nobody from the Cape has been reported missing for a long time. And she looked recently dead, didn't she?"

I glance up from my screen. "Huh?"

"I'm looking at photos in missing persons databases," she says. "Trying to figure out who the dead woman might be, but since nobody's gone missing from around here recently, I'm searching for people from other places. Because, in theory, she could have come here on vacation from anywhere."

"How can you tell from a photo?" I ask. "I have no sense of what she looked like before she died."

Nora's eyebrows lift as she continues to swipe at her screen. "I can picture her perfectly."

"How, though?" I say. "She was just so blank and pale and . . . I don't know . . . *dead*. And we couldn't see her eyes. How old do you even think she was?"

Nora sits up straight, folds her legs under her, and shuts her eyes. "She was twenty-seven or twenty-eight. Long, wavy dark hair. Like yours. She looked a bit like you, actually."

"Her hair was shorter than mine," I say. Mine is so long I can sit on it, which makes it longer than everyone else's. Plus, I don't want to look like a dead woman.

"She was willowy and graceful." Nora stretches her arms out like a dancer. "She loved music and art. And reading. She may have been a teacher. I think her name started with an *M*."

I shrug. There's no point in arguing with Nora when she gets like this. "We could ask my tarot cards about her. Not that they'll specifically tell us her name, but maybe we'll find out some more general details?"

Nora's eyes snap open. "Yes."

$$\sim \sim \sim$$

Two minutes later, she's sitting cross-legged on my quilt, the one my grandmother made for me just before she died three years ago. I take a wooden box from my bedside table, slide the lid open, and hold the blue-and-silver deck out to Nora.

"You're the one who feels the strong connection to her," I say. "You shuffle."

She shakes her head. "You're better at this than I am."

That's true, even if it's vain to admit it. I've been reading cards since I was thirteen. I put in the time and work to learn all the symbols and meanings of each card, all the subtleties and differences between each deck I own. My mom says tarot cards are purposely vague, so people are just seeing what they want to see, but mine have been uncannily accurate about a lot of things. Like the time I kept pulling the Tower, the card of sudden and total destruction, every day for a week, and then on Saturday night, my dad drank too many beers with his friends after work, crashed his car into a cranberry bog, and ended up losing his license.

Nora always reminds me that the Tower isn't necessarily a terrible thing, that there's no such thing as a bad tarot card. And I agree, to a point. After everything blows up, you have no choice but to start again from scratch, to fix whatever caused the disaster in the first place. My dad quit drinking after the accident and started going to AA meetings. It's been hard for all of us, and it sucks that we have to drive him places or he has to ride his bike for the next year, but I think the outcome was ultimately positive. In that case, Nora was right that sometimes you have to blow things up to fix them.

But it terrifies me that there's nothing stopping our lives from blowing up over and over, endlessly and forever. Yes, I stopped pulling the Tower after my dad's car crash, but I know it's lurking in there, waiting for the next big explosion. And sometimes you don't have any control over what caused it or what happens next. There's no way of knowing or preparing, and I hate not being prepared for everything.

"Let's do it together," I say, shuffling the cards a few more times, and then handing them to Nora. "Speak what you want to know."

"Who is the woman we found?" Nora shuffles once more.

"And what happened to her?" Using my left hand, I cut the deck into three piles, and Nora stacks them back up with the middle section on top. With a deep breath, I begin to lay them out.

The Moon. Secrets and shadows and hidden forces at work.

The Queen of Swords. A strong-willed woman, intelligent and decisive.

"That's her," whispers Nora. "Keep going."

The Three of Swords. Betrayal, sorrow, grief.

The Ten of Swords. Disaster, misfortune, deep wounds.

The Devil. Addiction, unhealthy relationships, entrapment.

"I guess that makes sense for a murdered woman," Nora mutters, but my skin is crawling. There might technically be no such thing as a bad tarot card, but together, these cards are unmistakably ominous. I might pull one or two of them in a reading, but never all at once. I flip over another card.

The Fool, reversed. Ignorance, unmindful choices, thoughtlessly leaping into situations.

A shudder slithers up the back of my neck.

"This is a warning," I say.

"Let's try again." Before I can react, Nora scoops up the cards and starts shuffling. "How can we help her?" she says. "What should we do next?"

She cuts the deck herself, then flips the top card. And there it is.

The Tower.

My skin goes cold. Deep down, I knew it was coming but kept desperately hoping it wouldn't.

There's a soft knock on my door, and we both jump. My mom pokes her tousled head in.

"Girls, I know it's been a long and terrible evening, but you're going to feel even worse tomorrow—or should I say, today—if you don't get some rest."

"Sorry if we woke you up," says Nora.

"Don't be sorry," says my mom. "Just try to sleep, okay?"

Nora and I exchange an uneasy glance over the Tower as my mom shuts the door.

"Should we try one more—" she starts.

"No." I bury the card deep in the deck before stowing the cards back in their box. Once the lid is closed, I finally stop shivering.

~ ~ ~

My eyes snap open. The digital clock on my bedside table reads two minutes past four. Beside me in bed, Nora is singing quietly in her sleep.

But singing isn't the right word for it. There are no words, just a strange, eerie melody that I'm sure I've heard somewhere before, but wish I hadn't. It makes every inch of my skin crawl.

"Hey," I whisper, patting her shoulder. "Please stop doing that."

Nora's breath catches. "So cold, she's so cold," she mutters.

"Shh," I whisper. "It's all right, you're dreaming."

"Mazzy, why is she so cold, though?" Her voice is taking on a frantic edge. "What's wrong with her?"

Because she's dead, is the first response that pops into my head, but I don't want to make her dream any worse, and I've heard you shouldn't try to wake people who are talking in their sleep. Or is that walking in their sleep?

"Just leave her alone," I say. "You're okay. Everything's okay."

A shudder washes over her, and she lets out a quiet cry, and I definitely should wake her from this nightmare, but then she rolls over to face me.

"Tell them I'm here," she says in a deep, croaking voice that does not belong to her.

My entire body goes cold. "Wh-what?"

"Tell them," she says again in that low, scratchy voice I've never heard before in my life. "They're waiting, you know."

With my heart in my throat, I switch on the reading light. Nora just lies there, breathing sleep-slow with her eyes shut, and I don't want to touch her with that voice coming out of her mouth, but I force myself to. I shake her. Maybe a little too hard, because she screams as her eyes fly open.

"What?" she says, thrashing away from my grasp.

"Sorry," I say. "You were talking in your sleep. It sounded like you were having a really bad nightmare."

"So you decided to scare me even worse?" Nora squints at the unexpected brightness of my lamp.

"No." I pause, unsure of whether to tell her she was just talking like some kind of demon. "It's just . . . I tried waking you gently and it didn't work. I'm sorry I scared you."

She flops back onto the pillow. "No, I'm glad you woke me up. It was a horrible dream."

"Sounded like it." I switch the light off and pull the covers over both of us, but I'm still trembling. Nora curls up so our knees touch, and I take one of her clammy hands and squeeze. "I'm here; it wasn't real. We're okay."

But in the predawn darkness full of shadows and nightmares and strange voices and songs, I can't quite shake the feeling that maybe that isn't true.

CHAPTER 4

A few hours later, I wake to the smell of bacon frying. Beside me, Nora is flicking through her phone. In my muddled state between sleep and wakefulness, I'm almost afraid to talk to her, scared that awful voice is going to come out of her mouth again.

"Are you . . . hungry?" I ask.

"Starving," she replies. "I was about to wake you up."

Her voice sounds perfectly Nora-like, and a bit of the crawling tension leaves my body. Everything seems less terrible in the daytime, although it's still dim in my room. Rain is pattering down outside, and I wish this weather had come a day earlier. It would have hidden the moon, and then we wouldn't have gone to the beach and found that body.

In the kitchen, my dad is pulling a massive, puffed-up Dutch pancake from the oven, filling the room with the drool-inducing smell of caramelized apple. Bacon sizzles on the stove, and the coffee maker gurgles. It's almost enough to erase the awful images of weedy hair and tangled limbs from my brain.

"Nora!" My brother, Henry, sits on the counter by the sink, legs kicking. He's got jam smeared in his scruffy brown hair, and his dinosaur pajama shirt is on backward.

"How's my honorary little brother today?" Nora tickles his round tummy.

"GRRARRR!" he yells.

"Did you two sleep okay?" My dad sets the skillet on the stove and starts laying the bacon out to dry.

Nora glances at me, wary, and I shrug. "Fine, I guess."

We set the table with plates and silverware, and soon the whole surface is filled with steaming food. Nora gets Henry settled in his booster seat, and my dad starts doling out slices of apple pancake.

"So, are you—" he starts to say, but Nora's ringing phone cuts him off.

"Hey, Mom," she says. "Yeah, I'm still here. I'm okay—we can still go to Grammy's. Um, I think so." She turns to me. "Mazzy, can you drive me home after we eat?"

"Sure."

"Thanks." She tilts her cheek back into her phone. "Yep, I'll see you soon."

I wait for my dad to continue asking whatever question he was in the middle of asking, but he just heads back to the stove to get the last batch of bacon. He's never been the most talkative person, but ever since he quit drinking, he gets these lapses where he just trails off and things feel heavy. I know he needs to work through whatever he's feeling, but I never know what to do when it happens.

"I found a couple of leads before you woke up," says Nora, leaning in close and dropping her voice. "None of them are from the Cape, but they've gone missing in towns around New England since July."

26

She pinch-zooms her screen and holds it up. The woman looks to be in her late twenties, with long, dark hair, but I still can't match her living face with that hollow, toothless one from last night.

"Maybe?" I say, and Nora pulls up the next photo. This woman is younger, with curlier hair and a beauty mark on her forehead.

"She didn't have a mole," I say.

Nora sighs. "You're right. I'm just not getting the right essence from any of them."

"Like their aura?" I ask.

"It's deeper than an aura. Even more intangible." Nora's dreamy expression turns slightly smug. "You wouldn't find it in any of your books."

Resisting the urge to roll my eyes, I take a large bite of bacon.

My dad drops into his chair and cracks his neck, making Nora and I wince. "What're you looking at?"

"Nothing," I say. "So, what are you doing today?"

He groans. "Everything I've been putting off for the past month. I have to break down all the cardboard and go to the dump. Kevin's giving me a ride, and then I told him I'd help fix his broken toilet."

"I'm gonna bring my tools and help too," adds Henry, through a mouthful of toast.

My heart sinks. I hate the idea of spending the day alone, but I hate the idea of following my dad and Kevin around while they dump trash and fix toilets even more.

"Somebody was singing a song last night," says Henry.

Nora's face goes greenish. "Was that me?"

"Um, maybe," I say.

"It was a good song!" Henry jumps down from his chair and belts out a few bars of the weird little melody. Sung in a kid's high-pitched voice, it's even creepier.

I set down my fork. My appetite is gone.

"Go wash your hands if you're done eating," my dad tells Henry.

"What else did I do?" whispers Nora, and I shake my head faintly.

"I'll tell you in the car."

~ ~ ~

Nora lives in a residential neighborhood like mine, several miles away from the beaches in West Yarmouth. That used to be far enough that the houses didn't get turned into vacation rentals, which bring in way more money in a single summer than most locals can afford to pay all year. Unfortunately, it's not far enough away anymore.

"I still can't believe I did that." She scrubs her eyes. "I have absolutely no memory of saying anything. I don't even remember my dream."

"It's probably a normal reaction after having something traumatic happen to you," I say, turning the windshield wipers up and slowing for a deep puddle. "Try not to worry about it."

But that song she was singing has been stuck in my head all morning. It's an eerie little earworm.

The shell driveway crunches as I pull up to Nora's small gray-shingled house. Out on the patchy sand-and-grass lawn, there's a FOR SALE sign. Nora and her mom have been renting this place since she was five, and their landlord always took care not to raise their rent too much. But now he's in his late sixties and planning to retire. Nora's mom had been hoping he'd sell her the house for a decent price, after all the years of money and repairs she's put into it. But then the housing market went sky high, and even the tiniest cottages in the worst neighborhoods started selling for over half a million dollars, and that was the end of that. Nora's mom was lucky to find an apartment she could afford in Dennis Port, still in our school district, but it's about half the size of this place, and there's no guarantee it won't get sold in the future too. They're moving in less than a month.

Not everyone's fortunate enough to have inherited a house from their relatives. I try not to feel bad that our mortgage is paid off and we can't get kicked out by a landlord—I lost my grandmother, who meant the world to me, after all—but the guilt is still there anyway.

"Who do you think she was talking about?" Nora asks.

I shift into park. "Who do I think *who* was talking about?"

"Her," she says. "The dead woman. She was using my voice because she wants us to tell someone about her. Who do you think she meant?"

It's lucky the car is parked, or I might have crashed it just now. "First of all, it wasn't the dead woman speaking. It was just you having a nightmare."

Nora folds her arms over her faux fur coat. "You don't know that for sure."

I want to snap at her that I do know for sure, but it isn't true. The voice that came out of her mouth last night was so strange, so wrong, so fundamentally *not* Nora. I don't even want to think about it. I want to pretend none of this ever happened.

The windshield wipers slash back and forth as rain pours down the glass.

"That would be so incredibly creepy," I say.

"It doesn't have to be," says Nora. "Maybe she just needs some help. Maybe we don't have to be so freaked out just because she's dead."

"Even if this person were communicating with you . . . or through you"—I shudder—"I don't think we should listen. It's not safe to mess with spirits. You know that."

We've had this argument a thousand times. Nora says my approach toward magic is too mild, too meek. She says I'll never gain any real kind of power, but that isn't my goal. I just want understanding, truth, a sense of control in a world that's increasingly spiraling. I want to avoid as many Tower-like explosions as possible.

The front door of the house swings open, and Nora's mom waves out at us. We wave back, and she points to her watch and mouths, *We're late.*

"Check the missing persons databases today if you have time, okay?" Nora says as she opens her car door. "I'll look too, and I'll text you later."

"But I still can't picture her face," I say.

"You'll know her when you see her," she says, hunching down inside her coat. "Don't pretend like you don't have a sixth sense too."

I let it drop. "Give your grandmother a big hug for me, okay?"

"Will do."

As she passes the FOR SALE sign in her yard, Nora gives it a hard kick.

CHAPTER 5

The weather just keeps getting worse as I leave Nora's neighborhood and head back across town. By the time I pull into my driveway, the rain is hammering down, turning the puddles into lakes. Steeling myself for the dash to my blue-shuttered saltbox house, I wonder if I'll ever shake the chill in my bones from last night. Absently, I start to hum, then realize it's that creepy song Nora sang last night.

My phone pings, and I pull it out, grateful for the interruption.

> Elliot: Hey

I almost drop the phone. He never texts me outside of our group chat with Nora.

> Me: Hi

Immediately, dots. My heart starts to race.

> Elliot: Are you and nora ok?

Of course he's going to ask about Nora, considering she was there. Considering she's the one who touched the body. But he's texting *me*. I wonder if he didn't notice that he's not on the group chat?

>Me: We're slightly traumatized but mostly ok
>
>You?
>
>Elliot: Same. I've never seen a dead body before
>
>Me: I have at wakes, but nothing like that

His next text is a photo of a sketch pad. The drawing is just a series of simple charcoal slashes, but I immediately recognize three figures standing over a fourth person lying by the tide line. I don't know how he managed it, considering nobody even has a face, but he's perfectly captured the bleakness of the night, the weight in our bodies, the sorrow of the moment.

>Me: That's exactly it
>
>How are you so talented

Last year, Elliot's final art project, a life-size mixed-media sculpture of a man growing into a tree (or out of it, depending on how you looked at it), made several people, including his teacher, cry. I'm certain he'll be famous someday.

I wait for more dots, but there are none.

>Me: Were you going to ask me something before we found the

Delete.

>Me: It seemed like you wanted to

Delete.

>Me: Does it feel like something is

Delete.

> Me: Do you want to

Delete.

A new text pops up, saving me from my downward spiral.

> Elliot: What are you doing

In my rush to write back, I keep messing up the words.

> Me: Noras going to hr grabdmothers and
>
> Im home
>
> Where are you

> Elliot: Work

"Dammit," I mutter.

> Elliot: It's dead here today
>
> not as dead as yesterday
>
> sorry that wasn't funny

> Me: It was a little
>
> I guess nobody wants to go out in the rain
> today

I'm doing it again. Making awkward conversation instead of asking him to hang out. It's just that I have no idea if this new . . . thing I'm feeling between us is real. If it's not and I say something to him, it'd create the world's most bizarre love triangle. Me liking Elliot liking Nora, and nobody liking the right person back. Just thinking about it makes me shrivel up inside. I'd be blowing up my very own Tower.

Still, he texted me on his break. Not Nora, not the group chat. I tap out another message and force myself to hit send.

Me: What are you doing later

Dots, then nothing. Then dots. Then nothing. I'm starting to sweat, despite the cold, and I might die of waiting.

Elliot: probably just going home

I wait for him to elaborate, but he doesn't. Either the conversation is over or he's doing some actual work. I have no idea if he just wants to go home and doesn't want to hang out later, or if he's telling me that he has nothing to do because he *does* want to hang out. Or maybe the idea of the two of us hanging out without Nora has never occurred to him. Last year, he swore he was over her, and then he went on a huge dating spree just to prove his point, but his longest relationship was a month-long thing with Gabriel James. None of them stuck, and I always wondered if it was because deep down, he still wasn't fully over her.

Me: ok

Before I can overthink anything else, I shove my phone back in my bag and dash out into the rain.

~ ~ ~

"Mazzy!" Henry sits at the kitchen island, surrounded by sheets of paper and markers. My dad is snoring on the couch. He's been napping all the time lately. My mom says his body is going through a lot of stuff as it recovers from addiction, so we let him sleep as much as we can.

"Hey, buddy," I say, putting a finger to my lips and lowering my voice. "What are you making?"

"Dad said I can watch TV later if I'm nice and quiet, so I'm drawing pictures," he says. "Can I have some toast?"

"Didn't you just eat like five pieces for breakfast?" I ask.

Henry shrugs and uncaps a red marker. "I like toast."

"Can't argue with that." I slot two pieces of bread into the toaster, then scroll through my phone while I wait. No more texts from Elliot, but there are a couple of articles and posts about the woman's body being found—apparently people have started calling her May, after Mayflower Beach. There's nothing about who she might be or how she was murdered, and no information about who found her, which is a relief. Nora and I already have a reputation at school for being witchy and weird. We don't need to make things weirder.

The bread pops out, and I jump. Henry laughs.

"Scary toast!" he says.

"Heart attack snack." I slather the two slices with butter and sprinkle cinnamon sugar on top. As I return to my phone, Henry crunches happily, scattering crumbs all over himself and the floor.

"Do you like this?" he asks, sliding his latest drawing across the counter.

"It's nice." I barely glance at the paper, but he shoves it closer and nudges my elbow.

"I did a good job," he says. "It looks just like her."

"Looks like who?"

As I fully take in Henry's drawing, a chill slides down my neck. A yellow line across the paper indicates the ground, and a stick figure is lying on her back, smiling up at the sky. Her weedy, black hair trails out in all directions. Just like the dead body. The woman they're calling May. There aren't hands on the ends of her arms, but given that she's a stick figure, maybe there aren't supposed to be.

"Who is this?" My voice shakes.

Henry climbs down from his stool, leaving his plate and the crumbs. "She's my friend."

I follow him into the living room, where toy trains are scattered all over the threadbare carpet. "What do you mean, your friend?" I whisper. "Is she a teacher at your school?"

"No." He sits on the floor and starts connecting wooden tracks. "She's just my friend. I don't know her name or where she works."

"Can you tell me anything about her?" I crouch beside him.

"She's good at singing," he says, rolling a red caboose over a bridge. "And dancing."

My scalp starts prickling all over. Nora said she was graceful.

"How do you know that?" I say.

Henry shrugs. "I saw her."

It feels like there are ants in my hair. "*Where* did you see her?"

"I don't remember." Henry hands me a green locomotive, and I absently set it in the bin. "Can I watch a show?" he asks.

"Did you see someone who looks like her on TV?" I ask, desperately hoping there's a simple, sensible answer to all of this.

"Yeah, maybe," he says. "Can I *please* watch a show now, Mazzy? Dad said I could."

It doesn't fully stop the crawling on my scalp, but he probably did see a woman somewhere who looked like her. I need to stop being so paranoid. It simply can't be the same woman in Henry's drawing. He wasn't there last night. My traumatized brain is just imagining things, weaving connections that don't exist because it's trying to process what happened. This is just a reaction. I have to keep reminding myself that it's okay to not be okay right now.

After turning on Henry's favorite cartoon with the volume low so it won't wake my dad, I grab half a lemon from the fridge and head to my room. Nora's song is still playing in my head over and over, making me feel less and less sane with each repetition. I keep catching myself humming it too.

After setting the half lemon in a shallow blue bowl—a handmade gift from Elliot—I sprinkle it with homemade sea salt, rosemary, and cloves. Then I poke a white charm candle into the lemon's center, anoint it with a few drops of lavender oil, and light the wick. I whisper a short incantation for safety and to reverse any negative energy, and then I take several slow breaths, letting the calming light and citrus scent wash away the eeriness that keeps slipping down the back of my neck like a draft.

Once I'm feeling a bit more centered, I take out my cello and start tuning the strings. Maybe instead of letting Nora's song torment me, I can make it mine. Everyone is always asking when I'm going to start writing original compositions. Nora says I need to stop following the notes printed on pages and screens and play from my heart. But whenever I try, I get lost, overwhelmed by all the possibilities.

This eerie little song isn't going away, though, and I may as well give it a shot.

As I'm plucking out the basic melody, my phone vibrates, but I ignore it. Once I've got the shape of the song down, I rosin my bow and then run through the whole thing a few times, smoothing it out and adding vibrato. And it's not bad. It's actually quite pretty, in a haunting way. I can do something with this.

My phone continues to vibrate intermittently as I play and stop, play and stop, going back and rephrasing and finessing. My head is swimming with the music, dipping and soaring, twisting and spiraling, and what I've crafted is so much more than what Nora sang, in the best possible way. Goose bumps cover my arms and legs.

I pour everything into the music. The fear and dread of finding that body in the sand. The shock of seeing her empty face. The deep sorrow for her poor, ended life. The gruesome stumps of her arms. The brutal nothingness of her now as a person. The senselessness. The never-ending void of death.

Why, why, why?

I finish the song, then immediately start from the beginning. Over and over and over, I move through the melody, sometimes slow and aching, other times frantic and frayed, and each time I think, *This is it. This is exactly how I feel right now.* My left fingers are numb from flying over the strings, and my right arm throbs from the exertion of bowing, but this song is the blood pulsing through my veins. The synapses firing in my brain.

I can't stop.

Behind me, the bedroom door swings open.

"Hang on, let me finish." I've got four measures left, and my right hand is cramping so hard I'm afraid I might drop the bow. It must be my dad, because Henry would have dashed in and jumped on my bed. I'm not one for sensing people's auras like Nora, but I can feel the wonder, the enjoyment radiating off him as he stands there listening. This song really is *that* beautiful.

I finish and turn around.

There's no one there.

CHAPTER 6

"Dad?" I say, peering over my shoulder through the half-open door. The hallway is empty.

I must not have latched the door all the way and it opened on its own, but I had such a strong feeling of someone standing there just now. Sweating, I lean the cello against my bed, then pick up my phone. I hiss in my breath. I've been playing for an hour and a half. My lemon candle is a burned-out stump. On my screen, there are four missed calls and a string of texts from Nora.

> Hey
>
> Where are you
>
> Answer meeeeeee
>
> Glenn and I are very disappointed

Underneath, there's a photo of Nora's guinea pig, Glenn, with her glaring face behind him.

I need to ask you something

??????

MAAAAAAAZZZZZZZZZZZZZYYYYYY

Dizzy and sluggish, like I'm deep underwater, I tap the screen to video call her. She answers in half a second.

"Why are you ignoring me?" she says.

"I wasn't; I was practicing." The music is still spiraling in my head, and I glance at the doorway again, but no one is there. "What's up?"

"I think we should go back to Mayflower," she says.

"Why?"

She closes her eyes and inhales deeply through her nostrils. "I don't know exactly. I just have this really strong compulsion that we need to go there. Like *she* wants us to. It feels like she's hovering close, like she wants to contact us, you know?"

I drag my hands through my hair. It's all too much, too unsettling.

"People are calling her May," I say.

Nora's too-close-to-the-screen nose wrinkles. "That doesn't fully resonate. I don't think it's her real name."

"Me neither," I say.

Part of me wants to stay home all day and work on this song, but I know I need a break. I've lost track of time while playing before, but never quite like that. I still feel so muddled, like I've been dreaming for the past ninety minutes. Leaning off-screen, I reach for the anti-anxiety spell jar on my bookshelf and give it a little shake to stir up the herbs and crystals inside. The wax seal on the lid is starting to peel, and things are looking dusty and brown inside—I should make a new one soon. Although the way this week is going, I should probably make an industrial-size anxiety bucket.

"Yeah, let's go to the beach," I say. If nothing else, it'll get me out of my own head, into some fresh air, and away from that song. "But we can only stay for an hour because I have a physics test tomorrow."

"That's fine. I need to work on my English essay," she says. College applications are coming up, and she'd never admit it, but even Nora is having anxiety over that.

"Sounds like a plan," I say. "See you in twenty minutes."

~ ~ ~

As soon as she gets in my car, I hand Nora the picture that Henry drew.

"What's this?" she asks.

"Henry made it today," I say, shifting into reverse. "He said it's his friend."

Nora is silent for a long while, staring at the picture as we drive.

"Who do you think it is?" she finally says.

We roll up to a stop sign; I hit the brake and turn to her. "Who do *you* think?"

She chews her lip. "Mazzy, I'm not being all woo-woo right now. I think it's her. May, or whatever her real name is."

Goose bumps break out all over my arms. "I think so too."

The car behind us beeps, and I realize we've been sitting at the stop sign for ages. With an apologetic wave over my shoulder, I hit the gas.

"Do you think he overheard us talking about her?" Nora asks. "I showed you some pictures at breakfast."

"Yeah, but they didn't look like her. This"—I point to the drawing—"really does look like her, in some way I can't explain."

"I know." Nora shudders. "I can feel her essence."

I'd like to argue with Nora that you can't feel someone's essence from a stick-figure drawing, but there's something unmistakable here. She recognized the woman before I even told her what I thought. Every hair on my body is lifting off my skin.

"Why do you think Henry said she was his friend?" asks Nora.

"Who knows with Henry?" I say. "He told me a tree was his best friend the other day, so maybe we shouldn't read too much into that."

Nora makes a soft *hmm* sound. "In all seriousness, though, I suspect May's spirit wants us to help find her killer."

"Seriously?" I say. "Even if you were having some kind of . . . spirit channeling moment last night, how could you possibly know who it was or what they want? You only said a couple of short phrases."

"You couldn't possibly understand," says Nora, "because it wasn't you."

"I was still there," I say. "I heard what you said. And you don't even remember it happening."

"Maybe not consciously," she says. "But it left a deep mark on me. I've been thinking about it all day."

I scrub my hand over my face because this has gone beyond arguable. "Why us, though? If that was really a spirit needing help, why would she ask two seventeen-year-olds? There are plenty of adults who find criminals for a living and actually know what they're doing."

"Well, yeah," says Nora. "But they don't have a connection with her like we do. She isn't communing with them like she is with us."

"You mean she's communing with you," I say, but Nora just flashes an all-knowing smile.

"She might speak to you too, if you let her," she says.

CHAPTER 7

I've been coming to Mayflower Beach my entire life. I've got so many memories of paddling around in tide pools with all the other preschoolers, of begging my mom for money to get an ice cream from the snack bar, of hopping from car shadow to car shadow in the parking lot because I didn't bring my flip-flops and the gravel was blisteringly hot. But the memory of what happened here last night has overshadowed all of those moments, compressed them into a tiny compartment of *then* versus *now*, where everything now is vaguely sickening.

I wonder how long that body lay on the beach, how long she floated before we found her.

The rain has cleared out, and the sky is now the same blue as the ocean. You'd almost be tricked into thinking it's a beautiful day if it weren't for the wet sand everywhere and the wind. Far away across the sandbars, whitecaps dot the sea. A woman and her dog are walking off to our right, and white bird with a forked tail swoops over them, heading out to sea. I twist my long hair into a bun to keep it from knotting up, and then Nora hooks her arm through mine as we head down the sandbar, our black coats billowing.

"Was it over there?" she asks, pointing to a spot strewn with slimy green seaweed.

"No." I say, steering us left. I recognize the sweeping curve of the tide line. I almost want to say it smells like the spot we found her, but that's not quite right. It's something more elusive, more indefinable. I feel it in my bones. Also, I recognize the boulder Elliot sat on while we did the ritual. Today, someone else is sitting on it, all bundled up in a long, hooded coat. As we approach, they stand and stretch, then head off down the shore toward Chapin Beach. For some reason, Nora and I both breathe a sigh of relief.

My feet are wet already, thanks to my shoddy Doc Martens knockoffs, and my ripped tights are doing absolutely nothing to keep my legs warm, but we keep walking, drawn closer by some deep need to stand in that spot again. A gull hovers overhead, shrieking into the wind, and a wave of dread and something like nostalgia washes over me. What a horrible, lonely end to someone's life that was.

A handful of tiny white shells glint at the edge of the lapping waves. I've never been much of a beachcomber, but something about them is drawing my eye. Something about them is off. I let go of Nora's arm and step closer.

They're teeth.

Human teeth: molars and canines and incisors. One has a silver filling. Gulping air, I back away and bump into Nora, who hasn't seen them yet. I want to turn her around, hurry her back to the car, pretend we never found this.

"What the—" she says, before I can pull her away.

"Don't," I say, but it's too late, and she's picking one up. "Jesus, Nora, don't touch them."

Nora opens her hand, tipping it left and right so the sharp little canine rolls back and forth on her palm, and I'm cringing so hard it hurts.

"These are *hers*," she says.

"Maybe that person dropped them," I say. "The one who was sitting on the rock right before we got here?" I scan the flats between here and Chapin, but there's no sign of them.

"Who brings *teeth* to the beach?" says Nora, and I have to agree that it's not a rational explanation. "They must not have seen them. But I'm certain with every fiber of my being that these teeth are May's."

I don't want to agree with Nora; I don't want it to be true. But May was missing all of her teeth, and now there are teeth here. Sour revulsion washes up my throat.

"If they are hers, you're tampering with evidence," I say.

"No, I'm not." Nora gestures at the sloshing ocean. "They're about to get washed away, so we have to pick them up."

She's right. If these actually are May's teeth, they could be the key to finding out who she is. Somebody could put these back in order and check them against dental records. Especially that one with the filling. Even though every fiber of my being is recoiling, I crouch down to help Nora gather them up.

It might just be that my skin is so frigid from the wind, but the first tooth feels hot. The second one too. Held loosely in my free hand, they click and clatter against each other, and I swear they're buzzing faintly with a weird energy. I want to drop them, but I don't.

"Do you feel . . ." I trail off, unsure of how to explain it.

"Yeah." Nora picks another tooth out of the sand. The knees of her black jeans are soaked, and her eyes are gleaming in a feverish way. "It's her."

I think of that gaping mouth, those sunken cheeks, those handless wrists, and the beach tips and tilts around me. That awful little song loops over and over in my mind, keeping time with the rushing waves. As much as I want to tell Nora she's wrong, I can't. There's no rational explanation for why these teeth, which somehow washed up in the same place as that dead woman, are buzzing like bees in my hand.

We gather the rest of the teeth and then rake our fingers through the sand, making sure we've found them all. Their humming vibration has traveled all the way up to my elbow, and my head feels buzzy too, like I've drunk too much coffee. I've never had such a sudden and visceral reaction to touching something—not that I've touched anyone else's disembodied teeth before.

"That's enough," I say as water swirls around our ankles, shocking my feet and making them cramp. Nora keeps digging, and I pull her up by the shoulder of her coat. "Come on, that has to be enough."

She blinks at me, like she'd forgotten I was here. "But—"

"No." I pull her away from the water. "The police will have to work with what we have. Did you get the one with the filling?"

Nora's hand shakes as she checks her gruesome collection, and I'm worried she'll drop them, but she doesn't. "Yeah," she says.

My teeth are chattering, and it feels like I'm walking on needles. "Let's go call the police from my car."

We wade back through the tide pools, a disturbing echo of last night. I try to drop the teeth into my coat pocket, but I can't unclench my fingers. I don't understand why we, of all the people who could've been walking on the beach today, found these. It's too much to be a coincidence. Everything is too much to be a coincidence.

There's a gray SUV with a Delaware license plate parked right next to my car, even though the rest of the lot is empty. Nora and I throw ourselves into our seats, and I turn on the heat full blast. She cups her hands together and blows into them, and the teeth rattle like a set of macabre dice. As I drop my own handful onto the lid of the center console, the buzzing in my hand and forearm subsides, and it's like a dragging weight has been lifted off me.

Seven shiny, faintly yellowing teeth. They're so much grosser when they're not in someone's head anymore. I'm still not fully onboard with Nora's story, that May's spirit is asking us for help from beyond the veil, but I have no other explanation. Clearly something very strange is happening here.

"What are we going to tell the cops?" I ask.

Nora rattles her handful again, making me shudder. "Maybe we could keep them for a day or two and then turn them in?"

"What?" I say. "Why would we ever do that?"

"We could try to contact her spirit." Nora stares out the windshield at the long, waving grass on the dunes. "We could use these in a ritual."

"Oh no." I pull out my phone. "No, no, one hundred percent no. Are you *kidding* me?"

Not a single one of my magic books would ever recommend reaching obliviously into the spirit world using random, washed-up teeth. Even Nora, with her spontaneous, whimsical, vibes-only sense of spell work, should know that's a terrible plan.

She winces. "It was just an idea."

"You said May wants us to help her, right?" I say.

Nora nods, her knee jittering.

"These teeth might be a key piece of evidence," I say. "And on a scale of one to ten—with one being the least helpful and ten being the most helpful—you and I doing a dangerous, made-up ritual is like a one or two, whereas the police checking her dental records has to be at least an eight or nine, right?"

"Point taken," says Nora. "You didn't have to yell about it, though."

"I'm sorry," I say. "We can still do a ritual to see if she really does need help, but we should do one without the teeth. A safe one."

"A boring one," she grumbles.

"Maybe we could find a medium who could help us reach out to her?" I suggest, leaving out how much I actually like the idea of doing it in a "boring" way. Hopefully, a medium can also shed some light on whether Nora is imagining this connection. It's impossible to ignore all the creepy things that have cropped up since last night, but that doesn't mean she's not jumping to conclusions.

Nora adds her handful of teeth to the collection. "That's actually not a bad idea."

"Okay, good." I'm relieved she's open to some less drastic options. Sometimes it's hard to talk Nora out of her wild ideas.

As I look up the non-emergency police number, she starts arranging the teeth on the center console. Incisor, canine, molar, incisor, canine, molar. It's even worse seeing them in a pattern that isn't how they'd be in a person's mouth. Nora sets the molar with the filling in the center.

"She only had one cavity," she says.

"Unless there are more that we didn't find." I haven't counted them, but it doesn't seem like quite a full set.

"May took good care of her teeth," says Nora in a weird sing-song voice that makes my skin crawl. "She learned her lesson after that first cavity. See how it's silver? That means it's old. She was just a kid when it—oh."

We both look up as a middle-aged man passes in front of my car, close to the hood. He's wearing a dark baseball hat and coat, and a grayscale tattoo of a thorn-covered vine winds up the side of his neck and behind his ear.

I drop my hand over the teeth, and they fizz like Pop Rocks against my palm. The man gives us a distracted half smile as he skirts into the space between our two vehicles.

"That's not the person who was sitting on the boulder, is it?" Nora mutters as he climbs into his SUV.

"No," I say. "That person had a totally different coat. Did he see the teeth just now?"

"I don't think so," she says as the SUV pulls away. "And even if he did, it's not like it's illegal to have teeth in your car."

"Just extremely fucking weird," I say, and we both laugh nervously.

Once the SUV is gone, I tap my phone screen, and the police line starts to ring.

CHAPTER 8

The sun is low in the sky by the time a black sedan pulls into the parking lot and takes the spot where the gray SUV was parked. A tall woman in her midthirties, dark hair pulled back in a sleek ponytail, gets out and peers into our car.

Nora hastily scoops up all the teeth again. "Is that a police officer?"

I take in the woman's tailored black pantsuit and subtle makeup. "She doesn't look like one, does she?"

The woman taps on Nora's window, and I lower it.

"Are you the person who called the police?" She has the faintest trace of an accent I can't place. Scandinavian, maybe.

Nora and I just gape at her, unsure of how to respond. With a flicker of irritation, the woman reaches into her jacket and pulls out a badge.

"I'm Detective Huld," she says. "With the police department. Did you call about finding something on the beach?"

My shoulders relax a little. The clothes make sense if she's a detective, not an officer. The badge looks real enough, and if she

52

didn't actually work for the police, she couldn't have known we'd called them.

"Yeah," I say. "We, uh, found some teeth in the spot where that dead woman washed up last night."

Detective Huld's eyes narrow. "Would you mind getting out of the car so we can talk?"

"I don't like this," mutters Nora, but we get out anyway.

"You said you found teeth in the location where a body washed up," says Detective Huld. "What makes you think that?"

"Because we were the ones who found the body last night," I say.

Detective Huld folds her arms over her chest. Inside the collar of her jacket, a silver chain glints. "What are your names?"

We tell her, and she nods but doesn't write anything down or call the station to check our identities, which must mean she's familiar with us already.

"And why are you here now?" she asks.

"The dead woman, she wan—" Nora starts, but I cut her off before we both get hauled in for a psychological evaluation.

"We were just trying to . . . process what happened last night," I say. "Retrace our steps, get some closure on what happened."

Detective Huld says nothing, like she's waiting for me to continue, but that's all I've got for an excuse.

"Do you have any leads on the victim?" I ask. "Who she was or where she came from?"

"Nothing I can share as of yet." The detective's expressionless face may as well be carved out of marble.

"We feel terrible about what happened to her." Nora stuffs her hand into her coat pocket, and the teeth make tiny clicking sounds. "And we thought maybe we could find some more clues to help with your investigation."

The frigid wind gusts, and I tuck my chin inside my coat's collar, but Huld looks entirely unfazed in her narrow-cut suit jacket. I can't quite make out the angular symbol carved on the silver pendant of her necklace, but it might be a rune.

"I appreciate your concern," she says, "but it's not helpful to interfere with an active crime scene."

I almost laugh, because even though I told Nora we shouldn't tamper with evidence, the police aren't exactly doing anything to investigate the crime scene right now. Besides, it's underwater half the time. This woman should be grateful we grabbed the evidence before it washed away.

"May I see what you found?" says Detective Huld.

Nora's shoulders hunch up, and I just know she's thinking about running away or jumping back in the car, so I nudge her with my elbow.

"Go ahead," I whisper.

She pulls her fist from her pocket and slowly uncurls her fingers. The teeth tip back and forth on her palm, glinting in the slanted sunset light. I watch Detective Huld for a reaction—revulsion, surprise, horror—but not a muscle in her face moves.

"Where on the beach did you find them?" she asks. "And what time?"

"Out on the sandbar, like forty minutes ago," I say. "We found them exactly where the body washed up. We know it's the same spot because there's a boulder near there, and it never moves. But the tide came in and it's covered with water now. That's why we picked them up, even though we know it would've been better not to touch them."

I'm rambling, and Nora is just standing there glowering, but I don't care if she doesn't want to give these teeth away. It's all so sinister and gross, and I want this situation to be over as soon as possible. I want to pretend I never felt those teeth fizzing, buzzing against my skin.

Detective Huld opens her trunk and pulls out a plastic baggie and a tag. "Put the teeth in here, please."

Again, I can feel Nora's resistance almost as strongly as if it were mine. But she does what the detective asks, dropping the teeth into the open mouth of the bag. The smallest one, an incisor, sticks to her skin like it doesn't want to go, but she brushes it off and then blows out something like a sigh of regret. Or maybe it's relief. I feel a little lighter now that those things are out of our possession.

Detective Huld seals the bag, and as she holds it up to inspect the teeth in the waning light, her silver pendant slides back inside her jacket collar. She mutters something unintelligible.

"Sorry?" says Nora.

The detective drags her gaze away from the evidence bag. "Is this all of them?"

I let out an awkward laugh. Knowing Nora, it wouldn't surprise me if she kept some for herself, but this woman doesn't know Nora.

"Of course it is," says Nora, and I nod, because I just want to get out of the cold, go back to my house and my physics textbook and my regular, safe, boring life.

"Is there anything else you'd like to tell me about this situation?"

Detective Huld's dark eyes bore into mine, and I get the uncanny sensation that she can read my thoughts. It feels like we've done something wrong—like we're *doing* something wrong—even though we've told Detective Huld all the facts. The things Nora believes about the dead woman, well, they're not facts. And there's no point in telling those kinds of things to someone in law enforcement, as if she'd believe us. I'm still not sure I believe them myself.

"Nope," says Nora, and I add, "I don't think so," so it sounds less rude.

Detective Huld pulls out two business cards and hands one to each of us. "If you remember anything else that's relevant"—her sculpted eyebrow lifts, like this is more of a *when* than an *if* situation—"call me."

"We will." Nora's already getting back in my car.

"Thank you for your help," says Detective Huld as Nora's door slams. "Whether or not these teeth are related to the case, I appreciate you turning them in."

"No problem." I'm about to head back to the car too, but she steps in close, and a feeling like spider legs crawls up the side of my neck. Huld smells faintly of leather and smoke.

"You two should stay away from beaches for a while," she says.

My skin is crawling so badly I can barely think, so I squeak out an "okay" and lunge for the door handle.

"I don't like her," says Nora as we pull out of the parking lot.

I glance in my rearview mirror. Detective Huld leans against her car, arms folded, watching us leave. "She was just doing her job, right?"

"Her essence was off," says Nora. "It was all coarse and gray. Like steel wool."

"Hmm," I say, flicking on my blinker. "Did you see her necklace?"

"Yeah, and I didn't like it either." Nora squints at the detective's business card in the dim light of my dashboard. "Eva Huld, I hope we never have to make your acquaintance again."

"Me too," I say, although I'm not quite sure why.

CHAPTER 9

Monday afternoon, last period. The dreaded AP physics test. I'm so exhausted, I'm barely functional. It was late by the time I got home and explained what happened to my parents. They were even more confused than I expected they'd be, and I'm now banned from going to Mayflower Beach. After a long conversation about safety and responsibility and limits, and then an even longer dinner, followed by mandatory cleanup, it was hours later than I'd initially planned to start studying. I couldn't make any of the words or numbers stick in my brain, but I forced myself to keep trying until after midnight.

As I lay in bed, that same eerie song played in my brain over and over, getting louder each time. At three a.m., fully convinced I was losing my mind, I put in my earbuds with white noise to block it all out, and, finally, I fell asleep. My dreams were scattered and brutal, although I can't remember a single one.

Across the room, Elliot sets down his pencil and flips his stapled papers around. This is the only class we have together, and he got here right before the bell. As he passes my desk to hand in his test, he waggles his eyebrows at me and my brain goes fully blank. I manage to waggle mine back, but it's too late and he's already gone past, and I curse myself for being such an awkward weirdo. His freshly washed hair looks soft, and there's a hole in the shoulder of his black shirt. I imagine pressing my finger to it, touching the skin underneath.

Once I've written, erased, and rewritten the last equation about seventeen times, I hand in my own test, then lay my head on my desk and listen to the clock tick, keeping time with the music in my head. This morning before school, I reworked our unsuccessful test-taking spell, adding twice as much rosemary for memory and some coffee for stamina, but it still didn't feel like it worked.

The bell rings, and Elliot is heading my way again. I force my face into what feels like a normal expression as I gather up my stuff.

"How'd you do?" he asks.

I shrug. "Okay, I guess. Considering everything."

His forehead creases with concern. "So, what exactly happened at the beach yesterday?"

I recount the day's sordid events as we weave through the chaos of the hallways, stopping at my locker and then his to grab our coats.

"You know the chances of them being that same woman's teeth are, like, infinitesimally small, right?" he says.

"I guess," I say as we step out into the parking lot. "But, at the same time, how many other people's teeth could possibly be out there, just rolling around in the ocean?"

"Honestly?" he says. "Probably more than we think."

I shudder. "Wow, I'm never going in the ocean again. Thanks for that."

"Sorry." Elliot grins, and I'm pretty sure he's not remotely sorry.

"Nora wanted to keep them," I say. "She wanted to use them for a ritual to contact the dead woman."

"Jesus," he mutters, and I feel bad for talking about Nora behind her back, but, at the same time, it's nice to have validation that that was an incredibly messed up thing to suggest.

"She's convinced that woman—May—is speaking to her," I say. "And, honestly, I'd say this is one of her usual overdramatic situations, but that voice she spoke in the other night was so wildly different from her normal voice. She couldn't have done that on purpose, and definitely not while she was fully asleep."

"Hold still." Elliot stops abruptly, tips his head, and leans in close, and for one wild second, every reckless possibility blows through my mind, but then he pulls something off my shoulder. A ladybug. He opens his fingers gently, the bug flits away into the sky, and I make a foolish wish.

"People do messed up stuff in their sleep," he says. "Some lady sleepwalk-murdered her husband and then had no idea what happened when she woke up. Allegedly."

"I guess you had to be there with us that night," I say. "But here's the thing. When we went to Mayflower yesterday and I picked up those teeth, it was like they were full of this strange, fizzy energy, and I just—"

Elliot's expression has shifted from confused to wary.

"—don't know." I trail off. He's never believed in our magic practice, and he's clearly not ready to believe in ghosts, which is absolutely fair. I don't want to believe in this particular ghost either. But after witnessing Nora speaking in that voice, then having that strong sensation that someone was watching me play my cello, and finally finding those teeth washed up on the beach, it's getting more and more difficult not to.

"Anyway, I convinced Nora to try a non-tooth-related approach to . . . all of this." I gesture vaguely around myself. "We're heading to Midnight Alchemy to talk to a medium."

Midnight Alchemy is our favorite local metaphysical store. Nora and I have been haunting the place ever since we got into tarot and spells and all things esoteric back in seventh grade. After years of patiently putting up with our endless questions, the owner, Ione, has basically become our adopted witchy aunt.

Elliot's eyebrows lift. "A medium? Like, with a séance and a crystal ball?"

"I don't know if they'll use a crystal ball," I say. "It's usually just someone who's attuned to spirits and can talk to them directly and safely. Someone who knows what they're doing."

A few years ago, Nora and I used her Ouija board to communicate with what she claimed was a spirit named Phillip who died in the 1960s. I swore she was moving the planchette herself, and I was pretty sure a ghost who died over sixty years ago wouldn't use the word "bro." But weird stuff started happening every time we used the board that I couldn't explain away. Her books would sometimes fall off the shelves, lights would flicker, and, once, her electric pencil sharpener turned itself on, even though that wasn't supposed to be possible without a pencil inside.

Spooked, we went to Midnight Alchemy and asked Ione for advice. She told us that when you invite the spirits in, it isn't always the one you invite that shows up, especially if you don't know what you're doing. And sometimes, she said, even the ones you think are friendly and safe can change. This was just one of many long warnings she's given us about getting involved in things that are, as she puts it, "over our heads."

After that, we threw out the Ouija board. I wanted to burn it, but Nora was afraid we'd hurt Phillip's feelings. I didn't care about Phillip's feelings, but I didn't say that out loud in her house.

"You know most of those so-called mediums are frauds, right?" says Elliot. "They prey on people who are emotionally vulnerable after losing a loved one, and they ask a bunch of leading questions to figure out details and manipulate them."

"Yeah, I get that, but some of them really do know what they're doing," I say. "Plus, Ione recommended this particular woman, and I trust her judgment."

Elliot shrugs. "It's your choice. Just don't give her a credit card number or let her talk you into signing up for extra sessions."

"We definitely won't," I say. "Nora thinks May wants to give us information about her death. Personally, I just want to find out whether an objective third party—someone who's got experience working with spirits—can tell if May exists."

Elliot chews on his thumbnail, which is drawing my gaze to his mouth and giving me reckless thoughts again. "Do you actually believe in ghosts?" he asks.

"I don't *not* believe in them."

I am, at heart, a raging agnostic. Nora says I can't be an agnostic pagan because that means I don't actually believe in anything, but that's not true. I believe anything is possible, but we can't possibly know the exact truth because it's all too vast, too complicated, too far beyond our comprehension as silly little humans. I believe there are ways to try and make sense of the unknowable, like with tarot cards and other divination tools, and I believe there are ways to exert small amounts of control, like with spells and rituals, but I could never begin to explain how or why they work.

"If this medium is scamming you, she might end up 'seeing' things that aren't there." Elliot makes air quotes around the word.

"Do you want to come with us?" I ask. "It could be helpful, since you were there the night we found the body, and you could keep an eye on the medium to see if she seems legit."

"I wish I could," he says. "But I'm starting back at the grocery store today—I've got three shifts lined up already this week."

"Wow," I say, trying to hide my disappointment. "Why so many?"

He grimaces. "My dad got laid off. Again."

"Shit." I blow out all my air.

"He's talking about looking for jobs off-Cape."

My chest seizes up. I cannot, *cannot* fathom Elliot moving away. Not to mention, he's only applying to fine arts programs, which means there's almost no chance of us going to the same college next year, and if we no longer have this shared base of Cape Cod to come home to, I might never see him again. I gulp down the sticky panic rising in my throat and make a mental note to burn a green candle for Elliot's family tonight.

"Do you think he'd commute from here?" I ask.

Elliot shrugs. "Depends how far away it is. Obviously, I don't want to leave."

"Me neither," I say. "I mean, I can't—"

I can't stand the thought of you leaving.

I can't stop thinking about you.

I'm tangled up in knots, wondering if you feel the same way, but I'm terrified to ask.

"Do you"—I swallow hard—"need a ride?"

Dammit, Mazzy.

He flashes a rueful smile that muddles my insides. "I rode my bike today, and I don't think it'll fit in your car."

It definitely won't fit in the trunk of my tiny Jetta. I should get a bike rack, but since I don't own a bike myself, that would probably look desperate.

"Oh, right," I say. "Sorry."

He shrugs. "Not your fault."

We're both quiet then, and I guess it's my turn to talk, but I can't shake the feeling that he's waiting for something else. Something more. I just wish he'd give me an indication of what that might be.

"Well . . . I guess I'll see you later," I say finally. "Have fun at work."

"Thanks," he says. "Text me if that medium ends up being a fraud—or if you find more teeth."

I shudder. "God, I hope not."

Furious with myself for being such a wimp, and also a little frustrated with Elliot for being so unnecessarily hot and confusing, I head for my car. In a completely un-stalkery way, I watch him wheel away. A few minutes later, Nora climbs into my passenger seat.

"Can we get a coffee on the way? I'm falling asleep." She adjusts the corset she's layered over her burgundy chiffon dress. Everything looks looser on her lately.

"Me too," I say. "What a nightmare day."

CHAPTER 10

Nora and I head west on Route 28, slowly caffeinating ourselves with giant iced coffees, even though my car thermometer says it's thirty-nine degrees out. This road is lined with hotels, motels, restaurants, mini golf courses, gift stores, and ice cream shops, and in the summertime, I avoid it at all costs. In November, though, it's a straight shot all the way to Hyannis. All the empty parking lots are slightly depressing in this windswept, gray weather, but it's a mixed blessing to be able to get where I need to go without hours of traffic.

Main Street, Hyannis, is a little busier, a two-lane, one-way road with smaller boutiques and bistros and more of a downtown feeling, rather than a sprawl of tourist attractions. There's an empty parking space in front of my mother's shop, with its pale purple facade and hand-painted sign that reads GISELE'S GIFTS. Gisele and my mom have been friends since high school. I basically grew up in that shop, and I work there too in the summer. My mom's car is parked two spaces ahead of us, although I can't see her inside the store.

I shift into park, wondering what this medium is going to tell us. I wonder if Nora's been right this whole time about May's spirit, if an undead woman really is trying to contact us from beyond the veil. I can't quite bring myself to believe it, and yet so many unbelievable things are happening all of a sudden. Now that we're here, I'm a little scared of the answers we might get.

Just as I'm about to shut off the engine, my phone rings, and I hit the hands-free button without checking who it is.

"Hello?"

"Mazzy? This is Detective Huld."

My stomach lurches. Nora swears, and I widen my eyes at her because we're on speakerphone, but she just sticks out her tongue at the speaker in my dashboard.

There's a long pause on the other end of the line.

"How is it possible for a person to be this awkward?" whispers Nora.

"Can I, uh, help you with something, Detective?" I ask.

"Yes, actually. I had a quick question for you and Nora," says Detective Huld. "Did I hear her voice just now?"

Nora groans. "Yeah, I'm here. We're in the car."

"Perfect," says Detective Huld. "This will only take a minute."

"Good, because we're going to be late for an appointment," says Nora.

"I've been looking through the reports from Saturday night, trying to paint a clearer picture of the lead-up to the body being discovered," says Detective Huld. "Don't worry, you're not in any kind of trouble."

Nora whispers, "If we're not in trouble, why is she asking questions like we might be?"

"Can you tell me again what time you arrived at Mayflower Beach?" asks Detective Huld.

"Around nine forty," I say. We already answered that question at least five times on Saturday night.

"And can you tell me why you went to Mayflower Beach, specifically?" says Detective Huld.

Another question we answered several times, which means she's trying to catch us in a lie. But I remember exactly what we told the police then, and I'm not veering from the story.

"We went to look at the full moon," I say. "We were bored, and there was nothing else going on, so it seemed like a fun thing to do."

Detective Huld waits, but I don't elaborate. Eventually, she clears her throat.

"One of the officers found a candle stump in a jar near the body," she says. "Was that yours, by any chance?"

Nora and I both freeze.

What do we tell her? I mouth, and Nora shrugs. My brain is whirling, trying to decide how to answer, but we can't possibly be murder suspects, and it's not like a candle could be used as a murder weapon anyway. "Um, yeah, that was probably ours. We must have dropped it in all the confusion."

"Right, of course. There was a lot going on," says Detective Huld. "And was that candle yours, Mazzy, or Nora's?"

"It was mine." Nora cuts in. "Did you have any other questions? Because we're officially late for our appointment now."

There's a sound of papers shuffling in the background. "That's all I needed to know," says Detective Huld. "Thank you again, girls."

"Sure, okay, bye." Nora reaches across me and hits the hang-up button before I have time to say goodbye.

"Nosy-ass bitch," she mutters.

Part me wants to tell her it's a detective's job to be a nosy-ass bitch, but part of me agrees. There's something about Detective Huld that rubs me the wrong way, and I can't put my finger on it. Why is she trying to catch us in lies? What does she think we could possibly have to do with a murder? And even if we'd somehow, inexplicably murdered that woman, why would we have called the police ourselves?

"Come on," says Nora, shoving her door open. "We're so late."

CHAPTER 11

As we step inside Midnight Alchemy, the sweet, chalky scent of incense fills my nostrils. The walls are draped with tapestries, the ceiling is painted night-sky blue with silver stars, and antique lanterns flicker on the tables and shelves. Quiet new-age music floats out of the speakers by the counter, where Ione is explaining different sets of oracle decks to an older woman. She's wearing a hand-knit sweater and a purple sugilite crystal necklace today.

"Mazzy, Nora," she says, tucking a strand of curly, chin-length red hair behind her ear. "I'm so sorry, but I just got a message from Jade that she can't make it in today."

My heart sinks. Jade is the medium we had an appointment with.

"Her sister is sick, and she had to fly out to New Mexico this afternoon," says Ione. "She won't be back until next week."

"Is there someone else we can see?" I ask.

Ione shakes her head. "I'm very picky about who I hire for that kind of work, and there's nobody else who could come in on such short notice. But I'll be happy to reschedule you for next week if you'd like? With a discount for the inconvenience, of course."

"I don't want to wait until next week," mutters Nora, loud enough for only me to hear. "May needs us now."

"We'll think about it," I say, tugging Nora toward the herb section at the back of the store. Ione gives us an apologetic smile and resumes her conversation with the older woman.

"Let's just contact her ourselves," says Nora.

I scrub my hands over my face. "Listen, I get how important this is to you." She opens her mouth to interrupt, but I talk over her. "And I'm not saying no, exactly, but every time I think about just reaching out into the ether, to someone we don't know, my intuition starts telling me it's a bad idea."

Nora's mouth snaps shut. She can't argue with intuition. It's got nothing to do with books or rules.

"There might be a safe way for us to do this on our own," I say, thinking of Elliot's question about crystal balls. "What if we searched for answers without asking May directly?"

"How, though?" Nora chews her lip, dubious.

"Scrying," I say, picking up an antique silver compact mirror from a table. We've dabbled in scrying before, usually by looking into the reflection of a bowl of water under moonlight or candlelight. I've got a book at home about the practice, and it seems like a much safer option. We'd just be using it like a window to see things, not to actually invite May's spirit in—or any other spirit that happened to hear our invitation.

"That might work." Nora checks the price on the back of the mirror and winces. "How much money do you have?"

"Like fourteen dollars for the rest of the week," I say. "We'll have to explain to May that we're on a budget."

"I'm sure she'll understand," says a raspy voice behind us.

Startled, I whirl around. It's Tina, one of the shop's regulars who seems to practically live here but never buys anything.

"So you're trying to find out more about her too, eh?" Tina's teal windbreaker crinkles as she folds her arms over her narrow chest. I've never been able to figure out how old Tina is. She might be in her fifties, or she might be in her thirties and just lived a really hard life. Her burgundy hair is pulled up in a messy bun, with half of it escaped and wafting around her neck.

"I mean, not really." I throw a glance at Nora, who is browsing the herbs and pretending not to hear us.

"Did you hear she was missing her hands?" says Tina. "And her teeth?"

"So they couldn't ID the body, right?" I say, and Tina leans in close. Her breath smells like wintergreen and cigarettes.

"They can test people's DNA nowadays. So why bother?" In true Massachusetts style, Tina drops the R off the end of the word. "If you ask me, she got murdered in a ritual."

"What kind of ritual?" Nora's at my elbow now, still holding the mirror.

Tina coughs, wet and crackling. "I've got a few theories."

I widen my eyes at Nora. Once, I made the mistake of asking for Tina's opinion on crystal pendulums, and it devolved into a twenty-minute rant about how the government has been secretly collecting magnetic dust from space and adding it to the public drinking water so we'll all become more receptive to the subliminal messages they beam at us from their satellites.

"Do you have any theories about who the woman is?" Nora asks.

"No, but I bet I know who killed her," says Tina.

"Who?" I should keep my mouth shut, but I can't help it.

Tina glances in Ione's direction and lowers her voice. "Have you ever heard of the Hand of Nephthys?"

Nora and I both step closer to shield our conversation from being heard.

"It's a secret group," continues Tina. "Named after one of the Egyptian goddesses of death. They've been practicing magic around the Cape for decades. It's dark sea magic. Baneful stuff. Dangerous stuff. Stuff that allegedly"—she peers over my shoulder to make sure Ione isn't listening—"involves necromancy and human sacrifice."

My scalp starts to prickle. "Why do you think they're linked to May?"

"Couple of reasons," says Tina. "First of all, they're called the *Hand* of Nephthys, right? And her hands are gone."

"Do you really think it'd be that obvious?" I ask, but Nora cuts in.

"Ooh, I bet you're right. And w—uh, the cops found her on a beach, which could fit with the whole sea magic thing."

"Her heart was missing too," says Tina. "And that sounds like something the Hand of Nephthys would do to their victims."

"How do you know about her heart?" I ask. "It wasn't mentioned in any of the news articles I saw." And we didn't see any evidence of it, although I'm not going to tell Tina we found May's body.

Tina shrugs. "I hear things through the grapevine."

This sounds just like all of her other wild theories, but Nora's eyes are gleaming in a way that makes me nervous.

"How can we find out more about them?" she asks.

"That I can't help you with," says Tina. "I've been told, 'You don't find the Hand of Nephthys. They find you.'"

Goose bumps wash up my arms.

"But they'd never be interested in somebody like me or you." Tina sounds almost rueful. "From what I've heard, they're only interested in . . . unique types of people, whatever that means."

Unique types of people who are into murder, apparently. I wonder how accurate her sources are about this group and about the woman's heart being removed.

"Usually, nobody finds the bodies of the Hand of Nephthys's victims," says Tina. "But something must have recently changed."

Nora and I lock eyes. Something like a spell to unearth hidden entities, conducted on a beach under a full moon. Maybe Tina's theories aren't so wild after all.

"Do you think—" Nora starts to say, but Tina makes a sharp cutting motion with her hand and widens her eyes. Ione is heading our way. The oracle deck woman is gone.

We're all silent for a moment, trying to decide whether to include Ione in this strange conversation about secret groups that might be conducting ritual murders and whether we might have just found one of their victims. But that's basically the embodiment of "over our heads," and I strongly doubt she'd approve of me and Nora getting involved. The prickling sensation in my scalp has crawled down my neck and shoulders, and I'm filled with a jittery sense of foreboding.

"Mazzy, the Irish folk magic book you ordered just came in," says Ione.

"Oh . . . uh, great!" I say, my voice slightly too high. "Can't wait to read it."

Tina slides away to look at incense; I take the compact mirror from Nora and set it back on the table. "Let's use something we already have," I say.

As we pick up my book and pay for some herbs and a package of divination-blend incense, my mind is racing. A dark, magical, murderous group called the Hand of Nephthys. A body washed up on a beach, missing its hands and teeth—and possibly its heart. A spell to reveal hidden things, and a dead woman revealed. A spirit who might be reaching out to Nora and me, asking for help. It's possible that this is all just a trauma reaction, combined with Tina's paranoid ramblings, but my intuition is positively screaming at me that there's something here. Something big. It's time to start asking questions, no matter what the answers might be.

CHAPTER 12

"Will you stop looking at that damn book?" Nora sits on the braided rug in her bedroom, setting up her altar for our scrying ritual. The low table is draped with a black cloth printed with silver moons in progressive phases. A square wood-framed mirror we found in Nora's attic sits in its center.

"Okay, okay." I shut the scrying book we picked up at my house, satisfied that I've got the basics down, plus several ways to keep this ritual safe. As Nora sets a ring of purple and black charm candles around the mirror, I peruse her crystal collection, then add smoky quartz, obsidian, black tourmaline, and selenite to the four corners of the mirror for protection. The black candles should also help.

My eye keeps getting drawn to an oil painting on the wall. It's one of Elliot's, a dreamy haze of blues and grays. In it, Nora and I stand holding hands, knee-deep in a stormy sea, and the wind is blowing my long hair in an exaggerated, twisty curtain behind the two of us. Tucked in the strands of it are tiny, glowing periwinkle shells and stars. It wasn't intended to be a gift for Nora, but as soon as she saw it at Elliot's house, she begged him to give it to her, and he did. I wish I'd been the one to ask for it.

"Ugh, this mirror still reeks," says Nora.

Not wanting to take any chances with a secondhand object, I washed it three times in a mixture of vinegar and cleansing herbs that my book recommended.

"You won't notice the smell once we light the incense," I say.

Nora grumbles something about how we're not making salad dressing, but I choose to ignore it.

"You don't think Tina made all that stuff up about the Hand of Nephthys, do you?" I say.

After we got back to Nora's house, I googled every possible combination of "Hand of Nephthys secret group magic witchcraft Cape Cod" I could think of, with not a single useful hit.

"Who even knows with Tina," says Nora. "But someone murdered May and cut off her hands. I definitely think we should look into it."

"Let's see if our scrying shows any overlaps with Tina's story." I sprinkle mugwort around the mirror to help with visions and clairvoyance, and black salt for another level of protection. Already, the air feels static-charged. We turn off our phones, Nora switches off the lights, and I shiver as darkness washes around us. She sprinkles sea salt in a clockwise direction around the candles, then lights them. I light a stick of divination incense and also run it clockwise, letting the curling smoke fill and cleanse the space.

As we begin to speak, one of the purple candles flickers and gutters, and I think it's about to go out, but then it flares high. Nora's hand closes around my wrist, and we both watch silently. It's not the first time a candle has done weird things during a ritual, but it's an interesting sign. A cool gust of air whispers around us. In the edges of the mirror, the bright candle flames waver and warp, and I soften my gaze, letting my eyes unfocus. The sweet smoke floods my nostrils, anise and sandalwood and mace, and I start to feel like I'm floating.

The room around me fades out as the candle flames bend inward, and each reflection becomes a dancing person in a long, dark cloak. Shadows skim their twisting bodies, and my heartbeat speeds up as the scene starts to unfold around me. I've never seen anything this clearly when scrying before, and I wonder faintly if I should make it stop. It's too real—it shouldn't be this vivid, but I'm so mesmerized, so enthralled. Nora's grip on my wrist tightens, and I wonder if she's seeing the same thing, but I don't want to speak and break whatever magic is at work.

The salty scent of the sea floods my nostrils. Nine hooded figures appear, dancing on a sandbar under the moonlight. The sand is soft and wet under my feet, and the air smells of smoke and brine, herbs and sweat. And faintly, underneath it all, something weedy and rotten. It turns my stomach.

Then, somehow, flames are licking across the tide pools all around us. The fire drifts across the sand and crawls up the robe of the person across from me, but they keep dancing, oblivious and seemingly in no pain. The robe of the person beside them catches fire, then the next one and the next, the flames leaping across the narrow gaps. Black smoke billows into the starry sky as the hooded figures begin to sing.

I know this song. *I know this song.*

One figure steps into the center of the circle, and it's only then that I notice the woman sprawled on the ground. She wears a long, dark dress, and her head is wrapped in white cloth. She's lying so still, I can't tell if she's dead or alive, but the shape of her body makes me think of May.

This is all connected. Nora wasn't being overdramatic. I want to scream, I want to break the circle, I want to run away, I want to save that woman. But I'm not in my body anymore—I'm seeing through the eyes of someone else, existing in their bones, and I can only watch, horror-struck, as the hooded figure kneels beside the woman and unbuttons the neck of her dress. The dancers move faster, and I'm moving with them, swirling and dipping, our flaming robes a blur. The figure in the center pulls a dagger from their robe. As they lift it over their head, the curved, silver blade glints in the moonlight.

"Girls?"

I jolt, and Nora shrieks. Light floods in from the hall. Nora's mom is standing in the doorway.

"Am I interrupting something?" She takes in the altar, the candles, the two of us sitting here holding hands, and her mouth twists in a wry smile. Nora's mother thinks our fascination with witchcraft is a silly little phase. My mom tries to be respectful about it, but I know she feels the same way.

"Yes," snaps Nora. "Can you please knock before you come barging in here?"

My heart is hammering. I don't understand what I just saw—or how. And it was more than just seeing. I heard the voices, I felt the cold, I smelled the smoke and salt and sweat. I, Mazzy Carlin, the person who secretly scoffs at her best friend for saying she can sense people's essences, just stepped inside what I can only assume was someone else's memory.

Over all these years, as Nora and I worked to expand our practice, to learn and strengthen our abilities, I've always had solid expectations of what might be possible, what we might achieve. Tarot has taught me about predicting, seeing, finding the hidden connections between unrelated objects and events. And lately, Nora and I have been moderately successful with our smaller spells, the ones I think of as metaphysical nudges. Like the time we wrote Kaitlynne Donner's name on a scrap of paper and stuck it in a glass of water in Nora's freezer, and she almost immediately stopped telling everyone that we were in a Satanic cult and drank blood.

But none of the expectations I've had about our practice have come anywhere close to watching a literal scenario play out through someone else's eyes. Ever since that night on Mayflower Beach, almost everything I thought I knew about magic has been proven wrong, and I wish I understood what happened, what changed. That song, *that song* is still looping in my brain, and I feel like I might burst into a million pieces.

Nora's mom clears her throat. "Mazzy, your mom just called to see if you were here. She's been texting you, but you haven't answered."

"I turned off my phone." In a daze, I pick it up from Nora's unmade bed. As the phone powers back on, images from that vision—or dream, or whatever it was—keep flashing back. The cold, smoky air. The flaming robes swishing across the sand. How did they not burn themselves? How did they set water on fire? What was I doing there? *Who* was I?

Three text messages from my mom pop up on my screen.

> Where are you?
>
> You said you'd be home for dinner.
>
> Did you turn off your tracking?

I shut off my location tracking weeks ago because I'm not a little kid and she doesn't need to know where I am every second of every day. I didn't tell her because I didn't feel like fighting about it. With a heavy sigh, I text her back.

at Nora's home soon sorry

As soon as Nora's mom leaves, I sit back down on the floor.

"What did you see?" I ask.

Nora's face is chalk-pale, and her eyes are watery. "Nothing. Did you see anything?"

"I saw a group of people dancing on a sandbar at night," I say. "They were performing a ritual, and the water and their robes were on fire. Nora, I . . . I think I may have just seen the Hand of Nephthys. I think Tina was right, which is just . . ." I mime my head exploding.

"Oh my God," says Nora. "Was May there?"

"There was a woman lying in the sand, and she had a dress just like May's, but her face was covered," I say. "One of the people was holding up a dagger, like maybe they were about to kill her—but then your mom came in."

"You really saw all of that?" There's a slight edge of jealousy to Nora's voice.

"Trust me, I wish I hadn't," I say. "I think you're right about May, though. About everything."

She cocks her head. "You didn't believe me before?"

"No, I did." I shake my head, wipe the sweat off my upper lip. "I just didn't realize how serious it was. How connected it all is. Those people in my vision were singing that same exact same song you sang in your sleep the other night."

Nora huffs. "I told you that was May's voice, not mine. You need to trust me more."

"Did you not see anything at all?" I ask.

Nora chews her lip. "No, but she was whispering to me. I could literally feel her breath in my ear."

I cringe at the thought of a ghost's mouth. Would it be rotten and festering? Or would it be a black void inside?

"What did she say?" I ask.

"It's hard to understand her," says Nora. "She speaks in fragments and pieces of thoughts, like a poem or a riddle. I asked her who killed her, but she just kept repeating, 'Couldn't see.'"

"Her face was all bound up in cloth." Goose bumps flood across my arms. "They must have kidnapped her and covered her eyes so she couldn't see where they were taking her. I don't know if her hands were still attached, or if she was conscious. I . . . God, Nora, I think I almost saw May's murder."

Faint irritation flickers across Nora's face. "May also said something about needing to do this faster."

"What do you mean, faster?" I ask, hugging my arms around my knees to fend off the lingering cold. "We're doing our best with a very small amount of information. Can't she give us a few more clues if she needs help?"

"I don't think she can. She's not fully human anymore, you know? But I can tell she's really upset. She said we need to hurry because *someone* already knows."

My throat goes tight. "Who?"

"Maybe the Hand of Nephthys?" Nora shrugs. "But who actually knows, because my stupid mom came in, and now May's gone. I can't feel her anymore."

81

"Do you want to try the ritual again?" As soon as the words are out, my phone starts buzzing. It's my mom again, and it's seven thirty, half an hour past dinnertime. She's going to kill me if I don't leave in the next two seconds.

"Listen." I take Nora's frigid hands in mine. "Tomorrow, after school, we'll do this ritual again. We can also do some more digging on the Hand of Nephthys. God, can you believe Tina was actually telling the truth?"

"I actually can." Nora's jaw is tight. "But I have color guard practice after school. I can't miss it."

"Then we'll go after that. Just promise me you won't do anything by yourself before then, okay?"

Her gaze slides away, and I squeeze her hands hard. "I mean it. It's a really bad idea. We'll figure everything out tomorrow. Together. I'll call you later, okay?"

"Okay," she says. "Love you, Mazz."

I hug her. "Love you too."

Even through a thick sweater, Nora's body is freezing.

CHAPTER 13

"It really isn't too much to ask for you to call if you're going to be late." My mom gestures to the messy kitchen, the pots on the stove. "I had to give Henry scrambled eggs and put him to bed. The carbonara sauce is completely congealed. I spent eight hours unpacking boxes at the store today, and I'm not running a restaurant on top of that."

It's true. It's all true. How can it possibly be?

"Sorry," I say, rubbing my eyes and trying to focus on her words instead of my whirling thoughts. "You didn't need to wait for me."

"Nora's mother said you were doing some kind of mystical . . . thing." She opens the refrigerator and ponders the contents. "Did you take the lemon that was in here?"

"Yeah. Sorry." I pull forks and knives from the drawer and start setting the table as a peace offering.

The spirit of a murdered woman is talking to my best friend, and now I'm having visions.

"How many times do I have to tell you not to waste food on nonsense like that?" My mom takes out the milk. "I had to put lime in the carbonara, and it's really weird now, on top of being congealed."

"Sorry." I want to tell her that protective spells aren't nonsense, but I'm so overwhelmed, so drained from that unsettling, impossible ritual, I don't have the energy to start another fight. It still stings every time she says something like that, though. I know she thinks it's just a phase, but she could at least try not to be so obviously dismissive.

My mom pours a glug of milk into the pasta. "Listen, I get it. You're trying to process what happened. It was absolutely terrible, and I can't begin to imagine how you and Nora feel. But I'm going to make some calls tomorrow, because I'd like you to speak to a therapist instead of trying to do magic and harping on that poor dead woman."

"We're not harping." My shoulders hunch up. "We're just trying to figure some stuff out."

If she had any idea what we're actually trying to figure out, she'd probably have a heart attack. Or, more likely, not believe us at all. Sometimes it feels like we're living in two completely different realities. Lately, even more than usual.

"Whatever it is, you need to stop." She jabs a spoon into the pot, spattering milky sauce onto the stovetop. "This isn't healthy. Let the police do their job. One of the detectives called me today, and it sounds like they're working really hard on this case."

I freeze. "Was it Detective Huld?"

My mom tastes the sauce again and frowns. "Yes. She wanted to know if I had any idea why you brought candles to the beach, and whether you and Nora practice witchcraft."

"What the—" I stop myself. Why is Detective Huld so interested in witchcraft all of a sudden? "What did you tell her?"

"I said you and Nora dabbled in that stuff, and that you were probably doing one of your little magic spells under the full moon."

It's so dismissive, so reductive, so embarrassing; I want to scream. Last time I checked, *dabbling* with *little magic spells* didn't mean you had conversations with the dead and full-blown visions of shadowy figures conducting murderous rituals.

"What did she say?" I ask.

"She said she figured it was something like that. Apparently, witchcraft is all the rage among teens these days."

I roll my eyes. "Did she ask you any other questions?"

"Not really." My mother sighs and pokes our dinner again with her wooden spoon. "This'll have to be good enough. Grab some plates, will you?"

Even though the food is borderline inedible and weirdly limey, I inhale it. It's like that vision has sapped all my energy, hollowed me out. I can't believe my brain is capable of transporting me to another time and place. Nora's constantly bragging about her own psychic abilities, but I always thought of myself as someone who just had really strong intuition. This new power—or capacity or whatever it is—is so far beyond anything I could have imagined, and I don't understand what's changed to make it possible.

"Have you been talking to your brother about any of this stuff?" My mom pushes away her half-eaten pasta.

"No," I say. "Why would I do that?"

"He said something about a lady in a long dress. And this afternoon, he made this."

She pulls a sheet of rumpled paper from a stack of bills and paperwork and hands it to me. My stomach drops to somewhere around my knees.

Henry's drawing is scrawled in heavy crayon. Two stick figures stand in the middle of the page holding hands. The person on the right is also holding a curvy, brown object, and the one on the left is wearing a gray dress. Her hair is long and stringy, and her black slash of a smile extends out one side of her head. The person on the right is smiling too, but black specks trail down from their eyes. They might be tears.

I set the drawing down before my mom sees it shaking in my hands. Drawing one picture of a strange lady is creepy and random. Drawing two is intentional.

"Is this Henry?" I say, pointing to the person on the right.

"I think it's you." She points to the brown object at the end of the person's way-too-long arm. "That looks like your cello."

My tongue is sandpaper in my mouth. Why does Henry think May and I are friends? And how did he know about the gray dress?

"He drew that same woman yesterday and said she's his friend," I say, "but I'm pretty sure she just looked like somebody he saw on TV."

Actually, I'm less and less sure of that by the second.

Please don't let her be talking to Henry too, I think. But he already told me that she did. I bite the ragged edge of my thumbnail.

"I'm getting a migraine." My mom sets her elbows on the counter and rubs her temples. "Mazzy, I don't want you dragging him into this nonsense."

"I'm not—"

"He's four years old," she interrupts. "His little brain is still developing. You could be doing serious harm by making him believe in ghosts."

"I swear I'm not," I say. The last thing I want is for my little brother to get caught up in any of this. But there's no reason for May to involve a preschooler in her murder investigation. Maybe he's just imagining her based on snippets he's overheard.

"I don't want to hear any more about spirits or ghosts or any of that stuff." My mom starts gathering up the dishes. "From you or from Henry. Do you understand?"

"Yeah." I grab my unfinished salad before she can take the bowl. It's not like I wanted to tell her about any of this stuff anyway. She'd just laugh at our witchy little nonsense. Still, I can't stop wincing every time I look at that drawing. I'd like to burn it.

"I'm not going to mention this to your dad," she says, piling everything in the sink. "He's got enough on his plate right now."

And if we stress him out too much, he might start drinking again. I know that's what she's thinking, even if she doesn't flat-out say it. Guilt pinches my insides, even though none of this is technically my fault.

"You can clean up," my mom says, gesturing to the stove. "And if you come home late again without calling, you're going to start losing privileges."

I can't stop the snort that flies out of my nose. Losing privileges, like I'm four years old too. Like that's the biggest of my worries right now.

"And cut the attitude." She takes her phone and heads for her room, leaving me with the kitchen mess and my anxious, tangled thoughts.

CHAPTER 14

In my bedroom, I sew four small drawstring bags out of purple fabric. Following a recipe from one of my oldest books, I add a pinch of black salt, blessed thistle, valerian, yarrow, and wood betony to each, then tuck a star anise and a couple of amethyst chips on top. Protective elements, plus a little something for good energy. After whispering a short blessing over each bag, I cinch them shut and put two in my backpack. The third one I slip under my pillow, and the fourth I take down the hall to Henry's room.

I linger in his doorway, making sure there are no ghostly women hiding in shadowed corners, but it's just Henry, snoring faintly in the glow of his star-shaped night-light. Quickly, I tiptoe to his bed and tuck the cloth bag underneath his mattress where no one will find it. He's probably overhearing random conversations and imagining things, but it's better to be safe than sorry. A spirit looking for help has no good reason to talk to a four-year-old.

I'm not going to bother sneaking one of these protection charms into my parents' room. If my mom ever found it, I'd never hear the end of it. Plus, I don't think May is remotely interested in either of them. I can just imagine my mom giving her a long lecture about stopping her ghostly nonsense and working on being more responsible.

My phone pings as I'm heading back to my room.

> Nora: Whoa look at this

Underneath is a link that takes me to an online forum called Mystical Mysteries. I scoff at the cheesy name, but as I scroll down through the thread, my breath catches.

> Black.cat57: Does anybody know anything about the Hand of Nepthis? Apparently it's a secret magickal society based somewhere on Cape Cod?

> Rowan_Tree: It's spelled Nephthys, and yeah, I've heard a few things.

> Black.cat57: @Rowan_Tree Are you willing to share what you've heard? DM is fine if you'd prefer.

> CrystalMama: The HoN are scary af. I wouldn't mess with them or even ask questions if I were you!

> *~moongoddess~*: allegedly the members of the HoN fake their own deaths before joining so they're completely untraceable. that's seriously metal.

> Black.cat57: @*~moongoddess~* I've heard their rituals involve human sacrifice.

My skin starts to prickle all over. I might have seen one of those sacrifices if Nora's mother hadn't interrupted. Although the more I think about it, the more I'm glad she did.

LisaLotus: I've heard that about the sacrifices too. A couple of years ago, five homeless people went missing on Cape Cod during the week of a total lunar eclipse. It wasn't really in the news because who cares about the homeless (/sarcasm) but my aunt works at a shelter and she told me all about it. I've heard that the HoN prey on people at the fringes of society, so nobody notices when they disappear.

Black.cat57: I've also heard that the members all live separately so no one can track them, and they only gather a few nights a year for their deadly rituals.

Black.cat57: @Rowan_Tree, I DMed you.

ProfessorTom: Nephthys, or Nebet-Het, is the lesser-known sister of Isis in Egyptian mythology. She slept with her sister's husband, Osiris, and then gave birth to Anubis. She's mentioned in the ancient Egyptian *Book of the Dead*, more specifically in *The Lamentations of Isis and Nephthys*. She was considered a friend and protector of the dead, bringing recently deceased souls to the afterlife and looking after them for eternity.

From what I've heard, the HoN believe they're doing Nephthys's work, ushering souls to the afterlife. But their goal is to figure out how to reverse that process, bringing them back, as well. Not sure if they've succeeded, but I'd steer clear of them if they're still in the experimental phase.

CrystalMama: I'd steer clear of them even if they weren't in the experimental phase! I've also heard that they target runaways, kids who are in trouble and looking to fly under the radar.

Rowan_Tree: Dead is way under the radar.

CrystalMama: Not funny.

Black.cat57: Worshiping an ancient Egyptian deity sounds like Kemetism. Are they like kemetic extremists or something?

LisaLotus: Please don't besmirch Kemetism like that. We would never associate with a group that performs ritual murder. Do some research and look up the Laws of Ma'at.

The thread ends, and I hit the call button. Nora picks up on the first ring.

"Did you read it?" she asks.

"Yeah," I say. "Sounds like they're even worse than we thought. Specifically targeting unhoused people and runaways?"

"Maybe May was homeless, and that's why we can't find anything about her going missing."

"She was definitely too old to be a teenage runaway," I say. "But my vision lines up with the kidnapping thing, with her blindfolded like that."

"Hang on," says Nora. "I'm going to make an account on this forum."

There's a scuffling sound, and some muttering. I put Nora on speaker and open the forum page again. A few seconds later, I hit refresh and a new message pops up.

May_be (New member): Has anyone heard of them cutting off people's hands in their rituals?

"The last message was two months ago," I say. "They're probably not going to write back straight away."

"True," says Nora, but we refresh our screens anyway.

"I almost forgot," I say. "Did Detective Huld call your mom?"

"What?" says Nora. "No."

"She called mine earlier today and asked why we had that candle at Mayflower and whether we practiced witchcraft."

"Seriously?" says Nora. "Who the heck cares if we did a ritual at the beach? What does that have to do with their investigation?"

"Right?" I say. "Why is she so obsessed with that?"

"She did have that rune necklace. So maybe she knows a thing or two about witchcraft."

"It might not have been a rune. And I can't picture a cop being into that stuff," I say, tapping refresh again. "The whole thing is just so weird. I wish I knew what she was after."

"Yeah," Nora says, and we both fade into silence. The short-lived burst of energy from my mom's lumpy carbonara is wearing off, and my eyelids keep drooping lower and lower. My brain is struggling to work through everything I've seen and learned today. Still, there's no response to our message, and my clock reads twelve fifteen. I have to get up in less than six hours.

"That's enough waiting for me," I say. "I'm going to bed."

No answer.

"Nora?" I say, louder this time. "Did you fall asleep?"

"Huh?" There's scuffling in the background. "No, I was brushing my teeth."

"I'll talk to you tomorrow," I say. "Text me if you hear anything, okay?"

"You know I will."

The house is dark now, and everything is silent except for the wind blowing outside and tree branches occasionally clacking against the roof. It's hard not to imagine they're the tapping fingernails of a spirit who's trying to come in.

Before getting in bed, I sprinkle black salt on the thresholds of all the doors, whisper a protective spell for the house, and set black tourmaline crystals on my windowsill and Henry's. I should have done this two days ago, back when May was speaking through Nora in my bed, but I didn't believe what was happening. I hope I'm not too late. I hope Henry really was imagining his conversations with May, as unlikely as that seems now.

My parents are both asleep, which prevents them from yelling at me for leaving the hall light on, so I do. I leave my door cracked open, and the long triangle of gold light stretching across the floor makes me feel one tiny degree safer. I get out my anxiety jar and give it a good, long shake before climbing into bed.

As I'm drifting off, I refresh the Mystical Mysteries site one more time. There are no replies to our message, but Nora has added another question.

May_be (New member): *Hypothetically* if someone were interested in joining the HoN, how would they go about doing that?

CHAPTER 15

The next day after physics, I catch Elliot up on all the new developments: Tina's story at Midnight Alchemy, the forum we found about the Hand of Nephthys, Detective Huld's unexpected questions, and our ominous scrying ritual.

"I realize I'm about to sound just like Nora," I say. "But that vision I had was one hundred percent real. It was like I was fully transported to a different place. I could hear things, feel things, *smell* things."

Elliot holds the door open for me as we head out to the parking lot. "Are you sure you weren't burning some bad combination of herbs that made you hallucinate?"

"We only burned incense," I say. "That's not going to give anybody a hallucination."

"Maybe you fell asleep and dreamed it?" he says. "Like some kind of sudden-onset narcolepsy brought on by . . . uh, frankincense or myrrh or whatever you were burning?"

"Listen." I stop at the edge of the lot. "I know it's hard to believe. I didn't necessarily believe Nora when this all started. You know how she gets."

"I didn't believe her either, but you've never gotten carried away like she does." Elliot's looking everywhere right now except my face, and I feel like I'm somehow letting him down, no longer being the rational one, but I can't pretend this isn't happening.

"That's why you have to trust what I'm telling you now." My cheeks are burning. He probably thinks I'm insane.

"Okay," he says, finally meeting my gaze. "So tell me what you think, and I'll try."

"I think May's spirit is real," I say. "I think she was kidnapped and then got murdered in some creepy ritual—most likely by the Hand of Nephthys—and she's asking us to help her. Why she thinks that we, of all people, can help her is unclear. And as for what we're supposed to do, I have absolutely no clue."

Elliot laughs. "That makes two of us."

"I know this sounds impossible, and I get it if you can't believe everything right away." I scrub my hands over my cheeks, wishing I could wipe the hot flush off. "I definitely didn't. But can you just try to be open to the possibility?"

He tips his head like he can almost sense the change that's humming around inside me. His gray eyes search my face, and there's something so unbearable yet so intoxicating about this. I want to hide, but I also never want him to stop looking at me.

"I made you something," he says abruptly, stepping back and unzipping his backpack.

This isn't the first thing Elliot's ever made for me, but knowing he's been thinking about me feels different now. My chest goes warm as he hands me a plum-size ceramic figurine, green and glossy. It looks like a cross between a troll and a frog, with squatting legs, a round belly, and a long, curly beard. It's wearing a tiny pair of overalls, and one of its buggy eyes is winking. It's exactly my style of whimsical and weird.

"I love it," I say, rubbing my thumb over the frog-troll's smooth little head. "Thank you."

"It's an incense holder," says Elliot. "For non-hallucinogenic incense, obviously. See the hole?"

On the ceramic frog-troll's chest, beside a tiny carved M, there's a hole that's just the right size for a stick of incense. Elliot's always noticed little things, but this proof of his thoughtfulness hits me especially hard.

Without thinking, I throw my arms around him. He tenses, and I think maybe this was a bad idea because Elliot and I don't really hug, but then he sinks into it with something like a sigh. His arms wrap around my waist and my face is so close to his bare neck. His body is lean and warm, and I just want to soak in the clay-dust scent of him forever.

But eventually, we do have to let go, and then I don't really know what to say, but it occurs to me that I also made something for him.

"Here," I say, pulling one of the protection bags from my backpack. "I know you're still working on believing, you know, everything, but this is a charm to keep you safe—well, hopefully *safer*, anyway. Don't open it; just keep it with you, okay?"

He tucks the sachet into his coat's breast pocket. "I feel safer already. Where is Nora, anyway?"

He's asking about her because she's our friend and it's a logical thing to wonder about. I don't have to read any more into that. I really don't.

"She has practice," I say, "and then we're going to her house to do some more research on the Hand of Nephthys. If people are talking about it on one forum, there has to be more information out there. We might do another ritual too."

I pull my phone out, and there's a single text from her, from about an hour ago.

> Mazzy

I tap out a reply:

> Nora

There's no immediate answer, which isn't surprising because practice will have already started by now.

"Do you want to come to Nora's later?" I ask Elliot.

"Yeah, sure." He rubs the back of his neck, and the silence stretches out between us.

"What are you doing in the meantime?" he says finally.

"I was planning to go home for a while and then come back to pick her up," I say. "Maybe start my homework or practice cello."

In truth, I can't decide if I want to play my cello or never touch it again.

"Do you want to hang out?" Elliot asks.

My mouth drops open, and it's possible I've forgotten how to speak English. I can count on one hand the number of times Elliot and I have hung out without Nora.

"Uh . . . yeah." This isn't usual. This is potentially huge. "What do you want to do?"

The sunlight glinting in his steel-colored eyes is so utterly distracting. "Want to get a coffee?" he asks. "Are you hungry?"

"I am, but I'm almost out of money," I say. "We could go to my house and make something to eat?"

Oh God, I've just invited him to my house. Where nobody else is home. I remind myself that nothing will happen, that there's still the whole issue of him liking my best friend. But he's still looking at me with that deeply curious expression, and if I weren't so paranoid that I'm imagining all of this, I'd wonder if something is already happening.

"Okay," he says.

Then, somehow, we're both walking to my car like I'm not about to leap out of my own skin.

As I turn the key in the ignition, music blares out of the speakers at full volume. Elliot and I reach for the dial at the same time. A static shock zaps us both, and I start to laugh.

"What?" Elliot's eyes are dancing, and I'm not imagining how elated he looks. Something is different, and he knows it too.

"I just . . . nothing." I turn the music back up and hit the gas.

~ ~ ~

We're pulling onto my road when my phone rings. It's Nora.

I tap the hands-free button. "Hey, what's up?"

Wind gusts against her phone speaker, filling my car with a loud rushing. I hear her voice in the background, but I can't make out any words. Elliot leans toward the speaker, straining to listen.

"Nora?" I say. "Can you hear me?"

More wind, more rustling, and I wonder if she butt-dialed me from practice, but I don't hear any band instruments or people talking.

"Hello?" I try again. "Are you there?"

"Mazzy." Her voice is shaky and broken, like she's crying. "Can you hear me?"

"Yeah," I say. "What's going on?"

Another gust of wind, and what might be a sob.

"I'm at Scargo Lake," she says.

"What?" I pull into my driveway but leave the car running. "Why are you there? Don't you have practice?"

"I didn't go," she says. "I'm at the lake. Mazzy, I—" Her voice breaks, and then the line goes quiet and I think I've lost her.

"I found another body," she whispers.

CHAPTER 16

Scargo Tower sits on top of a hill overlooking a lake and the wide ocean beyond. I haven't been here in years, and the round cobblestone structure is much smaller than I remember, only about thirty feet tall. When I was a kid, this felt like the top of the world. Now it just reminds me of my least favorite tarot card, a warning of collapse. At least this tower isn't on fire like it is in my decks, and nobody's falling out of the windows. Not yet, anyway. Considering the way this week is going, nothing would surprise me.

The parking lot is empty, and ominous clouds loom overhead. Elliot and I peer over the low fence that separates the lot from a steep, tree-filled embankment that leads to the lake. It's too far down to see Nora. I hope she's still there. My anxiety is ramping up to unbearable levels, making me dizzy.

"What is she even doing here?" says Elliot.

"I told you, May is talking to her." I swipe my hair out of my face, but the wind immediately throws it back. "Telling her to go places."

"I just . . . I don't know." Elliot kicks a pebble with his heavy black boot. "Do you think there's actually a body here?"

I press my lips together and nod. If there's one thing I'm certain of, it's that. Nora wouldn't lie about something so serious. We are in so deep over our heads right now.

"Hey, are you okay?" Elliot ducks to peer at my face.

"Not really," I say, swallowing hard. "Are you?"

He grimaces. "Maybe the second dead body won't be so bad. Now that we have . . . I don't know . . . experience?"

I try to laugh, but it comes out as a weird, high-pitched burst of sound. I'll never be ready to face another corpse. But it's Nora down there, and I'd face a hundred corpses if she needed help. I wanted to call the police on my way over, but she made me promise to wait until we got here and saw.

"You can wait up here and I'll go find her," Elliot offers, and his kindness makes me want to cry, but I shake my head.

"She needs me."

Not to mention, I don't want to stay up here all by myself. I pull my calf-length skirt up over my knees to clamber over the fence, and Elliot's gaze snags on my legs before he quickly looks away and climbs over too. Then we're scrambling and sliding in the dirt and leaves, grabbing at tree trunks and branches to slow our descent. There are so many other, easier ways to get down to the lake. I can't imagine why Nora chose this spot.

A whiplike tendril of thorns catches my ankle, and I yelp as I lose my balance. Elliot grabs my waist before I go tumbling down, and we both slide to a stop, breathing hard. His heart is thudding against my shoulder, and in some parallel universe where we weren't both covered in sweat and full of dread and about to find another corpse, this might've been my moment to tell him everything. But I'm too nauseous to even consider it.

The slope flattens out, and gray water gleams through the gaps in the trees.

"Nora?" I call. "Where are you?"

No answer.

Elliot gives a sharp whistle. "Hey, Nora!"

"I'm here," she calls, and we veer left, clambering over fallen logs and mossy stones. It's starting to rain, cold drizzle slipping inside the neck of my coat, and I just want to rewind time, go back to Saturday night. I'd come up with a better reason for not doing that spell at the beach. I'd drive Nora and Elliot to my house, and we'd have a movie marathon instead. Someone else would find the body, and none of us would be here now.

Just before the trees end, Elliot stops short, and I step on the heel of his boot. He's mumbling curses, and I don't want to look at what's ahead, but I do. On a narrow strip of sand beside the gray water, Nora kneels with her back to us. She's bending over what looks like a pile of rags. But I know what it really is.

The wind gusts, and the smell hits me, rotten and sweet, and I can't do this, I can't. I want to turn around and climb back up that hill, get in my car, drive away, and let the police deal with this.

But I can't just leave Nora here. With my hand pressed over my mouth and nose, I skirt around Elliot. She's humming quietly. It's a song we both know.

"Nora, hey." I edge closer. "We're here."

Her hands are tangled in the woman's long, blond hair, and I realize she's braiding a section of it. Elliot, who still hasn't moved from his spot, looks just as horrified as I am.

"I, uh—" I choke down the bile swimming up my throat. "I don't think you should be doing that."

102

"Doing what?" she murmurs, still twisting the filthy strands of hair.

"Touching her," I say. "The police will check the body for fingerprints, you know?"

"Oh, right." Nora lets go of the braid. "Oops."

"That's okay." I fight to keep my voice steady. "You probably can't get fingerprints on hair. Can you stand?"

It takes Nora a minute to notice I'm holding out my hand, but then she takes it and the tangled hair spills out of her lap as I pull her up. Snapping out of his own daze, Elliot hurries over to help.

"Are you all right?" I say.

Nora lets out a weird hiccup of a laugh. "I'm doing better than *she* is."

The dead woman gazes up at the sky with flat blue eyes. She's wearing a long, gray dress like May's. Her hands are gone too. Her teeth are still in her mouth, which should be reassuring, but isn't.

Nora whispers something I can't make out.

"Took her what?" Elliot's face is almost as pale as the dead woman's.

"Her heart," Nora mutters, picking up a stick. "Look."

She uses the stick to push aside the neckline of the dead woman's dress, revealing a puckered, stitched-up wound near the center of her white chest. I can't drag my eyes away from the wound. There's nothing surgical about those stitches, which are big and jagged and look like they were done with black sewing thread.

"Tina wasn't making that up either," I say.

"There's no blood," says Nora. "That means they did it after she died."

Elliot takes a big step backward. "Somebody's hunting these women down. Cutting them up."

"It's the Hand of Nephthys," I say, and his forehead creases.

"There has to be a rational explanation," he says. "Like a serial killer targeting women in the area."

"Or a bunch of serial killers who practice magic together," I say.

Elliot opens his mouth to respond, but his eyes cut to something across the lake. "Is somebody over there?"

"Where?" All I see on the opposite bank is trees and the occasional house, but there are thousands of hidden places in those woods. Shadows and hollows and holes where anyone could be hiding. Watching. Waiting.

"I thought I saw someone backing into the trees," says Elliot, and a full body shiver washes over me.

"Come on," I say to Nora. "Let's go back to the car."

Nora's shoulders hitch, but when she finally looks up, her face is composed, her eyes dry. "May's really happy that we found her."

"Great," Elliot mutters sarcastically, and I echo his sentiment. Tugging my coat tighter around me, I peer across the water, then down the shoreline and back up into the trees. I can't see anyone, but that doesn't mean there *isn't* anyone.

Elliot pulls out his phone, and as he leans over the body to take a photo, Nora grabs his arm.

"What are you doing?" she hisses.

"Just in case we need evidence," he says. "I don't trust anything about this situation."

"It's disrespectful," says Nora. "May doesn't like it."

I don't care what May thinks, but I keep that to myself. Plus, I agree with Elliot that we should document everything, especially with Detective Huld poking around, asking questions about us. I start to head back toward the hill, but Elliot and Nora just stand there, staring at the body. She's still clinging to his arm, and even though I know we're all dealing with a lot and I'm being unreasonable, my eyelid twitches.

"Guys?" I say. "Can we please go?"

Elliot glances down at Nora's hand like he's only just noticed it. His eyes snap to mine and I can't read his expression, but then she lets go and bends over the body.

"May your soul find peace," she murmurs, making an odd little sign of blessing.

And not start haunting us too, I think as we climb back up the hill.

CHAPTER 17

The three of us take the short flight of spiral stairs up to the top of Scargo Tower and stand there staring out at the vast, whitecapped ocean. I don't know what we're doing up here, but when we got to the top of the hill, we all just gravitated toward the tower instead of the car.

"How did you get here?" Elliot asks Nora.

"I took a cab," says Nora. "I left during sixth period."

"But why?" he says. "How did you know to come here? And why didn't you tell us you were leaving school?"

"Because May was screaming inside my head." Nora wipes her nose on her sleeve. "Literally screeching."

Dread seeps like cold mud into my stomach. This whole situation is spiraling. A range of emotions flickers across Elliot's face, and I know he's grappling with disbelief, but how else could Nora have known about a dead body out here in the middle of nowhere?

"I was just sitting there in English class, and all of a sudden, she started," says Nora. "At first, I thought someone was screaming out in the hall, but then I realized nobody else could hear it. It filled up my whole head, blocked everything out until I couldn't think straight. I went to the bathroom and texted you, Mazzy, but you didn't write back."

"I didn't see your message until after school," I say. "And I wrote back as soon as I could."

"Too late," murmurs Nora. "Way, way, way too . . ." She trails off and starts humming, and I never want to hear that god-awful song again in my life. Why, why, why didn't I check my phone between classes? I usually do, but I've been so preoccupied, so muddled lately. After fourth period, I walked face-first into an open locker door, and there's a bruise slowly darkening on my forehead.

"I'm really sorry." I pull her into a hug, and she sags against me as the wind throws my hair around us both.

"Is May still talking to you now?" Elliot asks.

Nora shakes her head. "She went quiet as soon as I found her sister. But I could feel that she was happy."

I think of the corpse's pale blond hair. It didn't look dyed. "They're sisters?"

"I think so. May was yelling and whispering and sometimes singing, and I couldn't make out any of the words except *Scargo Lake* and *my sister*." Nora sniffs. "I couldn't make it stop. I had to help her."

"That's weird if they're sisters," I say.

Elliot laughs. "Like any of this *isn't* weird."

"No, I mean—isn't it unusual for two adult sisters to disappear together?" I ask. "That's the kind of thing that gets big news coverage, but we haven't seen anything."

"Unless they were unhoused," says Nora. "Homeless people disappear all the time and it never makes the news."

"Even still, people would have noticed two sisters going missing," I say. "Something isn't adding up here."

"May definitely called that woman her sister," says Nora. "She said it multiple times."

"We can't tell Detective Huld about that, though," I say.

Nora jerks away like I just suggested we murder someone ourselves. "We can't tell Detective Huld anything!"

"Why?" I ask.

"I don't trust her," says Nora. "I keep thinking about that rune she wears and all the questions she's been asking about one measly candle. Why should it matter if we were practicing witchcraft on the beach? It shouldn't make any difference in a regular murder investigation. Are we even sure she's a real cop?"

"If she is, she'll be listed on the police website." Elliot taps his phone, and we wait in nervous, itchy silence while he searches. The frigid wind is like fingers in my hair, pulling and tugging and ripping.

"Is this her?" he asks. Filling the screen is a headshot of Detective Huld in front of a plain white background. Her hair is pulled back in the same pin-straight ponytail, and her mouth is set in a straight line. Even the photo of her sets my teeth on edge.

"Okay, so she's a cop," Nora says. "But she already suspects us of doing something sketchy at Mayflower, if not actually murdering May. Do you really want her to know we found another body in less than two days?"

She has a point. Detective Huld doesn't trust us either. The fact that we've just found another corpse might not be enough evidence to arrest us, but I don't want to find out.

"No," I say, "but we can't just leave the body lying there."

"And if there's a serial killer on the loose, we definitely need to tell the police," says Elliot.

"I know, I know," Nora says. "I'm not a complete monster. I just don't want to deal with Detective Huld, and even if we called the main police office, I bet they'd make us talk to her."

We lapse into worried silence again as a lopsided V of Canada geese traverses the wide gray sky. I keep irrationally thinking that the dead woman down by the lake must be cold. Her dress was wet and she didn't have a coat.

"What if we reported the body anonymously?" says Elliot.

I shake my head. "They'll be able to trace our phones."

"Does that old pay phone at Cumby's still work?" he asks.

I almost laugh, even though none of this is funny. "Have you ever used a pay phone before?"

"No, but I was just there the other day, and it's still on the wall outside," he says.

This is way too big of a problem for us to handle alone. But Nora is right that Detective Huld is suspicious, and there's no way the cops will believe that we just happened to find a second body. To be honest, even I'm starting to wonder if there are parts of Nora's story that she's not telling us.

Skin crawling with anxiety or intuition or both, I slide the phone back into my pocket.

CHAPTER 18

I park in an empty restaurant lot across the street from the convenience store, just in case there are security cameras outside. In the back seat, Elliot pulls up the hood of his coat.

"How much does it cost to call?" he asks.

"No idea." I rummage through the cup holder where I keep all my loose change. "Take four quarters, just to be safe. What are you going to tell them?"

"I'll say I was fishing at Scargo and I saw the body," says Elliot. "And then I'll hang up."

"Hmm," says Nora, who is braiding a red strip of her hair.

"Is that a good *hmm* or a bad *hmm*?" Elliot asks.

"It's neutral," she says. "May doesn't care what we tell the police. She only cares about her sister being found."

Elliot and I exchange an uncomfortable glance as he gets out of the car. His broad shoulders hunch as he tugs his hood lower and tries to make himself less obvious, but that's practically impossible for someone who's over six feet tall. Nora and I watch silently as he jogs across the road. The pay phone is on the outside wall of the building, a few yards from the entrance. He lifts the receiver and pushes coins into the slot, and I can't tell if it's working or not.

"I hate that May can get inside your head," I say.

Still braiding her hair, Nora shrugs. "She doesn't care if you hate it."

"It's getting worse, though," I say, fighting to keep my voice calm. "It was one thing when she was whispering or singing to you, but I think we can both agree that screaming inside someone's head to make them do stuff is crossing a line."

"Hmm," Nora says again in that infuriatingly vague tone, and I hate it. I want my best friend back. The funny, talkative, magnetic Nora who thinks she knows everything about witchcraft and is always dragging me along on weird adventures. Not the Nora who speaks with a ghost's tongue and runs away on her own to find dead bodies.

"I'm starting to wonder if May wasn't such a great person before she died," I say. "Not that she deserved to be murdered, obviously."

"It might just be that she communicates differently now that she's a spirit," says Nora. "She doesn't have the luxury of politeness when she's calling out from beyond the veil."

"There's politeness, and then there's manipulation," I say. "I think we should step away from her. Sever our connection."

Nora jolts, letting go of her hair. "How?"

"Let's do another ritual to block her from communicating with us. We can ask Ione for help. She'll probably be mad at us for getting so tangled up in this, but I bet she'll—"

"Don't you even *care* about helping May?" snaps Nora. "And her sister?"

"Of course I do," I say. "And we still can, but this is getting really dark, really fast. Aren't you scared she's going to fully take over your brain?"

"Hmm," she says again, and I'd like to shake her.

"I don't see why you should put yourself through torture for a complete stranger," I say.

"Mazzy." Nora glares at me with bloodshot eyes. "The Hand of Nephthys is out there murdering people. Not just May and her sister. All those homeless people and runaways and probably loads more people we don't even know about. We have information that nobody else has. That nobody else could *possibly* have. And you want to throw that away because you don't feel like dealing with the inconvenience of how May communicates with us?"

"That's not what I said at all." I sigh. "And I wouldn't exactly call her controlling you an *inconvenience*."

"But what if this is all we have?" says Nora. "What if the trail goes cold without May? Do we just give up and go home and let more people get killed?"

"No, but how do you expect this to play out? You won't even talk to Detective Huld," I say. "What's the endgame here? It's not like we can single-handedly take down a murderer—or a bunch of murderers—and drag them to jail."

"Elliot taking those pictures gave me an idea," says Nora. "What we need to do is collect as much evidence as we can, like completely irrefutable proof that these murders were done by the Hand of Nephthys. And then we'll take it to the police and show them before Detective Huld gets a chance to step in."

I drag my hands through my own wind-tangled hair, making it crackle with static. "Why does it matter if Detective Huld—"

"Look!" she interrupts, pointing across the street, where a gray SUV with a Delaware plate has pulled into the lot. In the summer months, at least half the cars in town are from out of state, but it's much less common at this time of year.

"Is that the guy who parked next to us at Mayflower?" I ask.

The man who gets out of the car is wearing a dark baseball cap, but it's too far away to see if there are tattoos on his neck. Nora snatches up her phone and starts snapping pictures. As the man disappears inside, Elliot hangs up the pay phone.

"Zoom in," I say, craning over to peer at her phone. The man's body fills the screen, and then she swipes up. A blurry gray smudge winds around the side of his neck.

"It's him," she whispers.

"It has to be a coincidence." I'm saying this because I want it to be, not because it actually has to be. "He's probably visiting for the week, and we just ran into him twice. It happens."

"Why would anybody come here in November?" Nora asks. "This place is dead."

"It's a lot deader than usual," I say, and we both cringe. "Maybe he has a summer home and likes the offseason?"

"Right, because who doesn't love freezing rain and everything being closed?" Nora rolls her eyes, and I'm relieved to see her old personality coming back.

The back door swings open, and Elliot jumps inside.

"It's done," he says, panting. "Go!"

As we swing out onto Route 28, Nora leans over me to snap another photo of the gray SUV.

"What did the cops say?" I keep an eye in the rearview mirror until the convenience store is out of sight.

"Not much," says Elliot. "I just told them about the body and then hung up when they asked for my name."

"Okay." I wipe one sweaty palm on my skirt, then the other. "Did you see that guy who went into the store just as you were leaving?"

"No, why?"

"He was at Mayflower the day we found the teeth," I say. "And he's got a Delaware plate on his car, which Nora and I find slightly suspicious."

"He might have something to do with the Hand of Nephthys," adds Nora.

"Isn't that supposed to be a local group?" Elliot asks.

"Technically," she says. "But if they're faking their own deaths, who knows what they might do to protect their identities? Or maybe he's a wash-ashore, and he just joined."

Nora snorts at her own joke and pulls out her phone. *Wash-ashore* is the term locals use for people who move here from other places. It's barely funny, considering everything that's washing up lately, but at least she's making jokes now instead of singing and braiding her hair.

"Ooh, somebody wrote back on the forum," she says.

"What did they say?" I ask.

"Somebody named Raven said they haven't heard of the Hand of Nephthys cutting people's hands off, but allegedly they carve a symbol into their victims' sternum during rituals."

"Nothing about them taking their hearts?" I ask.

"No," says Nora, still reading. "People are arguing about what the actual symbol is. One person says it's a tree, and somebody else says it's a falcon."

"There wasn't a carved symbol on the second body," I say. "It was a stitched-up wound. Did you notice anything like that on May's chest?"

"No," says Nora. "Her dress was covering it."

"Can't you just ask May how she died?" Elliot asks.

"That's literally what I've been trying to do all this time." Nora's voice is sharp with irritation. "*You* try understanding a dead spirit who's screaming inside your brain. You have no idea how hard this is."

"Okay, okay. Let's figure out a different plan," I say.

"If we hurry, we could go back to Scargo and check the body for symbols before the cops get there," says Nora.

"No, that's too risky," I say. "But hear me out." A plan is forming in my brain. A batshit plan, but everything is basically batshit at this point. "What if we went to the morgue and asked to see May's body? If there is a symbol on her chest—or if her heart was cut out—that's some solid evidence that she was killed by the Hand of Nephthys."

Nora sets down her phone, her whole face alight. "Yesss."

"Wait." Elliot squints at me in the rearview mirror. "Can you just show up at a morgue and do that?"

"No idea," I say. "But it can't hurt to try, right?"

My anxiety is gusting in like a windstorm, and I know we're pushing things way too far, but hopefully once Nora realizes we can do this investigation and gather real evidence without May's help, she'll be more open to severing their connection. This could be the key to fixing everything.

"Let's do it," says Nora. "The worst they can say is no."

CHAPTER 19

After a minute of internet research and twenty-five minutes of driving, we file through the front door of the Office of the Chief Medical Examiner. Inside the single-story building, it's bright and modern, but there's a faint scent of chemicals and an underlying sense of something dark and unsettled. This is the place where bodies get sent when their deaths are suspicious. This is where the recently murdered people end up.

A tired-looking woman behind the front desk glances up from her laptop. She frowns as she takes in Nora's smeared eyeliner and mud-spattered clothes.

"Can I help you?" she says.

I clear my throat. "We, uh, were wondering if it's possible to see the body of the woman who was found on Mayflower Beach?"

She stares at me like I've just sprouted a second nose. "It is absolutely not possible."

"Please." Nora plants her hands on the desk, and the woman leans back like Nora's goth-ness might be contagious. "It's really important. We were the ones who—"

"I'm going to stop you right there," says the woman, holding up a hand. "*If* there were a body here, that would be an active investigation, and nobody but staff and law enforcement would be allowed to go near the deceased."

Nora chews her lip. "What if we had a missing family member and we wanted to check if it was her?"

"Then you should speak the police first," says the woman. "Now I'm going to have to ask you to leave."

"Come on," mutters Elliot, heading for the door, but Nora doesn't move. Her lower lip starts wobbling.

Don't do it, I think as hard as I can. The last thing we want to do is make a scene right now, not when we're trying to keep a low profile. I'm about to take her arm and pull her out of here, but then she blinks and rearranges her expression into a smile.

"Okay, we'll do that." She brushes a fleck of dirt off her furry coat. "Sorry to take up your time."

"That's all right." The receptionist's sour expression says it's anything but all right as she rounds her desk and starts shepherding us toward the door.

"So, um, should we call the regular police, or maybe 911?" Nora is dithering beside an empty desk for some inexplicable reason.

"What is she *doing*?" whispers Elliot.

The woman doubles back for Nora. "Just call your regular police station's non-emergency number."

"Okay, and who should I ask to talk to?" asks Nora. "Is there, like, a detective or someone else I—oh!"

Somehow, Nora has managed to trip over the receptionist's foot, or the receptionist tripped over hers, and the two of them go sprawling. The woman catches herself on the corner of the desk,

117

but Nora bounces off and lands on her hands and knees on the floor.

"Jesus Christ," mutters Elliot as we help Nora up for the second time today.

"Oh my gosh, I am so sorry about that," she says as the receptionist stalks ahead of us and holds the door open. Elliot and I stagger out into the parking lot with Nora clutched between us.

"Do *not* come here again," says the woman, and right after the door slams shut, I hear the click of a bolt.

"Holy hell, Nora," I say. "What was that?"

"Just keep walking," she mutters.

Nora's got this odd, faraway look on her face as we cross the parking lot, and I'm afraid she's going to start singing and braiding her hair again, or tell us we have to run off and find another body. But as soon as we're back in the car and pulling out onto the road, she turns to me with a massive grin.

"Got it," she says, holding up a white access badge.

I swerve briefly into the wrong lane. Thankfully, it's empty.

"Please tell me you didn't steal that receptionist's badge," Elliot says.

"Um, no," says Nora. "She'd notice it was missing right away and know we took it. I grabbed this off that other desk when I 'fell.'" She makes air quotes around the word. "It's late, so whoever this belongs to probably won't be in the office until tomorrow. We can sneak in tonight and put it back on their desk."

"We can't actually sneak in there, though," I say.

"Why not?" she says.

"Don't they have security cameras?" Elliot asks.

"Probably," she says. "But I bet I can get around that."

"How, exactly, are we going to get around security cameras?" I ask.

Nora shrugs. "I found a new spell that temporarily disrupts electronic devices, and I bet it'd work on cameras."

Alarm bells start ringing in my brain. "Where did you find a spell like that?"

She waves her hand airily. "Yesterday. Online."

"It's not from the person who posted that moon shadow spell, is it?" I ask.

"Nope," she says, but I don't quite believe her. "Anyway, I tried it out on my phone, our TV, and our internet router. It's pretty simple, but it only lasts a few minutes, so we'll have to hurry."

The alarm bells in my brain turn to full-blown tornado sirens. This isn't how Nora and I practice magic—I can't begin to imagine having that kind of direct effect on the world. Considering we still haven't managed to pull off a spell to clear up acne, it makes no sense that Nora suddenly knows how to disable internet routers. It's not even in the same league as anything we've tried before.

"I have an extremely bad feeling about this," I say.

"Of course you do," says Nora. "But we have to do it anyway. May and her sister need our help. Listen—we know things that the police don't, right? But if we go to them now, they'll never believe a word we say. Once we've got enough evidence, I promise we'll give it all to them, but right now, we're just going to look suspicious. And we're going to attract even more attention from Detective Huld."

"But we're not actual murder suspects," I say. "They can't blame us for being at a beach with a candle, and they don't know it was us who found the second body."

"Who even knows what they can blame us for?" says Nora. "Anyway, if the spell doesn't work and the electricity stays on, we'll just leave."

"And if something goes wrong and the cops catch us, we'll tell them the whole truth?" says Elliot.

Nora's eyes slide sideways. "Sure."

I don't like the way she's practically vibrating in her seat right now, but I don't have a better option to get to the bottom of everything and make it all stop.

"All right," I groan. "But you promise that if we do get caught—"

"Then I swear we can come clean about everything. But we're not going to get caught," she says, and I wish I had half of Nora's conviction about literally anything.

I glance over my shoulder at Elliot. "If you don't want to get caught up in this mess, we totally understand. I can bring you home."

"Are you kidding?" he says. "There's no way I'm letting you two sneak into a freaking morgue without me."

Despite myself, I smile as I merge onto the highway.

CHAPTER 20

"Is this good?" I say, pulling so far off the road that branches crunch against the side of my car. My teeth are chattering, even though the heat is on and I'm wearing a heavy sweatshirt.

"If your goal is for me to not be able to get out, it's perfect," Nora grumbles.

"Just climb over and get out my side," I say. "I don't want anyone to see it parked here and call the cops."

"It's not illegal to park on the side of the road," she says, but she crawls over the center console anyway and takes the face mask I'm holding out. Elliot gets out of the back, carrying the big golf umbrella my dad put in my car for emergencies.

Nora laughs. "Are you expecting rain?"

He shakes his head. "I'm going to use it to shield us from security cameras while we look for the body."

"We're not going to need it," says Nora, "but okay, I guess."

"I still kind of hope the cops show up," he mutters, but I know that's not true. The idea of spilling everything to the police is appealing, but getting arrested isn't. Besides, Nora's right that we stand a better chance of being believed if we have more concrete proof about what's happening and who's responsible. I just wish the potential proof wasn't inside a morgue.

We pull up the hoods of our black sweatshirts and tuck the masks over our faces before ducking through the patch of woods that leads to the chief medical examiner's office. It's nine fifty-five. The night is cold and moonless, and there are no streetlights out here, so we switch on our phone flashlights. We haven't seen a single car since we got here, but I can't shake the feeling that anyone could be out there in the trees, watching.

The building is deserted and unlit, and as we tiptoe closer, the only sound is our nervous breath, coming fast. A tiny red light glows beside the entrance, and as soon as Nora flashes her badge at the card reader, the door clicks open and we slip inside, keeping our heads low.

"Stop here." Elliot opens his umbrella and we all duck underneath, and then Nora pulls out two mason jars. Whispering an incantation, she pours the contents of one into the other and gives them a little shake to mix. Instantly, a migraine stabs into the space behind my eye sockets. The glowing exit sign flickers out. The emergency lighting along the floor goes black. The low background hum disappears. It's as silent as a tomb.

"My phone just died," whispers Elliot. "Nora, are you *kidding* me right now?"

"Told you it'd work." Nora is positively dripping with smugness.

My phone screen is blank too, and uneasiness worms around in my gut. This shouldn't be possible. I wonder if having May inside her head is making Nora more powerful, if having possession of two minds gives her twice the intention to apply to her spells. Or if May is somehow changing her. The thought makes me nauseous. We know nothing about May, except that she's dead and she likes bending people to her will. It's not smart for Nora to just accept whatever she's giving her.

I take two flashlights from my bag and hand one to Nora. Even though the batteries are fresh, mine won't switch on, and hers flickers for a few seconds before dying. She pulls out a lighter and a small candle in a silver tin.

"I thought that might happen," she says. "Good thing I brought backup."

This building seemed so official and clinical in the daytime, but the faint candlelight and wavering shadows make it feel like a completely different place. A sinister place. The chemical smell reminds me of the frogs we dissected in ninth grade science class, all stiff and rubbery and wet, and I can't stop thinking of all the murdered people who have passed through here. I wonder where they came from, how long they stayed, how many of them gave up their secrets once they were sliced open.

Nora gives her spell jar another shake, and something inside catches my eye. I lean in to get a better look, and she snatches it away, but not fast enough.

"Is that a *tooth* in there?" I ask.

Nora pauses. "Maybe."

"Nora Hawthorne, tell me you didn't find a spell online that told you to use the tooth of a murdered woman," I say. "Tell me that did not seem the slightest bit suspicious to you."

"The spell didn't say to use the tooth." Nora clutches the jar to her chest, like I'm about to snatch it away. "I had a flash of intuition about adding it. And I was right. Look how well it's working."

"You were supposed to give them all to the police," I say.

Nora shrugs. "I'm sorry I didn't tell you I kept one, but this spell only lasts a few minutes, so can we talk about this later?"

"Fine," I say, but now I'm wondering what other things she's hiding from me.

Elliot's still staring at his blank phone, muttering about how all of this is literally impossible, and I nudge his shoulder.

"Are you ready?"

He blinks at me for a minute. "Yeah. Let's keep the umbrella in case there are backup cameras."

"Okay," I say, but I bet even backup batteries are no match for Nora's fun new spell that includes an actual human tooth.

Tucked under the umbrella, we creep into a room at the back. The candlelight glints on two long metal tables, empty and body-size. Behind them, there's a deep sink and a counter full of instruments and tools to dig out the secrets of the dead. We move toward a row of four wide metal drawers on the opposite side of the room. Only one is labeled.

Jane Doe

7842-96283-49

"That's her," whispers Nora. "Open it."

Just get it over with, I think, but I can't make my hand open the drawer.

"Let me." Nora passes me her candle, and I shrink closer to Elliot, who draws the umbrella lower over us. I try to let his calming energy soak into me, but it's useless. I cannot bear to see that bony, pale body again. That sunken face that's been haunting me for days. Those half-closed eyes.

A gust of cold wafts out as Nora tugs the handle, and all I can think of is May's rotten breath on my skin, her open, toothless mouth.

"Shit," Elliot says as Nora pulls the drawer all the way open.

It's empty.

CHAPTER 21

Not totally empty.

Something small and metallic glints in the back corner of the body-size drawer that May is supposed to be in but isn't. Nora snatches it up and holds it close to the candle.

The key is shaped like a horseshoe crab, with a rounded body tapering to a long, thin tail. Carved in the center of the body is a skeleton's face with empty eyes and a grinning set of teeth. The craftsmanship is ornate and macabre and oddly compelling.

"Can I hold it?" I ask.

The key is heavier than I expected, and a cool sense of calm washes over me.

"My headache is going away," I say, blinking at the loss of pain and pressure. "I wonder if it's the key or—" I glance at the spell jar Nora's holding.

"Crap, it's wearing off." She slams the drawer shut as something in the room starts to hum. The systems are coming back online. We're going to get caught. As much as I'd like to give up on this investigation and hand it all over to the police, this isn't the way I want it to happen.

"This way." Elliot drags us under the umbrella, and we hurry toward the emergency exit, tripping over each other's feet. More things are humming now, and there's a faint clicking sound coming from the other room. A light flickers as Elliot shoves the door open and we rush outside. Abandoning any effort to stay under the umbrella, we charge across the parking lot and into the woods.

None of us speaks until we're back in the car and speeding away with no police in sight.

"That key belonged to May. I'm sure of it. She's, like, *ecstatic* right now." Nora laughs like she's delighted too, and I press my lips together to keep from saying something snarky and resentful. It's not that I want a psychic link with a dead woman, especially one who'd scream at me inside my head. I just don't like my best friend having secrets and connections with someone else, on a totally different level than I'm even capable of. I feel like I'm slowly losing her.

"I swear I've seen that horseshoe-crab skull somewhere before," says Elliot.

"What the hell happened to May's body?" says Nora.

"Maybe someone claimed it?" I say. "Or maybe they moved her to a different facility."

"And what about her sister at Scargo Lake?" she says. "Wouldn't the police have brought her there too?"

"None of the other drawers were labeled," says Elliot.

"Maybe they didn't have time to bring her in yet," I say, but Nora shakes her head.

"You can't just leave a body lying around wherever. It has to be refrigerated."

"What do you think?" I glance over my shoulder, but Elliot is busy swiping through his phone.

". . . definitely seen that skull somewhere . . ." he's muttering.

"Something fishy is going on," says Nora.

After everything that's just happened, I can't help but burst out laughing.

"Oh, you *think*?"

"Yeah, just a *tiiiny* bit fishy." She's laughing now too. "A little . . . *horseshoe-crabby*, actually."

"What have we gotten ourselves into?" I wipe my eyes with my sleeve. "We just snuck into an actual morgue."

"And that wasn't even the weirdest part of our day," says Nora. "But in all seriousness, I think someone took May's body. And I bet I know who: Detective Huld."

"You think *Huld* took the body?" I ask. "Why would she do that?"

"Because she's in the Hand of Nephthys."

The top of my head starts to tingle. In the back seat, Elliot bursts out laughing, then stops when he realizes Nora and I aren't.

"Come on, don't you think that's kind of far-fetched?" he says.

Nora just shrugs. "This entire situation is pretty damn far-fetched. Maybe Eva Huld legitimately is a police officer, but that doesn't mean she's not also in the Hand of Nephthys. It'd be a pretty good cover. Nobody would suspect her, and she could sabotage any investigations into the group's murder victims."

"And she'd have access to the morgue," I say, slowly putting the pieces together. As wild as this theory is, I can't deny that something is off about Detective Huld. Nora's theory would explain why she's been asking so many pointless questions about us practicing witchcraft. Why she's so obsessed with learning how we found the body, rather than how May got murdered in the first place. If she were part of the group who murdered May, she'd already know the answer to that, and she'd be on a damage control mission.

"*We* just got access to the morgue," says Elliot. "It wasn't hard."

"Yeah, but she could take the body without raising any suspicions," I say. "She could make up an excuse about transporting it somewhere."

"Exactly," says Nora. "That's why we have to keep searching. We need to collect so much evidence that not even Huld can cover it up, and then we'll show the other cops before she gets a chance to step in. If we can find evidence of her being in the Hand of Nephthys, that's even better."

"We should have taken a picture of that empty drawer," I say.

"Yes!" Elliot yells, and I peer in the mirror, curious about his sudden attitude change. He zooms in on something on his phone, then holds it up. "Found it."

"Found what?" I can't focus on the reflected image and the road at the same time.

"The horseshoe crab with the skull face." He hands his phone to Nora. "I knew I saw it somewhere."

"Where is this?" she asks.

"Woodside Cemetery," he says. "It's carved on the door of one of the mausoleums."

Nora and I glance at each other.

"What time do you need to be home?" she asks.

"Eleven." My dashboard clock reads ten forty-one. "We don't have time to go to the cemetery now."

Plus, I've had enough of creeping around in dark places that belong to the dead. My nerves are shot, and my skull feels like a cracked egg after Nora's spell.

"Can we ditch school tomorrow morning?" Nora asks.

"I have a history test first period," says Elliot.

"Okay, then we'll go to the cemetery before school starts," she says.

"I still don't understand how you shut my phone off earlier," says Elliot. "The battery's at six percent now."

"Guess you need to stop underestimating my abilities," Nora says, and my stomach sours, because I'm certain there was more than just Nora's abilities at work tonight.

"Sooner or later, you're going to have to believe us about everything," she adds.

Slipping my hand into my coat pocket, I run my thumb over the skull face of the key. Somebody—possibly Detective Huld—is trying to cover up evidence. But they got sloppy and they dropped this key, or May left it for us somehow. We still have no concrete proof that May and her sister are the victims of the Hand of Nephthys, but I have a strong suspicion that this key might just change everything, connect it all, if we can just figure out what it leads to. As wild and improbable and eerie as everything is, it feels like we're on the brink of discovering something massive. We have to keep going.

I'm not sure we have a choice, anyway.

~ ~ ~

After washing up and brushing my teeth, I crawl into bed with my phone and open the Mystical Mysteries forum. There's one new post. Someone has responded to Nora's question about joining the Hand of Nephthys.

Anon09: Nobody "joins" the HoN. It's not a club. If you prove you're worthy, they find you.

Shivering, I tug the blankets up under my chin. Seconds later, I get a text.

Nora: Did you see the forum???

Me: Just saw it now, seems ominous

Nora: Ominous like how

Me: From a victim standpoint, they FIND you?? No thanks

Nora: Tina already told us that, remember?

But now I'm wondering about the changes we've been seeing in May. The screaming, the manipulation, the nasty little elements of her personality slowly slipping out.

Me: Do you think it's possible May and her sister went looking for them? Like trying to join?

Nora: ooooohhhh and maybe that's what they mean by nobody finds the HoN, because they kill you if you get too close

Me: Or May and her sister failed some initiation test and the penalty was death

Nora: Could be

I wonder how you prove yourself

Maybe you could do it

> Me: What

Nora: That vision you had, maybe it's the kind of thing they're looking for

Maybe you're **special** Mazzy

> Me: No

Nora: I wish it had been me

> Me: You have a literal psychic link with a dead lady
>
> If anybody's *special* it's you

Nora: I guess

> Me: Anyway, it's not a compliment to be chosen by a murderous cult

Nora: We should try the ritual again

> Me: I'm so tired I can't even think about that
>
> Let's talk about it tomorrow

Nora: ok

> Me: Do not do that ritual by yourself
>
> Promise me

Several minutes go by with no response, and I'm starting to wonder if she's already setting up her altar, if she's calling May's spirit into her room as I sit here waiting, but then dots appear on my screen.

Nora: I promise

CHAPTER 22

The sky is barely starting to lighten when we get to the cemetery, just a smear of orange along the horizon under charcoal clouds. Elliot leads the way, his dark coat flapping behind him as we file through the open gate and skirt along the fence that runs parallel to the road.

"Do you remember that night we came here and played Ghost in the Graveyard?" he asks. "With Allie and Cam and those kids from Barnstable?"

"How could I forget?" That was one of the creepiest nights of my life—until this week, anyway. It was late, and Elliot's friend Cam banned everyone from using flashlights. Nora swore she heard a voice whispering underneath a crooked old gravestone, and one of the girls from Barnstable said she could hear it too. Then we started the game, and Elliot went missing and Cam fell into an open grave. Luckily, the hole was still empty, waiting for someone who was going to be buried the next day. Nora said it served Cam right for not letting us use our flashlights.

"We never figured out where you hid," she says to Elliot. "I thought we'd lost you to the spirit world forever."

134

"I was over there." Elliot points to the far side of the cemetery, where we're heading. "Taking pictures of that door."

The hill looks like a normal part of the landscape until we get to the other side and the perspective changes. A stone door cut into its side turns the grassy mound into a tomb. Elliot was right. Carved into the center of the door is the same horseshoe crab with a skull face, and underneath there's a tarnished silver doorknob and a keyhole.

I slip my hand into my pocket where the key rests, cold and smooth and full of secrets I'm not sure I want to know. Something is coming. Something big is on the other side of that door. I feel it in my bones. Elliot and Nora step aside to let me approach the mausoleum, and this is my last chance to turn around and go back to the car, to not use this key. I swear there's a low humming sound coming from the other side of the door, and the key is faintly buzzing like those teeth we found on the beach.

It's still so dark, and the cemetery is blanketed in shadows. Somewhere in the trees, an owl hoots three times, and then an answering call floats over the graves. My scalp is crawling, my palms are damp, my heartbeat is throbbing in my ears as I step forward and pull out the key.

"Do it," whispers Nora.

A wave of foreboding hits me as I push the key into the lock. I almost hope it won't fit, but it does; the lock clicks and the door creaks open. A puff of dust stings my eyes.

"Whoa," says Elliot, peering into the pitch-dark space. I should turn on my flashlight, but I can't quite make myself move. Nora nudges me aside and shines hers into the depths of the tomb. The bright beam darts over a cobwebby ceiling and two walls of stone drawers for keeping bodies. On the floor in the back lie six wooden coffins. There are no lids.

"I hate absolutely everything about this," I say.

"Me too," says Elliot.

Even though the space doesn't smell like bodies or rot, it smells *off*. Like the time I had Covid and everything tasted like ashes. This place reeks of cinders, with a faint, sickening floral undertone. I'm certain terrible things have happened here. The awfulness hangs thick in the air.

Nora steps inside, and I'm too late to pull her back. She heads straight for the coffins, and a fresh wave of nausea hits me as she bends low, shining her flashlight inside one.

"They're empty," she says, and that should relieve me, but I'm so deep in fight or flight mode that all I can do is nod and try not to throw up on my shoes. After all the things we've seen in the past few days, I don't know why I'm having such a sudden, visceral reaction to an empty tomb. Maybe it's a delayed reaction, or maybe it's the cumulative effect of everything that's happened, but this place has pushed me over the edge. My skin is coated in cold sweat, and my ears are ringing so loudly I can barely make out what Elliot is saying. He leans in close.

"Do you need to get some air?"

It's even harder to think straight with his face this close to mine, but I'm mostly just afraid of vomiting on him. I swallow hard and press my hands to my eyes, letting the cold soak in.

"We're already outside," I manage. "This is ... all the air there is."

We both laugh, and I can breathe a little now. Everything is still swimming, but maybe I'm not going to throw up.

"Guys," says Nora from inside the mausoleum. "Come look at this."

Elliot's jaw tightens. "Can you just describe it to us while we wait out here?"

"No," she says. "You have to see it. May is *really* happy about this. She's, like, vibrating with elation."

"Great," I mutter. The things that make May happy are getting more and more hideous.

"Let's get this over with," says Elliot, and then somehow, his fingers are intertwined with mine. His hand is warm and dry, and I should be freaking out that we're actually, finally, holding hands, but it has the opposite effect. I feel calmer. Safer. He bumps his shoulder against mine and smiles grimly.

All of the outside sounds—the wind, the owls, the distant traffic—go silent as we step inside the tomb. The ashy, sweet scent fills my nose and mouth, and I tighten my grip on Elliot's hand. His flashlight beam dances around the tight space and lands on Nora crouching in the back.

"Look." She hefts open a trapdoor, revealing a square hole in the concrete. Metal rungs lead down into blackness. "Where do you think this goes?"

A rusty creaking sound cuts through the silence, and we all freeze. Swearing, Elliot drops my hand and dashes for the door. He catches it just before it slams shut, then shoves it all the way open and sags against the frame.

I cannot begin to think about what almost just happened. And I cannot spend another second in this tomb. I run for the door and throw myself out into the cold gray of the cemetery. Sweat coats every inch of my skin.

Elliot stoops to pick something up from the ground. "Was this here before?"

He holds up a weathered old Polaroid. In it, a woman with her back to the camera is walking into a shop with big plate-glass windows. To her right is a wicker chair, and to her left, an umbrella stand holding tall staffs that look like driftwood walking sticks. Dark hair tumbles down her back, and she's wearing a long, loose dress.

"Mazzy." Nora's voice is low and shaky.

Our eyes meet, and I don't have to say anything, because we both somehow know. It's the same exact feeling I got when I saw Henry's drawing.

The woman in the picture is May.

"Hey!" A man's voice calls out from somewhere on the other side of the hill. "Who's over there?"

The three of us freeze. Nora's eyes flick to the mausoleum.

"No," I hiss. Hiding inside that hellhole is not an option. "Shut the door!"

Elliot tugs it closed, and I pull the key from the lock.

"Hello!" comes the man's gruff voice again. "I know you're back there, so you better come out. I saw you on the cameras and I found your car."

"The cemetery has cameras?" mutters Nora.

"This way," I say, gesturing around the opposite side of the hill. We skirt back through the graves, then cut up the driveway, trying to look nonchalant—which is difficult when you've just been inside a tomb.

Under a gnarled old oak tree, a man stands holding a shovel. His face is covered with a surgical mask, and a wide-brimmed hat is pulled low over his eyes. I don't know why he's wearing a mask all alone in a cemetery, but maybe he has allergies. Or maybe he put it on when he discovered we were here.

"I'm not going to find any spray paint on the graves, am I?" His voice is weary. "You kids have no respect for the dead."

We have more respect than we probably should, I think.

"We, uh, were just visiting my grandma's grave," says Nora.

The groundskeeper takes in my long black coat, the steel spikes in Elliot's ears, Nora's multicolored hair. He grunts. "Shouldn't you be at school right now?"

"It hasn't started yet," says Nora. "We just wanted to stop by for a quick visit before we go."

The man folds his arms. "What's your grandmother's name?"

"Ffflorence," says Nora. "Florence . . . Welch."

She presses her mouth into a tight line, refusing to look at either me or Elliot, and I desperately hope this groundskeeper has never heard of Florence and the Machine.

He lowers his shovel. "I better not find any trash or graffiti back there. This isn't a party spot."

"Trust me, we were *not* having a party," I say. Nora chokes back a laugh, and I'm so close to laughter too, even though this is deeply unfunny.

"We're leaving now," says Elliot.

As we pass through the cemetery gate, I mutter, "Florence Welch," and Nora and I break into quiet giggling that quickly turns into full-blown, high-pitched laughter. That man is going to think we were taking drugs in his graveyard. For some reason, this makes me laugh harder, until tears are dripping down my cheeks. We've got dead bodies missing from drawers and skull keys and coffins and deep, dark holes. Polaroids that magically appear on the ground, right after we almost get locked in tombs. It's getting wilder and stranger and more dangerous by the second. I'm sure if I stop laughing, the panic will flood in, so I don't stop.

"Keep it together, you two," Elliot mutters.

I'm wheezing, Nora keeps tripping on the hem of her dress, and I'm not sure if we look more like drug addicts or two Victorian ladies having a hysterical breakdown.

"Bye, Grandma!" calls Nora from the middle of the road, waving over her shoulder.

"Watch out!" I tug her backward as a delivery van zooms past, narrowly missing her. The driver beeps but doesn't slow, and the laughter dies in my throat as the taillights disappear down the road.

The near miss is a stark reminder—nothing about this is funny, and it's dangerous to even pretend it is.

CHAPTER 23

As I pull out onto the road, Nora is scrolling on her phone and Elliot's busy examining the Polaroid in the back seat. I can't believe we're supposed to go to school right now and act normal.

"Who else thinks that wasn't really the cemetery groundskeeper?" he says.

I glance at him in the mirror. "Really?"

"That shovel was lying on the ground when we got there," he says. "I bet he just picked it up and pretended it was his."

"Right after he tried and failed to shut us in the mausoleum." My skin is crawling. "Or do you think May did it?"

"She wouldn't do that," says Nora.

"I wouldn't put it past her." It sounds exactly like May's brand of creepy behavior.

"Is it possible the groundskeeper was actually that guy from Delaware?" asks Nora. "I couldn't see his neck or any tattoos."

"His SUV wasn't on the road or in the graveyard," says Elliot.

"I think it's safe to assume that whoever tried to shut the mausoleum door also left the Polaroid," I say.

"Or they dropped it by accident," says Elliot.

"No, the Polaroid is from May," says Nora.

"But you don't think she tried to shut the door?" I ask. "Why?"

"Well, we agree that this is a photo of her, right?" says Nora.

Elliot shrugs; I nod.

"And we know May wants us to help her," Nora continues. "So this must be a clue that she wants us to have. We need to figure out where the picture was taken and then go there."

"Why wouldn't she just yell at you where to go, like she did yesterday?" I ask. "Why start leaving cryptic clues all of a sudden?"

"I don't know, but she's been muttering something about honey and flies today," says Nora.

"As in, you catch more flies with honey than vinegar?" says Elliot. "Does that make us the flies?"

Like flies on a corpse. I force the mental image out of my head.

"Whoa." Nora points to something ahead. "Look."

Parked on the side of the road is a black sedan that looks awfully familiar. I slow to a crawl as we pass, and the person in the driver's seat looks up. Her dark eyes lock on mine, and my teeth clamp together.

Nora sucks in her breath; I swear and hit the gas.

"That nosy, skulking stalker," mutters Nora, checking her mirror.

"Who?" says Elliot. "What just happened?"

"That," says Nora, "was Detective Freaking Huld."

"What was she doing there, though?" I ask. "Did she know we were at the graveyard?"

"Maybe *she's* the one who tried to shut us in the mausoleum," says Nora, and my neck starts to prickle.

"If she did, why would she run off and then park right where

142

we'd see her afterward?" says Elliot. "Anyway, cops don't usually go around locking people in tombs."

"But she's not a normal cop," says Nora. "She's hiding something. And I'm just saying that if she *were* in the Hand of Nephthys, locking us away in a mausoleum would be a quick and easy way to get us to stop meddling in their business."

Elliot groans. "But why would she leave the photo outside? Why give us extra clues?"

"I told you, the photo's from May," says Nora.

"Or it was the groundskeeper's, and he didn't mean to drop it," says Elliot.

"Hmm." Nora pulls a white feather from her pocket and twirls it in her fingers.

"Where did you get that?" I ask.

"I found it in one of the coffins," she says. "Don't worry, I asked permission from the dead before I took it out of the cemetery."

"Let me guess—that's from May too?" I can't keep the biting tone out of my voice. Taking things from random coffins is not a smart choice, whether you asked permission or not. Nora's never been the most sensible person I know, but this is stretching it, even for her. She knows better.

"Possibly." Nora tucks the feather behind her ear.

"Anything else you've taken that you want to share?" I say. "Because that's two things now, and neither of them was a good idea."

"Can you just drop it?" snaps Nora. "I'm allowed to take things I find in public."

"Actually, you're not," I say. "We're digging ourselves deeper and deeper into a hole, and stealing things from tombs isn't—"

"Guys, hey." says Elliot. "Look at this. There are some letters over the door." He holds the Polaroid up. *"I-Q-U-E-S."*

"I bet that's antiques." I flick on my blinker. "Do either of you recognize the store?"

"Nope." Nora folds her arms over her chest and stares out the window.

"We can probably use a reverse image search to find it," I say. "I'll do some research at lunch."

Nora pulls out her phone, and I wonder if she's already searching for the antique store or if she's just using it as an excuse not to talk to me. I feel a little bad for yelling at her about the feather, but I'm starting to wonder if I even know her anymore.

As we pull into the school parking lot, the morning bell is ringing, and the last few stragglers are hurrying inside. Thankfully, there's an open parking spot near the back, and we throw our bags over our shoulders and race across the pavement.

"Let me know what you find out," Elliot calls as he veers off toward his homeroom.

Frowning at her screen, Nora gives us a distracted wave as she heads to class.

CHAPTER 24

I'm sitting alone in the back corner of the cafeteria with a bagel, an open calculus book, the Polaroid, my phone, and a massive headache. It turns out that balancing a heavy load of AP classes—along with solving the mystery of two murdered women and dealing with the undead spirit of one of them—is a lot.

Someone drops onto the stool beside me, and I startle, then immediately break into a grin when I realize it's Elliot, holding a library book.

"What are you doing here?" I ask. It's been the bane of my existence that none of us have the same lunch period this year.

He waves a bathroom pass. "Thought I'd stop by and see if you found anything."

"Not yet," I say. "I tried taking a picture and reverse image searching, but nothing matched. So now I'm looking up all the antique stores on the Cape one by one and checking their street views."

"That's going to take forever." Elliot leans in closer, and I tilt my screen so he can see. A strand of my hair static-sticks to his shoulder, and a warm sensation spreads like sunlight across my skin. He notices it too but doesn't brush it away.

"Hopefully not," I say, forcing myself back to reality, where it would definitely not be acceptable to bury my face in Elliot's paint-flecked hoodie and inhale. "It's just super boring. Look what else I noticed, though."

I point to the white border under the image, where a letter is written in smeared black ink.

"Is that a *V*?" asks Elliot.

"Or an *M* that the edges got smudged off," I say. "Obviously this woman's real name isn't May, but that's kind of interesting, don't you think?"

Elliot nods. "Speaking of letters, I went to the library during my free period, and I saw this." He holds up the book so I can read the title: *Ancient Egypt and the Afterlife*. "There's some interesting stuff about Nephthys in here."

I cock an eyebrow. "Does this mean you finally believe us about everything?"

"I'm working on it," he says. "Want me to read this to you while you look for antique stores?"

"Sure," I say. If nothing else, it'll keep me from falling asleep.

Elliot opens the book to a scrap of paper he's tucked into the pages and clears his throat. "Nephthys, one of the earliest goddesses of Egypt, was a member of the Ennead of Heliopolis, a group of nine powerful deities. Often called the Mistress of the House, she is associated with both death and childbirth, as well as healing and magic. She is traditionally depicted as a hawk or kite—the bird, not the toy—or a woman with wings."

He flips the page.

"The book talks about a lot of stuff we already know, like how she was the sister of Isis and the mother of Anubis, and how she welcomed the recently dead and helped them travel to the afterlife. She's quoted in *The Lamentations of Isis and Nephthys* as saying, 'I am with you, your bodyguard, for all eternity.'"

A shivery sensation whispers through me as I tap a photo of an antique shop in Chatham to enlarge it. But the storefront is all wrong, with narrow windows and red brick walls. "What does it say specifically about the afterlife?"

Elliot flips back to the index, then shuffles through pages. "There isn't much about Nephthys in the actual afterlife, but when someone dies, they travel to an underworld called the Duat. They stand before Osiris and forty-two divine judges, and they recite something called the Negative Confession." Elliot skims the page for a few seconds. "It's a list of sins you have to say you've never done—stuff like stealing and murder and adultery, but also some really specific things like interfering with cattle that belong to the gods and diverting the flow of water. Also, no eavesdropping."

"Yikes, we'd never make it to the afterlife," I say, and Elliot laughs.

"Then they take the dead person's heart and put it on a scale, with the white feather of truth, called Ma'at," he says.

"Nora just found a white feather," I say, nerves crawling. "What do they use it for?"

"If the heart is lighter than the feather, the person gets to go to a place called Aaru, or the Field of Reeds, where they'll spend their eternity in happiness. If the heart is heavier than the feather, then the goddess Ammit eats it with her crocodile mouth, and the person is stuck in the Duat forever."

"Ouch," I say.

"That's why the heart always got left in the mummies of

ancient Egypt, even though they took out all the other organs," says Elliot.

"But it seems like the Hand of Nephthys are removing their victims' hearts," I say. "Why would they do that?"

Elliot shrugs. "They must be using them for something else."

"I'm working on a theory that May and her sister were looking for the Hand of Nephthys before they got murdered," I say.

"Why would you think that?"

"I just keep coming back to the fact that two sisters got murdered and then washed up in very similar ways," I say. "It's strange, right? And May had a key to that mausoleum, which is also strange."

The side of Elliot's mouth quirks up. "We hang out in cemeteries too. But we *are* pretty strange."

I groan. "Playing Ghost in the Graveyard and owning the key to a mausoleum aren't exactly the same thing."

He takes my phone and starts scrolling. "I still don't get how this is all connected."

"Now that May's in her head, Nora can do spell work that's way beyond her normal abilities," I say. "That makes me think May practiced witchcraft before she died, and she was good at it. So my theory is that May and her sister were searching for the Hand, possibly trying to join."

"So they were sociopaths too?"

"I mean, look at the way she was screaming in Nora's brain," I say. "It's definitely plausible. But the saying goes, 'Nobody finds the Hand of Nephthys. They find you.' They don't *want* to be found. If May and her sister got too close to finding them— especially if they started uncovering some of their secrets—I bet the Hand killed them. And what better way than to sacrifice them in a ritual? Then they sunk the bodies in the ocean and in Scargo Lake, but something made them—"

The rest of my sentence disappears as I spot the image Elliot has just opened on my screen. I grab the phone, my fingers wrapping around his.

"Oh my God, that's it," I say.

The text above the image says **The Magpie's Nest: Curiosities and Antiques.** In this image, there's no woman walking through the front door, but the windows are the right size and shape. Elliot holds the photo up beside it, and we compare the details. The same flowers are carved into the peeling paint on the doorframe, and the lettering on the sign matches perfectly. The umbrella stand is there too, although it only holds one walking stick.

Elliot extricates his hand from under mine, and my cheeks go hot as I tap the link under the photo, then scroll through the website. "Fifty-six Hallet Street in Eastham," I say. "They're open until five. We can go there after school."

Elliot groans. "I just got a message from the grocery store. Somebody called in sick, and they want me to pick up the shift this afternoon."

"What time do you finish?" I say.

"Not until seven," he says. "I'll call them back and say I can't do it."

"No!" I don't mean for it to come out sounding quite so frantic, but the last thing I want is for Elliot's family to run out of money and have to move. "Nora and I can go, and we'll catch you up as soon as you're done working."

"Are you sure?" He chews his lower lip, and I so badly want to kiss that mouth, even though we're in the middle of the cafeteria and our lives are in absolute chaos.

"I think we can manage on our own. No umbrellas necessary today."

Elliot laughs as I bump my shoulder against his, and I wish I could keep making him laugh forever.

The bell rings, and the noise of the cafeteria rises to a crescendo as everyone starts packing up.

"Shit, I lost track of time." Elliot jumps up and grabs his book. "Mr. Markham is going to take away my bathroom privileges."

"Sorry to get you in trouble," I say, even though I'm not actually sorry for distracting him.

"You're worth losing bathroom privileges over." He holds my gaze for a beat too long, and I lose all my words.

"That's the nicest thing anybody's ever said to me," I finally manage, and it's meant to be sarcastic but comes out sounding mortifyingly sincere.

Elliot grins. "Talk to you later."

I watch him join the mob leaving the cafeteria, and I wonder if I'll ever find the courage to tell him how I feel. It's just that I've imagined the scenario with a tragic outcome so many times. He learns the truth but doesn't like me back, and so he starts avoiding me. Then when we're forced to interact at school, he gets this look on his face, this excruciating blend of embarrassment and pity. A world where Elliot feels that way about me is simply not an option.

As soon as he's gone, I gather my stuff up and text Nora the plan for this afternoon. She's on her way to lunch now, so hopefully she's checking her phone—if she ever stopped.

Immediately, a response pops up.

Nora: Ok

I'm sorry i yelled at you

I don't feel like the best version of myself lately

    Me: I'm sorry too

    And I totally get it, all this stress is turning me into a bitch

Nora: You're not a bitch

Detective huld is a bitch

See you later xo

CHAPTER 25

Nora and I have driven up and down Hallet Street four times now, and each time the GPS on my phone has told me the antique store was in a different place. The first time it was on the left, then the right, then the left two more times, but all I see is a café, a closed saltwater taffy shop, and a bank, and I'm getting increasingly irritated each time the robot voice tells me to turn around. It's not even four p.m., but the daylight is fading fast.

"Pull in here," says Nora, pointing to the taffy store parking lot. "Your chaotic U-turns are making me seasick."

"I think the word you're looking for is *carsick*," I say.

"You have arrived at your destination," says the unhelpful GPS.

"Thanks so much," I mutter, wishing it were possible to punch a computer-generated voice.

My phone rings for the third time since we left school. **Eva Huld**, says the screen, and I let it go to voicemail once again. I don't know where she got my unlisted phone number from in the first place, and I don't think she's supposed to be calling minors to question them without their parents present. My stomach cramps up each time she calls.

"What's over there?" Nora points to a narrow drive that curves behind the building.

"Only one way to find out," I say, shifting back into gear.

The driveway winds around a dumpster and then leads to another parking lot on the back side of the building. Even though the shop is smaller than I expected, and more run-down, I recognize the carved doorframe and the cursive sign immediately: *The Magpie's Nest: Curiosities and Antiques.*

This is where May went—at some unknown point in time before she died. This is where someone photographed her, whether she knew it or not. My skin goes chilly as I pull into a parking spot and we silently take in our surroundings. There's just one other car: an old, blue Camry beside the bushy pines that flank the back of the lot.

"This is definitely it." Nora holds the Polaroid up. "And that's definitely an *M* underneath. I *told* you her name started with an *M*."

The Polaroid shakes a little in her hand.

"Are you scared?" I ask.

"No." She shoves her door open. "Come on."

The sign says the store is open, but it's dim inside. Warily, I push on the door, and as it swings open, Nora and I both pause. I don't know what we're waiting for.

"May wants us to go in," she says.

"Is she talking again?" I ask.

"No, but I can feel her. She's excited."

I don't like the idea of May being excited about anything anymore, but we're here now, and we may as well go in. The store smells like dust and mildew and something vaguely tangy. It reminds me of a very old person's house. A house they died in.

As our eyes adjust to the lack of light, we shuffle forward. The shop is positively stuffed with antiques. Porcelain statues and wooden knickknacks piled on tables, stacks of books on the floor, scarves and necklaces and hats hanging overhead. The walls are covered with dusty old paintings and tapestries. A narrow path cuts through the clutter.

"Hello?" I call.

Silence. There's a counter to our left, stacked high with boxes and bags, but nobody behind it.

"Excuse me? Are you open?" I say, but again, no one answers.

"The sign says they are," says Nora. "Maybe they're in the back."

I'm not usually claustrophobic, but the sheer volume of junk and dust in this place is making me feel like I can't breathe.

"Come on." Nora heads down the path, pulling me along. "There must be something we're supposed to find."

"How can we possibly find anything in here?" I ask.

"May will help us." Nora stops short, and I trip over the heel of her boot. She takes a deep breath and sways a little, then spins ninety degrees to the left.

"I'll look over here," she says, heading for a table covered in antique cosmetics. As she shifts through the silver lipstick tubes, the ivory powder boxes, the mother-of-pearl compacts, I wander over to the opposite side of the store, where boxes of records are lined up by the wall.

In the corner, on a table all by itself, sits an old phonograph player with a big trumpet-like speaker. Something about it is oddly magnetic, almost compelling, and as I drift closer, I start to wonder if it's compelling for a good reason or a bad one. I'm getting traces of that panicky wave I felt yesterday in the tomb, but I can't stop my feet from moving closer to the phonograph. There's a record on its turntable. Without thinking, I reach for it, then freeze.

The player's tarnished metal crank is carved in the shape of a horseshoe crab. Two wide eyes in the center of its body, two rows of grinning teeth.

"Nora," I say, but she's distracted, rummaging through a box.

I don't want to turn the crank, but macabre curiosity makes me do it anyway. I need to stop, I should definitely stop, but then it's done, the record starts to spin, and I'm setting the needle down. A static crackle, and the music begins.

It's May's song, played slowly on an out-of-tune piano.

Somehow, I'm not surprised. Somehow, this was inevitable.

Nora lets out a cry and drops something, and I wonder if whoever works here will come out now that we've made all this noise, but there's still no sign of anyone else existing inside this place. May's song keeps playing, scratchy and soft, the notes slightly broken, and I swear I can feel her breath on the back of my scalp.

The music slows, the record comes to a stop, and then Nora is standing beside me.

"How did you know?" She pulls the record off the turntable and inspects the label, but there's nothing written on it.

I point to the horseshoe-crab crank, but Nora isn't paying attention.

"Where's the cover for this record?" she asks.

I shift things around on the cluttered table and find a square white envelope with a hole in the center. It's the sleeve that protects a record inside its cardboard cover, and it's blank too, but then I turn it over and discover two tiny letters printed along the bottom edge.

K.M.

The bell on the front door jangles, and Nora and I jump. There's a big rack full of fur coats between us and the entrance, blocking our view, but Nora puts her finger to her lips and edges slowly sideways until she can see around it. She tips her head, listening, then creeps closer. I want to drag her back.

"There's no one here," she says.

"Seriously?" I say. "You heard the bell, right?"

"Maybe it was the wind." Nora winds her way through the clutter to peer through the window, but it's so dark, I don't know what she could possibly see out there. She stoops down by the door.

"Oh," she says quietly.

"What is it?" My mouth is bone-dry.

"Another one."

She holds up a Polaroid.

CHAPTER 26

I dash over to where Nora's standing, nearly toppling a hat rack and a grandfather clock on my way.

"Did you see who left it?" I ask.

"No," says Nora. "But I heard a car drive off just now."

She holds up the Polaroid, and I lean my chin on her shoulder so we can both look. A blond woman I instantly recognize stands with her back to the camera. In front of her is a white slash of beach and a roiling, gray ocean. Her right arm is outstretched; she's holding a white cup, and a dark liquid is pouring out onto the sand. It might be blood, but it's impossible to tell in the faded black-and-white image. In the border under the image is the letter *I*.

"May's sister," whispers Nora.

The air around us is staticky with an eerie sort of energy, and I don't need Nora to tell me that May is excited. I'm not going to acknowledge it out loud, though, because the last thing I want is for May to start speaking to me too.

"Why do you think there's an *I* underneath?" I ask.

"If the other one has an *M*, and May's real name also starts with *M*, then this woman's name must start with an *I*." Nora closes her eyes and rubs her temples. "I think it's either Isobel or Isabella."

"Maybe." I'm unconvinced, but I don't have any better alternatives. "Who do you think took these pictures? It doesn't look like she knew she was being photographed."

"I bet it was someone in the Hand of Nephthys," says Nora. "Maybe Huld, maybe someone else. They must have stalked their victims before killing them."

"But if you're so sure May's giving these to us, how did she get them? How is she physically moving them around if she's just a spirit?"

Nora shrugs. "I don't have the answers to absolutely everything, you know."

"It makes no sense," I say. "She could have just yelled 'Magpie antique store' in your head if she wanted to come here, like she did with Scargo Lake. I think someone else is leaving these for us. Someone who wants us to know more about the murders."

In the back of the store, there's a click, and the phonograph trickles out a few more notes of May's song. Absorbed in the second Polaroid, Nora barely seems to notice, but I'm ready to crawl out of my own skin.

"Let's get out of here," I say.

"Hang on," she murmurs. "I think I saw that cup."

Before I can respond, she dashes off and starts shifting things around on a table that's piled high with teapots and mugs.

"Got it." She holds up a small white vessel the size of a shot glass. "Whoa, come feel this thing."

I'm reluctant to touch the cup, which looks like it's been carved from ivory or bone and feels dangerous in a way I can't explain. As soon as my finger brushes it, my skin buzzes in a worryingly familiar way.

"This looks like a ceremonial vessel," says Nora. "May and her sister must have been practicing magic too."

"That's exactly what I've been thinking," I say.

Nora holds the cup to her nose and inhales. "This thing reeks of magic. Maybe they were in a rival coven or something?"

"I hadn't thought of that," I say. "But if they were in another secret society or coven, Ione might know about it. Seems like she knows all the various magical stuff that goes on around the Cape."

"Let's ask her." Nora checks her phone. "If we hurry, we can get to Midnight Alchemy before it closes."

A floorboard creaks behind us, and we both whirl around, but no one is there. No one we can see, anyway.

"Hello?" My voice cracks.

The crystals on an antique chandelier shimmer and tinkle. The rest of the store is silent. I still can't make out a single thing outside the black window. For all we know, the person who left the Polaroid is right on the other side of the pane.

"We need to leave *now*," I say. "How much is the cup?"

Nora checks the sticker on the bottom. "A dollar."

Something carved out of real bone or ivory should cost more than a dollar, but I don't care to stand around worrying about it. Just in case the phonograph counts as evidence, I snap a quick photo, and then one of the doormat where Nora found the second Polaroid. The chandelier is still swaying and clinking, and I cannot wait to get out of this place crammed full of dead people's things, hiding so many secrets.

I leave a dollar bill on the counter for the bone cup I wish we'd never found. We race out to the car and throw ourselves inside, and I don't stop shuddering until we're halfway to Hyannis.

CHAPTER 27

Even though Nora and I agreed on the way here that we'd only tell Ione some of what's happened, it's not as easy as we thought. After a few raised eyebrows and pointed questions from her, we break and spill absolutely everything. By the time we finish showing her the Polaroids, Ione's face is almost the same shade of green as the wool shawl draped around her shoulders. She pulls out a stool behind the counter and drops heavily onto it, then wraps her shawl tighter around herself with a shudder.

"What spell did you use that first night on the beach?" she says.

I glance at Nora, whose shoulders have gone into a guilty hunch.

"Um, it didn't really have a name," she says. "I saw it in a video online."

"Who posted it?" says Ione. "Do you still have the video?"

Nora pulls out her phone and swipes and taps for a while. She blows her hair out of her face. "Looks like it got deleted, but hang on, I downloaded a copy."

While Nora searches, Ione turns to me.

"You've always been so cautious with your practice, Mazzy. Why did you go along with this?"

"I—" I break off. Because Nora is my best friend in the world and I'd do anything to help her, to protect her, to get her out of trouble. Because it feels like our spells are finally, *finally* working and there's something so intoxicating about that. Because as much as I'm fighting it, that vision unlocked something inside me. Because I want to figure out what happened, make sense of this sordid mess, find justice for those dead women. Because I want it to be over so I can move on too. And maybe because I'm a little tired of being so cautious all the time.

"I don't know," I say.

Nora sets her phone down on the counter. "It's gone."

"What do you mean?" I ask.

"The video is gone," she says. "I looked everywhere, even in my deleted files. The thing has basically evaporated."

"Why am I not surprised?" mutters Ione.

"I'm not lying!" says Nora, and Ione shakes her head.

"I didn't think you were," she says. "I'm just not surprised the file is gone. To put it plainly, girls, this is *not good*."

Ione picks up a basket and heads for the back of the store, where she starts pulling herbs from the shelves.

"So, what do we do?" I ask. "How do we fix this?"

"For starters, you need to stop everything you're doing," says Ione. "Stop communicating with May, or whatever her real name is. Stop trying to figure out what happened to her, and above all, stop trying to find out about the Hand of Nephthys."

"But May needs—" Nora starts.

"May does not need anything," interrupts Ione, dropping a leafy bundle into her basket. "She's dead, and you can't fix that. Do you have any idea how many people the Hand of Nephthys have murdered over the years?"

"No," Nora and I say at the same time.

"At least fifty." Ione heads for the candle display. "Probably more, since they prey on people who are already on the fringes of society."

"Why aren't the cops looking for them, then?" I ask.

"Because nobody ever finds the bodies." Ione places three black candles in the basket. "And nobody finds the Hand of Nephthys."

They find you, I think with a shudder.

"So how do you know that all those people died?" asks Nora.

"I have my methods of seeing things," says Ione. "Let's just leave it at that."

"What *is* the Hand of Nephthys, though?" I ask. "Is it a coven?"

"They're devotees of the ancient Egyptian goddess Nephthys, or Nebet-Het," says Ione. "But they've taken all of the history and the ancient texts and manipulated them to fit their own twisted agenda. There's nothing in the Egyptian *Book of the Dead* about mortals coming back from the afterlife, but that doesn't matter to the Hand of Nephthys. They think they can force deities to bend to their will—or bribe them with sacrifices. Personally, I don't see how that could ever work, and a lot of people have ended up dead as a result of their experiments and rituals."

Nora and I exchange a look as Ione skirts behind the counter again and starts rummaging in the shelves beneath it. It sounds like we were right about a lot of the things we've been speculating on.

"It's a huge, horrible mess of cultural and magical appropriation," continues Ione. "The Hand of Nephthys steal and borrow and twist and warp any traditions they think will serve them—

even if they're closed practices they have no business touching. The result is terrifying, and highly unpredictable. A stitched-together jumble of unrelated, chaotic elements of power."

"Sounds like Franken-magic," says Nora.

"That's exactly what it is." Ione pulls out a spool of black thread and a notepad.

"Speaking of Frankenstein, are the Hand of Nephthys actually cutting people's hearts out?" I ask. "And does that have anything to do with Osiris weighing hearts on a scale?"

Ione pauses, tapping her pen on the notepad.

"I can only assume that as devotees of Nephthys, they believe you need your heart to pass on to the afterlife. They've probably got something twisted and terrible planned." She trails off, looking pensive for a moment.

My phone buzzes, and I don't even bother to check who's calling.

"Do you think there's any chance that one of the members could have infiltrated the police?" Nora says.

Ione tips her head. "How do you mean?"

"There's this detective who's allegedly working on the murder case," I say. "She's been following us everywhere, and we're suspicious about her motives."

"What's her name?" says Ione.

"Eva Huld." I pull out my phone and tap her name into the search engine to show Ione her photo on the police website.

"She wears a rune necklace and keeps asking us about the spell we did at Mayflower," says Nora. "She knows more about magic than she's letting on."

Ione takes a long look at Detective Huld's headshot, then

shakes her head. "I can't rule anything out completely, but she seems legitimate. If she were in the Hand of Nephthys, that would be incredibly difficult to pull off, since they fake their own deaths. She'd have to be using an alias and be pretty damn confident that nobody would recognize her from her previous life."

"What if she's using some kind of glamour magic?" says Nora. "And she has an accent, so she's probably from a different country, which would make it easier to hide from her past."

"With everything being online these days, it's not that easy to hide," says Ione. "You found her photo in about ten seconds."

"But what about our intuition?" Nora's voice is taking on a shrill edge. "Mazzy and I both feel like something is very off with this woman."

Ione holds up both hands in an appeasing gesture. "Listen, I'm only saying it's highly unlikely, not impossible. And it could be that your intuition is warning you about other things you haven't considered."

"Like what?" I say.

"It's possible she thinks you're somehow involved in the murders," says Ione.

"We've been wondering that too, but why would she think that?" I say.

"Who knows what she thinks?" Ione shrugs. "But in my opinion, the best way for you two to stop looking like murder suspects is to stop hanging around the crime scene. And also morgues and cemeteries."

Nora starts grumbling under her breath, but Ione continues talking.

"Once you sever your connection with May, this will all be

much easier. So let's talk about how to do that. Do you still have the bone cup?"

"I left it in the car," says Nora.

"What about the tooth?" says Ione.

"Um, it's at my house," says Nora, and I'm not sure I believe her. It wouldn't surprise me if she carries that gross little thing around in her pocket.

"That's fine," says Ione. "Just make sure you destroy them both tonight. Smash them with a hammer. Make sure they're pulverized, and bury the dust somewhere deep in the woods."

I nod, but I can feel Nora cringing beside me.

"Now, tell me as much of the original spell as you can remember," Ione says, uncapping her pen.

CHAPTER 28

Nora and I recount everything, from the snail shells to the sand dollar to the barnacle-crusted rock and the candle. Then we tell her all the words we can remember from the incantation.

"Okay." Ione stares into the space above our heads for a few seconds. "I'm going to write you a counter-spell and an unbinding spell to sever your connection with the dead woman." She starts writing in loopy, fast cursive.

"But what about all the other victims?" says Nora. "Are we supposed to just give up on finding justice for them?"

Ione's pen pauses as she stares at Nora. "Yes. That's exactly what you're supposed to do. You're seventeen years old, you are not an arbiter of justice, and there's no way in hell you can stop the Hand of Nephthys."

"Mazzy will be eighteen in January," says Nora.

Ione sets her pen down. "Do you have any idea how much danger you're potentially in right now? Or do you just not care?"

"We do care," I say. "But I'm not sure if we can *not* be in danger at this point. I mean, we've found two bodies, and May's been inside Nora's head. This doesn't feel like something either of us can just let go of."

Especially Nora. Whether she's connected to May or not, I can't see her just walking away from this whole mystery.

A flicker of worry flashes over Ione's face, but then her green eyes go steely. "You can absolutely let go. And then you move on with your life, and you hope the Hand of Nephthys either hasn't noticed you yet or loses interest."

Nora's hand squeezes into a fist; she tucks it into her coat pocket.

"Are you going to do the ritual with us?" I ask Ione.

She shakes her head. "You need to do it under as similar conditions as possible to the original spell. The moon phase, unfortunately, can't be helped, but bring the same people, wear the same clothes, find the same spot on the sandbar, and perform the ritual at the exact same time." She taps her chin with the pen. "Actually, the tide is more important than the time, and low tide will have shifted by now, so you'll have to look up a tide chart. Can you manage that?"

I can tell by Nora's expression that she's about to fire off a snarky response, but a sudden whooshing sound comes from the back of the store.

A . . . toilet flushing?

The door that leads to the back room swings open, and Tina emerges, looking sheepish. One side of her burgundy hair is all rumpled, like she's just woken up. But why would she be sleeping in the bathroom? Or was she sleeping in the storage room and then woke up and went to the bathroom? She doesn't work here and has no reason to be hanging out back there.

What the . . . Nora mouths at me.

"Hey there, girls." Tina's words are slurred and her pupils are the size of bus wheels, and I wonder, not for the first time, if she's using drugs. Maybe that's why she fell asleep in the bathroom.

167

Ione's mouth flattens into a thin line. "The shop closed twenty minutes ago," she says.

Tina rubs her eyes and yawns. "Sorry about that. I, uh, had some bad shrimp for lunch."

Nora's nostrils flare in disgust, but I feel bad for Tina. It's so clearly a lie. I hope she's getting help for whatever addiction she's dealing with.

Ione heads for the medicinal teas and pulls a box from the shelf. "Take this," she says. "It's on the house."

"Thank you," Tina says, looking guilty. "I'm really sorry about that."

"No worries." Ione leads her to the door and holds it open. "I hope you feel better soon. Call me if you need anything."

As we wave goodbye to Tina, Nora leans in to whisper, "Do you think she heard us talking?"

"I think she was passed out in there," I say.

"As much as I hate to agree with Mazzy, she's probably right," says Ione, shutting the door and sighing. "Tina's struggling again. I've tried to help her several times, but the thing is, she has to want to be helped."

I think of my dad, and my stomach knots with guilt. There has to be more you can do when someone is suffering like that. I just don't know what or how, and it still shocks me that most adults don't know how to fix it either.

"Anyway, I don't want you girls worrying about Tina," Ione says, returning to the counter. "You have more pressing matters right now. Do you know how to look up the tides?"

"Yes," says Nora.

"Good. Call me straight after you do the ritual." Ione writes her phone number at the bottom of the page, then tears the sheet off the pad and hands it to me. "And listen. I am very, deeply sorry that this is happening to you. All of it."

My laugh comes out shaky. "We thought you were going to blame us for doing that spell in the first place."

"Well, yes, that wasn't ideal," says Ione. "And I wish you'd told me what was happening much sooner, but none of this is your fault, and I hope you understand that."

My throat goes tight, and I don't know how to respond. It still feels like all our fault. Even though we didn't murder anybody or ask for any of this. We should have stopped as soon as it all started spiraling out of control. But May hasn't given us much of a choice.

"We were just trying to help," says Nora.

"I know." Ione rounds the counter and pulls us both into a hug. Through my coat I can feel her heart pounding. "But everything that's been done can be undone. We're going to fix this. It might get a little ugly, but as they say, the only way out is through."

I desperately want to believe her, but there's a tiny, unmistakable note of doubt in Ione's voice.

CHAPTER 29

"Is this the right size?" Crouched beside a silver tide pool, Elliot holds up a dripping rock.

"No, it needs to be smaller and rounder," says Nora, who's up to her elbow in another pool. "This one will work."

I'm kneeling by our circle in the sand, setting out the ritual items in my best approximation of their spots from last time. Nora places her barnacle-crusted rock beside the sand dollar and pulls the spool of black thread and a pair of scissors from her bag. Following Ione's instructions, we wind the thread around the candles, the stone, the shells, and the sand dollar until everything looks like a messy spiderweb. Then, using an eyedropper, Nora drips an oil blend that Ione gave us all over the thread.

The moon, no longer full, keeps slipping behind clouds, and my stomach is sloshing with nerves. I can't wait to be done with May, with all of this, but some tiny part of me is scared to let it all go and I don't know why.

"Now the mirror," I say, reading from Ione's instructions, and Nora takes our scrying mirror from her bag. This time we won't be using it to scry. In this ritual, the mirror will reflect everything

170

back to where it came from. I wedge it into the sand so it's upright, reflecting the altar and facing out to sea.

"Okay," I say, scanning the paper one last time. "Now we begin."

"Are you sure you have everything you need?" Elliot paces back and forth outside the circle. His hair is a tangled mess from the wind and from his constant tugging on it. I'm trying not to notice that he looks inexplicably hotter like this, in a distracted, tortured artist kind of way.

"Yes," snaps Nora. "I just looked at the list, and I'm sure Mazzy's checked like forty-seven times."

"It's going to be okay," I say, wishing I believed that myself. We're all desperately hoping we're not going to conjure up another dead body at the tide line if this goes wrong.

Elliot climbs on top of the boulder and swings his flashlight in all directions. "Nobody's out there. Dead or alive."

"Good," says Nora. "Now, can you please sit down? Your palpable stress is disrupting my intention."

I bite my lips together, because if Elliot's stress is palpable, mine must be positively chewable.

Muttering a sarcastic apology, Elliot sits and tucks his knees up, just like he did that first night. It feels like a lifetime ago, and once again, I wish I could go back in time and stop everything before it happened. But as Ione said, the only way out is through. The only direction is forward.

It takes me four tries to get the lighter lit, and then the wind keeps blowing the flame out before I can get it to the first candlewick. I'm trying not to read into that, because it's not like the wind ever stops, but I can't stop thinking that it's May blowing out the flame, that this is her last-ditch effort to stop us from banishing her.

"I'm sorry," I whisper, flicking the lighter again. "But we have to."
Again, it blows out.

"Here." Nora wedges the candle deeper into the sand and shields it with her hand, and finally, we get it lit.

"Remember not to look in the mirror," I say, pointing to Ione's note where it's been underlined and circled.

"I'm not going to look," Nora huffs. "Can we do this already? I'm freezing to death."

If I'm having guilt about severing this connection, I can't imagine how much worse Nora's feeling right now. I almost can't believe she's actually going along with this. We kneel in our spots, and together, we read the words Ione wrote. Our voices are shaky and faint, and the wind—or May—still seems intent on snuffing out our candles. But as the oil-anointed thread catches fire, the flame spreads to all of our ceremonial items. Our words grow stronger, louder. I'm starting to feel a sizzle in the air, a fizz of magic, and my pulse is speeding up.

The wind gusts hard, the candle flames stretch skyward, and I catch their reflection in the mirror. Quickly, I look away, but the afterimage of nine dancing flames is already seared in my brain. I try to focus on the ritual, the words, the steps—I've always been so careful about following the rules—but I can't stop myself from stealing another glance.

The flames become shadows, drawing inward from the edges of the mirror, growing larger and larger. I need to look away, but I can't, and then it's filling my vision until it's all I can see. Nine swaying, circling figures. The wind roars again, and inside the wall of sound, a woman is singing, her soprano voice soaring in a language I've never heard before.

The shadows become figures in long cloaks with white flames licking up from their hems. The singing continues, an invocation in that same indecipherable language, and other voices join in. I'm mesmerized, overwhelmed. A sudden feeling of delight hits me, an urge to laugh, to join in. The dancing figures warp and weave and bend like they're made of flames, and then, somehow, I'm singing too, in words I don't understand.

Now I'm standing in the center of the circle, and one of the cloaked figures is moving toward me. Their arm reaches out, and inside their wide sleeve, the silver handle of a dagger glints. I'm so close to being able to see the face tucked inside that hood, but smoke billows over us, blotting it out. We're all still singing, and I know, somehow, that I'm supposed to take the dagger. I don't want to, but my hand is reaching for it anyway.

Suddenly, a baritone voice roars, and my vision goes black. I topple backward, and the cloud-smeared night sky—the real one—appears. Nora is curled up in the damp sand beside me, sobbing.

Elliot stands in the center of our circle, shoulders heaving. The sand dollar and shells are crushed under his boots, and the mirror is gone.

CHAPTER 30

"Holy shit, holy *shit*," Elliot says. "What the hell was that thing?"

"What thing?" I feel like I've just woken from a coma and am struggling to understand reality.

He points his flashlight across the sandbar, where the mirror lies shattered.

"The wind cut out and the air went totally still as soon as you both started chanting," he says, "and then huge waves started rolling in. I thought we were going to get washed out, but neither of you even noticed, did you?"

I shake my head, and he continues, his eyes wild.

"It was like you went into a trance, and then Nora started singing in some weird language." He wipes sweat off his upper lip, his breath coming hard. "You started to sing too, Mazzy, and then this . . . this *hand* came reaching out of the mirror."

A dull roar fills my ears.

"What kind of hand?" Nora drags herself up to sitting. She looks like she's been hit by a bus.

"It was all gray and withered," says Elliot. "It looked like a corpse, but the fingers were moving." He gulps hard. "You started to reach for it, Mazzy, and I panicked. I grabbed the mirror and threw it."

I gulp down a mouthful of bile. Nora and I were so caught up, we had no idea what was happening. How is it possible that I almost touched a dead-looking hand that I somehow conjured *with my mind*? I can't imagine what might have happened if Elliot didn't break the connection with whoever . . . or whatever that was. Casting a horrified look at the two of us, Elliot walks over to the mirror and starts kicking sand on top of it.

"God, Nora," I say. "What did we just do?"

Her teeth are chattering. "Did you look in the mirror?"

I could lie. I *want* to lie. I never mess up like this.

"I'm so sorry," I say. "I didn't mean to."

Swallowing a sob, I duck my head and wait for one or both of them to yell at me. It's what I deserve. Something almost came crawling out of that mirror, and it was all my fault.

"It's okay," Nora wraps her arms around me. "Nothing happened. We're fine."

"We're *fine*?" A trail of snot flies out of my nose. "Ugh. Sorry," I say, wiping it away.

"I might have looked a tiny bit too," says Nora.

I sputter out something like a laugh. "How are we so *bad* at this?"

"I don't know, babe," she says, squeezing me tighter. "But I'm pretty sure we didn't stand a chance of not looking."

"Did you cut the thread?" I ask. It was the last step of the ritual, also underlined in Ione's notes.

Nora shakes her head. "I blanked out too, and now it's all burned away."

"Do you think burning it is just as good as cutting it?" I ask.

"Maybe." Nora doesn't even try to sound hopeful.

"Ione has way more faith in us than she should," I say, wiping my face on my sleeve.

"Who is this woman, anyway?" says Elliot, still kicking sand. "Obviously you know her from the shop, but what else do you know about her? What if she set you up to fail with this spell?"

"She lives in Centerville," I say. "She got divorced a couple of years ago, and she's one of the kindest people I know. I can't imagine she'd ever lie to us or trick us into doing dangerous spells."

"Let's call her." Nora pulls out her phone.

"That doesn't sound like a good idea," says Elliot.

"She told us to. Let's just see how she reacts when we tell her what happened." Nora taps in the number from Ione's paper, and Elliot exhales loudly and turns his back.

"Hey, Ione," she says, hitting the speakerphone button. "It's Nora."

"Can you hear me?" Ione's voice is scratchy and faint. "You sound like you're in a wind tunnel."

Nora switches off speaker and holds the phone to her ear. "Is this better?"

I pace the sandbar as Nora recounts everything to Ione. Elliot's still piling sand on the mirror. He must be horrified after what he just saw me do. After what I made happen. I hate, hate myself for being so weak. It wouldn't have been so hard to just shut my eyes, look away, stop the ritual—literally anything other than what I did. I'd like to dig a deep hole in the sand and bury myself, let the tide wash over me.

"No, you don't have to apologize," Nora says into the phone.

"We messed up too. I—yeah. We won't. Yeah, first thing after school. We could come earlier if—okay, sure, afterward. Ione, it's really fine, I swear. Nobody died."

My stomach flops. Several people have died. Just not us—yet.

"Okay," says Nora. "We'll see you then."

She hangs up and turns to me and Elliot. "Ione apologized like ten times for asking us to do that spell without her. She wants us to come to the store tomorrow after school so we can regroup."

"Are you sure you want to go back there?" says Elliot. "Look what just happened when you followed her instructions."

"It happened because we *didn't* follow them," I say, and guilt sucker punches me in the gut again. "She gave us all the right instructions, but we screwed it up by looking in the mirror."

"I don't think this is anyone's fault, really," says Nora. "Let's go talk to Ione tomorrow and figure things out from there."

Elliot looks like he's holding back about a thousand words. My head is pounding and my chest aches, and I just want to crawl into bed for the rest of my life.

"What did Ione say to do with the mirror?" I ask, eyeing the pile of sand.

"She said to smash it up—pulverize it and bury the dust, like with the bone cup," says Nora.

"I'll do it," says Elliot.

"Are you sure you want to?" I don't like the thought of any of us touching the shards.

"I'm the safest person to do it," he says. "There's zero chance of me hallucinating or getting sucked into a hypnotic trance. Plus, I've got tools for breaking down and recycling clay."

"Do you want to take the bone cup and the tooth too?" I say, but Nora shakes her head.

"I left them at my house when we stopped to get the ritual stuff," she says. "But don't worry. I'll smash them myself. It's not dangerous."

"I wouldn't bet on that," I mutter.

Leaving as much sand as possible on top of the mirror shards, we slide them into Nora's tote bag and I tie the straps tightly together.

Elliot reaches for the bag, and his cold fingers brush mine, but he doesn't make eye contact. I seriously contemplate flinging myself into the ocean, but I've caused enough drama for one night.

"May's not happy about this," says Nora as we make our way back across the flats. "She's positively *radiating* frustration right now."

"Good," I say, and for the first time in a long while, I think we might be making the right choice.

CHAPTER 31

Elliot has barely said a word since we left Mayflower and dropped Nora off at her house. I should have taken him home first, but I kept hoping I'd think of something to say once we were alone, find some way to explain what happened, to convince him that I'm still the same person, even though I just summoned an undead entity out of a mirror.

The problem is, I'm not sure I actually am the same person. I don't understand what's changed inside me, what makes me capable of these visions, these conjurations. My old self from a week ago couldn't have conceived of the things I'm suddenly doing. Is May's will leaching into mine now too? Have I somehow been infected with the Hand of Nephthys's magic? I don't want any of this.

We're turning onto Elliot's road now. I haven't thought of a single way to explain what's happening, and it's probably for the best. It's safer for him if he stays far away from me. I've never lost control like that, and I'm afraid of myself right now.

Something darts out from the side of the road, and I hit the brake. The car behind us screeches to a stop, barely missing our bumper. An opossum scuttles across, its uncanny little eyes gleaming in my headlights.

"Those things are so freaky," I say.

"They can't help looking like that," Elliot says, and my throat goes tight because I can't help what I'm like now either. I'm the last person who should be calling anything freaky. Nora and I are becoming unrecognizable, strange and dangerous, and I don't know how to make it stop.

As we pull up to Elliot's crooked little two-story house, motion sensor lights flick on, and I blink hard so my tears won't leak out.

"Hey, are you okay?" He turns in his seat, his voice soft with concern. His hair is still an inexplicably beautiful mess.

"Yeah." I press my lips together and swallow. "The lights are just too bright."

"Give it a few seconds and they'll go off again," he says.

We wait, and I'm sure he can hear how shuddery my breathing is, but I can't make it stop.

"I can't believe I messed that ritual up so badly," I say.

The spotlight clicks off, bathing us in darkness again.

"It's a hundred percent not your fault," he says. "Nobody could have predicted that a crusty old zombie hand was going to come out of that mirror." He pauses. "Right?"

I try to laugh, but it comes out more like a sob. There aren't words for how messed up this all is.

"And hey, if it makes you feel any better, I believe you and Nora about everything now," says Elliot. "I feel pretty stupid that it took me this long."

"Better late than never," I say, and he sighs.

"Listen, I know you and Nora trust Ione, but I just keep wondering if she knew this would happen," he says. "Isn't she supposed to be, like, this huge expert on witchcraft?"

"I don't think anybody has any clue what to do in this situation, including Ione," I say. "But we've known her for so long, and she's spent so many years teaching us how to stay safe in our practice, I just don't believe she'd intentionally hurt us."

Elliot doesn't look convinced.

"I'm glad you're letting me take the mirror," he says.

"Are you sure you're okay to smash it on your own?"

"Do you have any idea how excited I am to pulverize that thing?" He flashes a wicked grin. "I've been fantasizing about it the whole way here."

My lizard brain snags on the word "fantasizing," especially with the dark gleam in his eyes, but I force the unhelpful mental images away.

"You still have that protection charm I made you, right?" I say.

He pats the breast pocket of his coat, right over his heart. "I'm keeping it forever."

My own chest goes fluttery-warm, and maybe, just maybe, he doesn't think I'm a monster after all.

"I just—" I start to say, but Elliot speaks at the same time.

"Do you remember that night when we played Truth or Dare and you kissed Asher's dog?"

I laugh, startled by this sudden turn in the conversation. "Um, yeah, I guess? Eighth grade, right?"

"Ninth grade," he says. "Jessa dared you to kiss me, and you said you'd rather kiss Toby the beagle. And then you actually did it."

"Not on the mouth, on his nose!" I say, but my face is hot and

I'm kicking myself for not realizing how things would change. What if I'd just kissed Elliot then, instead of making a big fuss and kissing a dog? Would I have realized the truth? Was there something lying dormant inside me, even back then? Is that why I reacted in such an over-the-top way?

"I guess I just didn't want to make things awkward for you in front of Nora," I say.

"Nora?" Elliot looks puzzled. "What did she have to do with it?"

"Come on, we all know you've been in love with her for years."

He gapes at me. "Why would you think that? Because of that crush I had on her when I moved here?"

"Well, yeah," I say.

Elliot groans. "Okay, I did like her, but that only lasted a couple of weeks. Then I started getting to know both of you, and things... uh..."

He clears his throat and rubs the back of his neck. We're both leaning in so close we're almost touching. I can smell the salt on his skin, the sweetness of his breath. My heart is in my throat.

"Things what?" My voice cracks.

Sudden, bright light fills the car, and the thudding bass of a stereo shakes my seat. Elliot and I lurch away from each other as his older brother's giant pickup truck pulls in beside my car. The motion sensor lights flick on again, fully destroying any trace of the quiet, dark, honest... something that was happening between us. Elliot's brother, Aaron, jumps out of the truck, then stoops to peer inside our car.

"Nice," he mouths, widening his eyes and flashing a thumbs-up at Elliot.

"Jesus," mutters Elliot as Aaron heads inside the house. "Sorry about that."

THINGS WHAT??? I want to scream, but the moment is gone, and instead I say, "Don't worry about it."

Elliot picks up the tote bag from the floor, and I cringe as the mirror shards clink inside.

"Please, please be careful with that," I say, but he just smiles.

"When I get done with this thing, it'll be broken down into molecules."

"Text me once it's done, so I don't have to worry about you," I say. "I won't be able to sleep."

"Okay." He opens his door, and I want to pull him back inside and demand that he tell me what he was about to say, but considering everything that's going on—and the fact that he's about to destroy a mirror that an undead being tried to crawl out of—it'd be ridiculous for me to even consider kissing him now.

Ridiculous, but still permanently stuck in my brain, as I wave goodbye and back out of the driveway.

CHAPTER 32

An hour later, my phone vibrates.

> Elliot: IT IS DONE

Underneath is a flash-lit photo of a hole in the ground with gray dust inside.

> Elliot: No hands came out, no hallucinations or singing either
>
> I filled in the hole after I took this picture
>
> Me: Thank you for doing that
>
> Elliot: Hopefully you can sleep now

I wish it were that easy. I send him a heart.

> Me: You're the best

Dots, then nothing.
Then dots.

> Elliot: Do you ever feel like maybe we're cursed
>
> Me: Like, me and you?

Delete.

> Me: What do you mean

> Elliot: I don't know

obviously everything is kind of cursed right now

> Me: I don't want me and you, like the
> possibility of us, to be

Delete.

> Me: But did you mean

Delete.

> Me: We'll be ok i think

> Elliot: yeah

> Me: What were you going to say

Delete.

> Elliot: ok good night

> Me: I just

Delete.

> Me: night

As I'm plugging my phone into the charger, I scroll through the list of missed calls from Detective Huld, starting at three p.m. and ending at nine. She's left three voicemails. I call my inbox.

3:05 p.m.: "Hello, Mazzy. This is Detective Huld. Could you give me a call when you get this message? Thanks."

5:32 p.m.: "Hi, Mazzy. Detective Huld again. I need you to call me as soon as possible. It's important. Thanks."

8:57 p.m.: "This is Detective Huld. I didn't want to have to say this in a voicemail, but it seems you don't want to return my calls. I'm going to be frank here. You and your friends are messing with things that need to be left alone, and if you keep this up, you're going to end up in far bigger trouble than you can imagine. Just stay out of it. All of it. I'm trying to help you here, but I can't be responsible for your safety if you don't listen. This is the last time I'll call you, Mazzy. You need to make a choice. I hope you'll make the right one."

"End of new messages."

The automated woman's voice is so jarringly pleasant after what I've just listened to. Detective Huld knows we're investigating the Hand of Nephthys, and she's threatening us, in no uncertain terms. Ione was wrong about her. Maybe Huld faked her death back in her home country and had reconstructive surgery to change her appearance. Or maybe she got an exception to the death-faking rule because the Hand of Nephthys needed her to go undercover. Whatever she did, we are not safe.

I call Nora, but she doesn't pick up. I text her, but the message sits there unread. Hopefully, it's only because she's asleep. Even though Detective Huld said she wouldn't call again, I can't stop worrying about it, so I switch off my phone. It's past midnight and I need to sleep, but I can't calm my turbulent thoughts, can't stop hearing that emotionless, accented voice repeating her message.

You need to make a choice.

I want to trust that we actually have the ability to choose our actions, but after what happened tonight, it's getting harder and harder to believe we can control anything.

CHAPTER 33

The next morning, as soon as Nora's front door swings open, I know everything is not okay. She's wearing gray sweatpants and a hoodie, there's not a speck of makeup on her ghost-white face, and her hair hangs limp and greasy. Regular Nora would never set foot outside like this.

"What's wrong?" I ask as she gets into the car.

"What *isn't* wrong?" she says, taking a gulp from a travel mug that smells like coffee.

"You never texted me back," I say.

"Sorry," she says. "I had a big fight with my mom and she took my phone away for the night. I just woke up like ten minutes ago, and I feel like trash." She sets her coffee down and drags her hands through her dirty hair. "Do you have a hair tie?"

I pull mine off my wrist and hand it to her. "Detective Huld called me a bunch more times last night," I say. "And she left the creepiest voice—"

Nora lets out a sudden, strangled yelp and hunches forward, almost slamming her forehead into the dashboard. Her travel mug lands on the floor. Quickly, I pull over to the side of the road.

"What's happening?" I ask. "Are you okay?"

Her back is heaving, her breath a high-pitched wheeze.

"Do you need me to call 911?" I'm starting to panic. "Should I drive you to the hospital?"

She shakes her head *no*, then makes that strangled noise again and claps both hands over her ears. I want to cry. I want to call my mom. I want both of us to be anywhere but here.

"Can you not hear that?" Nora gasps.

"Hear what?" I lean in close, but all I hear is the ticking of my blinker and the intermittent roar of cars passing us on the road.

"*Her,*" says Nora, and my stomach clenches.

"May, leave her alone," I say, but I doubt the dead woman cares what I want. When Nora told me about May screaming inside her head, I had no idea it was this visceral, this painful. What kind of monster does that to someone?

"We need to go . . . to the marsh . . . near Grays Beach," wheezes Nora.

My gut is churning. There's no question of why May wants us to go there.

"What if we don't want to?" I slam my hand against the steering wheel. "We're not your puppets, May." And Detective Huld warned us in no uncertain terms to stay away from all of this.

With a howl, Nora doubles over again, clawing at the sides of her head with her fingernails.

"Stop it." I try to pull her hand away. "You're hurting yourself."

I wrack my brain, thinking of herbs, of protections, of banishing words that might get rid of May, even for a few minutes so Nora can breathe, but this is so far beyond anything I've ever studied in my spell books. I hate May for this, especially considering everything we've already done to try to help her.

"We just . . . need to go." Nora is wheezing now, her face slick with sweat.

Shakily, I shift the car into drive. "If we do, will she stop this?"

Nora lets out a guttural groan.

"May," I say, easing back out onto the road. "We're going there now. Stop whatever you're doing to Nora. Let go of her. This isn't okay."

Slowly, Nora's wheezing fades. As she uncurls her body, I find myself wishing May was a corporeal being so I could wring her neck.

"My coffee spilled on the floor," Nora says. "Sorry."

"That is literally the least of our worries," I say. "Are you all right?"

She picks up her travel mug. "I don't feel like my head's about to explode anymore, but she's still here."

I swear under my breath, wondering how we let things spin this wildly out of control. I never should have listened to Nora when she said we should let May in. We never should have done any of those rituals. We severely underestimated this woman. She's a vengeful spirit, an unstoppable force, and she must have been a hideous human being before she died. It's too bad the Hand of Nephthys killed her, because she would have fit right in with them.

"Can you call Ione?" I ask.

Nora nods and pulls out her phone.

"Straight to voicemail," she mutters, tapping out a text message. Even with my eyes on the road, I can see her hands shaking.

At the next traffic light, I waver. If I turn right, we can get to Midnight Alchemy in less than ten minutes. It won't be open yet, but Ione might go in early. We could park outside and keep calling until she either answers or shows up for work.

The light turns green, and I start to nudge the wheel right.

Nora screams. The sound coming out of her mouth is agonizing, broken, terrifying.

"Sorry, sorry," I say. With my heart in my throat, I cut the wheel left and head for Grays Beach.

CHAPTER 34

It's raining again by the time we pull into the parking lot, the droplets tiny and slushy. I start to drive toward the water, where a long boardwalk stretches out over the marsh, but Nora shakes her head and points in the direction of the playground and barbecue pavilion.

"She wants us to go that way. To find another sister."

Swallowing a mouthful of bile, I circle around and park beside the bathrooms, then shut off the car.

"Let's call 911," I say, "Let them find the body."

But Nora just shakes her head like she's too worn down to fight anymore. Like she's resigned to being May's puppet. Watching her break down like this is almost more horrifying than finding another corpse.

"Hey—" I start, but she just gets out, leaving the door open, and starts walking across the lot. The wind howls, covering Nora's empty seat in icy raindrops, and I can't let her do this alone. Muttering curses at May and her entire bloodline, I climb out, slam both doors, and follow.

Nora cuts through the playground, and I wonder if the next body is somewhere here—laid out under a picnic table or propped up on a swing—and my stomach lurches. But then she veers right, toward a narrow trail that cuts into the woods. I just want to drag her back to my car, lock her inside, and drive far, far away, but we'll never escape May. Instead, I hurry to catch up, and I take Nora's freezing hand in mine and squeeze. She squeezes back.

The path meanders through a small forest of gnarled trees, the dirt soft under our feet. Then the woods end, and a wide marsh opens up. It smells of low tide, dank and pungent and mucky. A boardwalk runs over a narrow channel of water, and as we trudge across the wooden planks, the dread in my chest gets heavier and tighter until I can barely draw a breath. When will this ever stop? How do we make it stop?

Nora pauses at the end of the boardwalk and lets go of my hand. She closes her eyes and sways with the wind, and I swear I hear a voice in between the raindrops, whispering something I can't quite understand. Something I don't want to understand.

With her eyes still shut, Nora steps off the path and wades into the grass, but I hang back. We're not supposed to go off the path. It's bad for the whole ecosystem because the grass is holding the soil in place, preventing erosion. Not to mention the mud is deep in places, and the low-tide muck smells like a toilet.

Nora's in the channel now, up to her knees in water, wading back toward the boardwalk. Eyes still fully closed.

"Please, get out of there." I double back across the planks to meet her. She takes a deep breath, and for one horrible second I think she's about to dive in, but she leans down and pulls something out from under the boardwalk.

A wrist. Attached to a long, white arm. Filthy lace. No hand.

"Don't," I say as Nora continues to pull, slowly dragging the woman's body out. "Nora, stop!"

Her eyes snap open, and she stares at me, but I'm not sure she actually sees me.

"Nora Elise Hawthorne," I say. "Listen to me."

She pauses, still holding that sawed-off stump of a wrist, and I want to vomit.

"Leave her there," I say again, forcing steadiness into my voice. "It's enough that you found her. It's all May wants."

She doesn't answer, but she stops pulling. I hurry to the end of the boardwalk, wade through the boggy grass, and jump into the channel. Instantly, my feet and calves cramp, but I keep wading until I've got Nora and then I pry her fingers away. The arm flops into the water with a splash. This woman was decades older than the others when she died. Her sunken face is creased with wrinkles, and her long, gray hair is streaked green with seaweed.

"This can't be May's sister," I say. "She's too old."

"That's what she called her," says Nora. "She said it multiple times."

I mull over the word, and all the things it might mean. "I think we were right about them being in a rival coven," I say. "They're sisters in that sense, not the biological one."

But Nora just turns away and starts whispering to herself, something fast and repetitive and panicky.

"Come on," I say, pulling her back to the muddy shore. She slips in the grass and lands on her knees. Her sweatpants are coated in foul-smelling mud, and her nose is running. She still keeps whispering, even as I drag her onto the boardwalk.

"She's laughing," says Nora. "May is *laughing* right now."

I'm about to be sick, right here on the boardwalk. If this is funny, what kind of sick game is May playing with us? I pull out my phone, but Nora slaps it out of my hand. It skitters across the boards and almost lands in the water.

"What the—?" I say.

"We can't call the cops," she says.

"I was going to take a picture of the body."

"My fingerprints are on that arm," says Nora. "I've found three dead bodies in less than a week. I'll go to jail."

"I wasn't calling the cops, and they're not going to put you in jail," I say, picking up my phone, which is miraculously unbroken. "There's no proof that you did it. Unless you've got murder weapons stashed somewhere in your house?"

It's meant to be a joke, but Nora's eyes dart sideways.

"What if they found one in my house, though." She doesn't phrase it like a question.

"But they wouldn't." The world is starting to go all fuzzy around me. "They wouldn't, Nora. Right?"

She shrugs. "It's such a mess with all the moving boxes. It'd be so easy to hide things."

This whole conversation has taken a sudden and bizarre turn.

"Do you think someone is framing you for these murders?" I ask.

"No."

"Then why are you talking about hiding murder weapons?"

She clenches her fists and starts whispering again, but I can't hear her words over the sound of my teeth chattering.

"What?" I say.

"I said, what if we're next?" A tear slides down Nora's cheek. "What if that's why we keep finding these bodies?"

Fear spreads like ice through my veins. Whether that idea is coming from May or from Nora herself, it's horrifying. She's nearly hyperventilating now, and I try to put my arm around her, but she won't let me.

"We need to go to the . . ." I trail off as the enormity of our situation hits me. Detective Huld's voicemail last night. Her threats of bad things happening to us if we didn't stop meddling. And now we've meddled again, and another body has turned up. *I can't be responsible for your safety if you don't listen,* she said, and we didn't listen. But what choice did we have? I'm certain Nora would have ended up in the hospital with brain damage or an aneurysm if we hadn't followed May's orders.

All I know is that we can't keep doing this on our own. It's long past time for us to talk to our parents. Even if they don't know exactly what to do. Even if it makes my dad start drinking again. We need practical advice on how to handle this situation with the authorities, not just magical help from Ione.

Nora's gasping breath slowly eases, and her eyes drift shut. I desperately hope this doesn't mean May is back. Carefully, I reach my phone over the side of the bridge to take a photo of the dead woman, but she's drifted underneath again, and there's no way I'm getting back in that water to pull her out. I can just make out the bottom of her shoe, so I snap a photo of that, for whatever it's worth.

"Come on," I say, taking Nora's elbow. She's shivering and drenched, her boots squelching. "Let's go to the car. We'll drive to your house and get cleaned up, put on some dry clothes, make some tea, and we'll just talk for now. We'll figure something out, okay?"

"The police can't help us," she whispers. "Ione can't help us. Nobody can help us. I think maybe . . ." She trails off and starts twisting a strand of her hair.

"Maybe what?"

"Nothing," she mutters.

~ ~ ~

The whole way to her house, Nora scrolls on her phone. Half of me is irritated that she's ignoring me, and the other half is relieved that she seems to be disconnected from May—for now. She's still shivering so hard I can hear her teeth clattering, but being cold is a simple thing we can handle. Once she puts on dry clothes, it will go away. May, on the other hand . . .

"Can you text Elliot?" I ask. "See if he can leave school and meet us?"

"Elliot can't help us either," she says, but she taps out a message anyway.

Seconds later, her phone vibrates, and she catches her breath.

"Is that him?" I ask, relieved that Elliot is checking his phone during school.

"Who?" Nora doesn't look up.

"Elliot. Did he write back?"

"Um." Nora's thumbs fly over her screen. "No."

"Who are you messaging, then?" I ask.

My only answer is the rapid clicking sound of her keypad.

"Hey," I say, turning onto her street. "Who are you writing to?"

Nora sets her phone face down on her leg. "Nobody."

It's so obviously a lie. I wonder how long she's been lying to me.

CHAPTER 35

While Nora showers, I change into a pair of her leggings and grab dry socks from her dresser. There's not much I can do about my soaked boots—she wears a smaller shoe size than I do—so I prop them up beside her heater. Warm and damp is better than cold and damp, at least.

The shower's still running as I head for the kitchen in search of a shopping bag for my wet clothes. The whole room is stacked with moving boxes, some open, some filled and sealed, some empty. Nora's refusing to pack until the day before they leave. She says she doesn't want to feel like she's camping in her own house, even though it's not going to be her house for much longer.

Hoping her mom hasn't packed the shopping bags yet, I pull open the drawer beside the fridge. It's still stuffed with paper bags, but my clothes will soak right through those, so I keep digging. At the bottom, I find another one of Nora's witchy tote bags, this one printed with skulls and moths. It's surprisingly heavy.

As I pull the bag out and peek inside, I almost drop it. There's a meat cleaver inside. The blade must be six inches wide, and twice as long. My mouth goes paper-dry. This thing could take someone's hand off, if you really wanted it to. But no, I'm letting my imagination run wild. The blade looks clean, and there's no sign of blood on the bag. Maybe Nora's mom put it in there so it wouldn't cut anything when they packed it. But why put it in the bottom of a drawer instead of a moving box?

"Nora?" I call, tapping on the bathroom door. "Are you almost done?"

No answer. The shower is still running, and she must be out of hot water by now. I rub the goose bumps off my arms and knock on the door again. "Hey, are you okay in there?"

"I'm fine!" she calls.

Back in her room, I set the bag on her rumpled bed. We have to talk about this before we even consider going to our parents. She was so unhinged in the marsh, and now there's a huge knife in her bag. I'm grasping for a rational explanation here.

What if they found a murder weapon at my house? she said.

Nora could never murder someone. Surely that's obvious. But she knew exactly where these bodies were, and if I remove May from this equation, there's no rational explanation for knowing that. Our parents aren't going to believe us about May speaking to her, and I can't exactly blame them. It was hard for me to believe at first too.

Even now . . .

I've never technically heard May speaking. Only Nora has. What if we've all been imagining her? Or what if Nora's been—I don't want to finish my next thought. It feels like a boulder is crushing my lungs. I wonder who Nora was messaging in the car on the way here. I wonder if they know something I don't.

My eyes stray to her laptop on the desk. The shower is still running. On silent feet, I cross the room and flip the screen up. Her password is the same as it's always been. Cringing at this breach of trust, even though she's absolutely been lying to me, I open her internet browser.

Mystical Mysteries

She's still logged in, and there's a new private message in her inbox.

"Sorry, Nora," I whisper as I click the mailbox icon, then gasp at the screen full of messages between her and some stranger she's never once mentioned talking to. I scroll up and start reading somewhere in the middle of their conversation.

Anon09: Now that I've answered your questions, it's your turn to answer mine. Why are you so curious about the HoN?

May_be: no specific reason, i'm just interested in occult stuff

Anon09: There's something more. I have a strong sense about you. Does this have to do with that woman who washed up on Mayflower Beach?

May_be: how did you know?

Anon09: Your username might have something to do with it :)

May_be: oh right, yeah i guess i do feel a connection to her

Anon09: I knew it. And unusual things are happening, aren't they?

May_be: more than you could ever imagine

"Jesus, Nora," I mutter. Every nerve in my body is crawling. "Why are you talking to this creep?" I tiptoe to the door to make sure the shower is still running, then hurry back to the laptop.

Anon09: Is she speaking to you?

It's all I can do to keep from slamming the laptop shut. Everything about this is terrifying.

There's a lag of several hours before the next message.

Anon09: Is she?

May_be: i don't want to answer that

Anon09: What spell did you use to find her?

May_be: i also don't want to answer that. i don't know you.

Anon09: And yet here you are, asking for help from strangers on the internet. Do you think anybody else on this forum has any idea what's happening to you? I do. I can help.

May_be: the dead woman talks to me sometimes, and i had a vision that i think was about her

"That was *my* vision," I whisper, irritated that Nora's taking credit for it, even though the last thing I want is to impress some nosy creep on the internet.

Anon09: Fascinating. Tell me more.

May_be: i don't really want to share private stuff on here

Anon09: If you tell me more, I'll tell you more ;)

May_be: are you actually in the HoN or something?

Anon09: Anything is possible.

"Nora Hawthorne!" I yell. "Please tell me you have not been actively messaging the Hand of Fucking Nephthys behind my back."

The water is still running in the bathroom.

May_be: are you trying to trick me into becoming your next sacrifice victim?

Anon09: Believe me, if the HoN knew someone like you existed, someone who had visions of the dead and could speak with them, you'd be the last person they'd sacrifice. They'd love to have you as a member. You have a rare gift.

May_be: i wish i could return this gift

Anon09: It's getting worse, isn't it? It's only going to keep getting worse. Do you think you can stand it?

Anon09: I'd really like to help you.

Anon09: I'll text you a time and place. You can think about it.

May_be: thanks but i'm all set. anyway you don't have my phone number

Anon09: I might ;)

There's a loud crash in the bathroom. I dash into the hall and bang on the door.

"Hey! What just happened in there?"

No answer. I knock again.

"Nora? Answer me!"

Nothing. Panic hits me like a cannonball.

"Nora!" I scream, pounding on the door. "Open up!"

But the shower just keeps running. I grab one of my boots from Nora's room and shove it onto my foot, then run back to the bathroom and kick the door hard. It crunches and springs open, and I rush inside. Instead of the steamy warmth I was expecting, it's cold and oddly windy.

The shower is still running. The tub is empty. There's a broken candle jar on the floor, and the window beside the toilet is wide open.

Nora is gone.

CHAPTER 36

"Nora?"

I poke my head out the window; she's not in the backyard. Her wet clothes lie crumpled up on the bathroom floor, but I remember that she brought dry ones into the bathroom with her, and those are gone. I don't know if she has shoes. I really hope she does.

"Nora!" I call, but there's no answer, so I head for the front door, let myself out, and do a circuit around her house. My car is still in the driveway, there are no vehicles on the road, and Nora has definitively vanished. I try calling her, but she doesn't pick up. There's no sound of her phone ringing anywhere in the house, and I can't find her wallet either. Kidnapped people don't usually take their stuff with them. That should make me feel better, but it doesn't.

I try calling Elliot, but he doesn't answer because he's still in class.

Call me it's an emergency, I text him.

Swearing, I pace up and down Nora's hall. Did she run away, or was she taken? Either way, I should call the police. Or should I call

Detective Huld? That's probably a terrible idea, considering those voicemails she left. On the other hand, she might be the only person who actually knows where Nora is.

Maybe she's Anon09.

The thought knocks all the wind out of me, but this is not the time to have a panic attack. I need to think, need to figure out what to do before it's too late. If Detective Huld is Anon09, I absolutely cannot call her. If Detective Huld is a kidnapper, I have to trust the other police to handle this.

I dial 911 for the second time this week. That's two times more than I've ever called in my life.

"What's your emergency?" says the woman on the phone.

"My friend is missing," I say. "Her name is Nora Hawthorne, and she's seventeen years old. She has black-and-red hair and she's about five foot three."

"How long has she been missing?" asks the woman.

"Somewhere between twenty minutes and an hour." I cringe at how ridiculous it sounds.

"I'm sorry, but that's not enough—"

"No, you have to understand." I cut her off. "There's more to this story. We . . ." I gulp, take a deep breath. "We found a dead body earlier today. But we didn't report it."

Complete silence.

"And I'm worried that she's in serious danger as a result." My voice is wobbling so hard I can barely get the words out.

"May I have your name, please?" says the dispatcher.

"It's Mazzy Carlin."

"Is that your full name?"

"Yes."

"And what's the address where you are right now?"

"Twelve Burke Lane, in West Yarmouth."

"Are you currently in any danger?" she asks.

"I . . . don't think so." Honestly, I have no idea anymore.

"We're sending an officer."

CHAPTER 37

Forty minutes later, a cruiser pulls up in front of Nora's house, and as a male officer with bristly gray hair and mirrored sunglasses gets out, I hurry down the front steps to meet him. I'm irritated that it took him so long to get here but also grateful that Detective Huld didn't come.

"Are you Mazzy?" he says, and when I nod, he continues. "I'm Officer Geary. Tell me what's going on."

I launch into the whole story, starting from Nora going missing and working backward. It's confusing, even to me, but the words are tumbling out so fast I can't stop. At some point, Officer Geary stops taking notes and just stands there staring at me.

"You're the ones who called in the false report of a body at Scargo Lake?" he says, propping his sunglasses on top of his head.

"It was our friend Elliot who called—but wait." The full meaning of his sentence sinks in. I take a step back and bump into the FOR SALE sign. "What do you mean, *false* report?"

"There was no body at the lake," he says. "We found footprints all over the sand in the spot he mentioned, but there was no sign of a corpse anywhere."

"Did you search the water? Maybe she . . ." I trail off. It's not like there's a tide in a lake that could have pulled the body back in. And it's not like she rolled into the water herself. The thought makes me nauseous. "Look," I say, pulling out my phone. "This is the body we found today. It's not a very good picture, but this is her foot."

Officer Geary squints at my screen as I zoom in, but the shoe is barely visible and looks more like a submerged rock than anything.

"Elliot has a better photo of the body at Scargo," I say. "He's at school now, so he can't answer his phone, but you could call the school or we could go there."

Officer Geary doesn't acknowledge the suggestions. "We sent divers into Scargo Lake, but they didn't find anything. So we assumed it was a prank call from some kids who heard about the woman washing up on Mayflower—"

"Whose body is *also* missing now," I interject.

Officer Geary's gray eyebrows go sky high. "Excuse me?"

"I . . . uh, heard the body went missing from the morgue," I say.

He regards me evenly. "Where did you hear that?"

"It's just a rumor going around," I say. "Where's Detective Huld? She's usually the person we talk to."

"She's not working today," he says.

"Isn't she the main investigator, though? Could she not come in on her day off for a literal dead body?"

"It's not your business what she does on her day off," says Officer Geary.

I don't even want to think of all the things she could be getting up to.

"Listen," I say, squeezing my hands into fists and forcing my voice into a reasonable tone. "Nora was messaging someone online about this group called the Hand of Nephthys, and I'm worried it was actually Detective Huld. Do you want to see the messages on her laptop?"

Officer Geary pulls out his notepad again. "What did you say your friend Elliot's last name was?"

"Winters," I say. "Can I go inside and get Nora's laptop? Detective Huld was acting suspicious and kept calling us, and a couple of days ago, Nora joined this message board called Mystical Mysteries—"

"You kids aren't messing around with satanic stuff, are you?" Officer Geary asks.

"What?" I say. "No. We're pagans, not satanists."

He takes in my fake Doc Martens, my all-black clothing, the skull pin on the lapel of my coat, and I doubt he knows or cares about the difference between the two groups. But it doesn't matter. I don't actually care what anyone thinks; I just need them to find Nora.

Officer Geary's radio chirps, and he pulls it out. "Excuse me for a minute."

He gets into the cruiser to speak to someone, and I dash inside and grab Nora's laptop. When I come back out, my mom's car is pulling into the driveway. She and my dad both get out, and I groan as Henry waves from his booster in the back seat. When I texted her, I wasn't expecting the whole gang to show up.

"Mazzy!" My mom rushes over. "What's going on? Did they find Nora?"

I shake my head, blinking back tears. Every second that I'm

stuck here talking is another second for Nora to be getting further into trouble.

My dad pats my shoulder awkwardly. "They'll find her. Or she'll come back on her own."

"Did you two have an argument?" my mom asks.

"No," I say, but before I can elaborate, Officer Geary emerges from the cruiser. His face is pinched with irritation.

"They checked the boardwalk at Grays Beach, and there was no body there either," he says.

"What do you mean?" says my mom. "Who's looking for a body?"

"It wasn't the main boardwalk," I say. "It was the boardwalk on the trail by the playground."

"Yes." If Officer Geary's jaw gets any tighter, he won't be able to speak. "They looked under both boardwalks, actually."

"Did they check the water near the trails too?" I say. "Maybe the tide went down and she floated away?"

"They searched everywhere," he says, but there's no way they had enough time to conduct a thorough search of the whole area. I want to scream.

"Okay, but can you please look at this?" I almost drop Nora's laptop as I try to open the Mystical Mysteries page. Everyone waits as I balance the computer on the stair railing and then click the mail icon in the corner of the page.

"She was talking to—" The rest of the sentence dies in my throat.

The conversation between Nora and Anon09 is gone.

CHAPTER 38

My knees go wobbly, and I sit down hard on Nora's front steps. Again, I refresh the page, but the message chain simply isn't there. I try closing and reopening the window; I click on her browsing history. Nothing. It's like it never existed.

"No, no, no," I mutter, clicking frantically.

"Mr. and Ms. Carlin, can I have a word with you?" says Officer Geary. "Alone."

I glance up. "Why alone?"

"Why don't you go sit in the car with Henry?" my dad says gently. "He's looking pretty lonely back there."

I'd prefer to stay and listen to whatever they have to say, but they all just stand there, waiting in silence, until I close the laptop and walk to my mom's car.

"Fuuu—fudge," I mutter, sliding into the back seat and dropping my head into my hands.

Henry perks up. "Does the police officer have fudge?"

"No, buddy," I say. "It's just an expression."

"Did they find Nora?" he asks.

I shake my head, and a tear falls onto her laptop.

"It's okay," he says. "The lady said she'd take care of her."

I sit up. "What lady?"

Henry laughs. "You look like a possum."

"I . . . what?" I wipe my eyes, and my hand comes away smeared with eyeliner. "Oh, do you mean a raccoon?"

He nods. "Or a badger!"

"Henry." I lean in close. "What lady are you talking about?"

"You know," he says, widening his eyes conspiratorially. "That lady I drew a picture of."

I'm about to lose the contents of my breakfast, right here in the car. "Were you talking to her?"

"A little." He shrugs, like that's a perfectly normal conversation to have.

"When did you talk to her?"

"Hmm." Harry taps his nose. "I can't remember."

I bite my lips together to keep from screaming.

"What did she say?" I finally manage.

"I already told you. She said she'd take care of you and Nora."

"Me and Nora? You never told me that."

"Yes, I did." Henry has the absolute gall to look annoyed.

Take care of us. That could mean two very different things. I hope she's not "taking care of" Nora right now. I need to get out of this car and get some air—right now.

As I shove the door open, another car pulls up. Nora's mom jumps out and hurries over to my parents and Officer Geary. Not caring whether I'm not supposed to overhear, I follow her.

"Mazzy." Nora's mom turns to me. "What did Nora say to you right before she disappeared?"

"I can't remember exactly," I say. "Probably something like 'I'm getting in the shower now'?"

"Were you fighting?" she asks.

"We had a . . . disagreement over how we should handle what was going on."

Nora's mom squints at me. "Is this about the body you found at Mayflower?"

"We found another one. Two, actually. There are three in total now." I'm fully aware of how absurd it sounds, of how everyone around me tenses. "I swear I'm not lying. Elliot has a photo of the second one on his phone."

My parents and Officer Geary glance at each other. Officer Geary clears his throat.

"Just to be clear, no bodies were found today," he says.

My mouth falls open. "But we saw it, I swear! Call the school. Elliot will show you."

He shakes his head. "The search team didn't find any forensic evidence of a corpse in either location."

I'm starting to wonder if he's gaslighting me, if there's some reason why the police are covering this up. It makes no sense—unless they're all in league with Detective Huld, and by extension, the Hand of Nephthys. Maybe Huld doesn't actually have the day off and Officer Geary is lying about absolutely everything. I contemplate telling him about the Polaroids, but I'm afraid he'll confiscate them and I'll never see them again.

Nora's mom sighs. "I've been working too much lately, and Nora's so upset about us moving. She and I had a big argument last night, and I bet she ran off to her dad's house in Falmouth. It wouldn't be the first time she did this to punish me."

"This isn't some petty punishment!" I feel like I'm losing my mind.

Nora's mom ignores me and heads toward the house, tapping on her phone.

"She was talking to someone online," I say, "but the conversation got deleted, and I think it might have been Detective Huld."

"Sweetie." My mom tries to put her arm around me, but I twist away. "You and Nora have been through so much this week, and I blame myself for not making you a therapy appointment."

"That *detective* has been calling me for days," I say. "And she left me a super-creepy voicemail. Listen."

I pull out my phone and call my voicemail.

"You have no new messages," says the automated voice. "You have zero saved messages."

"Are you kidding me right now?" I hang up, then try again, but still, there are zero messages in my inbox.

"Mazzy, look at me." My mom holds up her hands like I'm afraid she'll hurt me. "This is a trauma response. I know it's scary, but we're going to get you some help. We'll work through it together."

Over by the house, Nora's mom is pacing back and forth, saying things like "uh-huh" and "yeah" and "exactly" into her phone.

"Go talk to Elliot," I say. "Please. I'm not lying."

"Okay, okay." Officer Geary is now wearing the most patronizing smile I've ever seen. "We'll talk to him. In the meantime, why don't you head on home with your parents? I promise I'll let you know if anything happens."

"I don't want to—" I start, but Nora's mom cuts in, pocketing her phone.

"Nora's at her dad's house," she says. "Just like I thought."

"What?" My brain is spiraling out of control. "How do you know?"

"I just spoke to him," she says. "She took a cab there. Everything's fine. She just needs a break from . . . everything for a couple of days."

Her gaze lands on me, not unkindly but not warmly either. I don't see how Nora possibly had enough time to get to her dad's house, unless the cab sped the entire way. And I can't believe she'd just run off like this in the middle of everything that's happening.

Actually, I *don't* believe any of it.

CHAPTER 39

I don't know who Nora's mom just talked to or why they're lying, but something isn't lining up. I pull out my phone again, but before I can text Nora, my dad lays his hand on my wrist.

"Come on," he says, tipping his head toward my car. "I'll ride with you."

I'd like to think he's coming with me for moral support, but I suspect they're all worried I'm a flight risk. As we head down the driveway, I hear Officer Geary asking Nora's mom if it's possible we're involved with a satanic cult.

Once I'm in the car, I send Nora a text.

Are you actually at your dads

No answer. The message isn't read. I jab my key into the ignition.

"Hey," says my dad as we back out onto the street. "I'm sorry I can't drive right now, and I'm sorry Nora ran off on you. That must have been really scary."

Scary doesn't begin to describe it. I feel like I've been hit with a sledgehammer. Nora is gone, Detective Huld is gone, and the police either don't believe us about the bodies or they're covering something up. There's a solid chance Nora is with the Hand of Nephthys at this very moment, and before that, for some reason, she stashed a huge meat cleaver inside a bag.

A bag that's now tucked under a blanket in the trunk of my car. I grabbed it before Officer Geary came, because I decided I didn't know enough about what happened and I don't want Nora getting blamed for anything, just in case.

"I wasn't lying about the bodies," I say. "We really did find them, but I think somebody's taking them as soon as we find them."

He's silent for a minute, and I'm worried he's about to give me the same lecture on trauma and hallucinations or whatever they all seem to think this is.

"Why do you think somebody would do that?" he asks.

"It has to be the Hand of Nephthys," I say. "It's this secret magical cult. They didn't want anyone to find the bodies of the people they killed, so they're hiding them again. Or . . . disposing of them in some other way."

My dad shakes his head. "I don't know, Mazz. It all just seems a little—"

"I'm not making this up!" I say. "Nora thought Detective Huld was secretly a member of the Hand of Nephthys, and I didn't believe her, but now I do. And now I'm starting to wonder if the whole police department is in on it. Why else would they say they didn't find any bodies when Nora and I clearly saw them?"

I hit the brake too hard at a stop sign, and my dad braces his hand against the dashboard.

"Sorry," I say. "It's just so incredibly frustrating when nobody believes you about something this massive."

"I do believe you," says my dad. "Seriously, I agree that something is going on here. But I think you might be letting your imagination run a little wild here."

"I *swear* we found those bodies," I say.

"And I'm not saying you didn't," says my dad. "But let's slow down and think about this, okay? Do you honestly think the entire police department is in a secret magical cult? Can you picture Officer Geary hanging out with his buddies, lighting incense and collecting crystals and whatnot?"

The mental image is so ludicrous, I can't help but laugh. "Okay, no."

"Me neither," says my dad. "And I can't see why they'd be covering up murders for a bunch of mystical people either."

"Unless they were afraid of getting murdered by them," I say. "Or they were being blackmailed or something."

"Mazz, really?" My dad sighs. "The *entire* police department? With all the resources and weapons they have?"

The tension in my jaw eases a little, because what he's saying does make sense. "Okay, that *is* somewhat unlikely. But I still think something fishy is going on with Detective Huld."

"Could be," says my dad. "But I'm not sure she kidnapped Nora. You heard her mom talking to her dad just now. He wouldn't lie about her being there. Don't you think he'd be just as upset as you if she actually went missing?"

"I guess," I say. Something tells me that wasn't actually him on the phone, but I don't know how to make anyone believe me. I've got no proof of anything.

"And it doesn't make a lot of sense for a police detective to kidnap someone," says my dad.

He's right. It makes zero sense. But none of this has made any sense, right from the beginning. It's possible Detective Huld and Anon09 are two different people, but I still have this nagging feeling that a lot of things about Nora's situation aren't adding up.

"I'd feel a lot better if I could just talk to Nora," I say.

"Give her some time," says my dad. "I bet that girl won't make it two hours without texting you."

I want to laugh at his joke, but I can't stop thinking that she *can't* text me, wherever she is.

"I'm really sorry for all of this," I say. "We never should have gotten wrapped up in any of it, and this is the last thing you need to be dealing with on top of . . . you know . . . everything." My voice goes all weird and warped at the end, and my eyes are threatening to start leaking again.

My dad touches my shoulder, gently so it won't affect my driving. "Mazz, I'm not made out of glass."

"I know," I say, wiping my stupid eyes with my sleeve. "But I just don't want you to get so stressed out that it makes you want to drink."

My dad laughs, but it's a soft laugh. A kind one. "I want to drink all the time. That doesn't mean I'm going to. And it also isn't your problem to worry about. It's mine, okay? Please let that be my problem."

I nod, wishing it were that easy to shut off the worrying and the guilt that are sloshing around in my stomach like a soup of acid and rocks.

"Listen, I want you to stay home for the next couple of weeks." My dad holds up a hand to stop the protest that's about to fly out of my mouth. "I'm not saying you're grounded, but I want you to

218

stay the hell away from beaches or water or anywhere else bodies might wash up, just to be safe. Don't go out at night, lay low, and stay out of trouble for a while. Let the cops do their job."

I nod, because even after everything he just said, I don't want him to worry about me. But that doesn't mean I'm going to listen. The cops don't believe Nora is missing, which means they won't be looking for her. Either she's been kidnapped by the Hand of Nephthys or she intentionally ran away with them. I can't decide which is worse, and I can't just sit around waiting for everything to work out. Maybe some things aren't my problem to worry about, but others absolutely are.

This is on me now.

CHAPTER 40

I'm sitting on my bedroom floor with my hair draped around my shoulders like one of Ione's shawls. In front of me is a black bowl of water surrounded by candles. Beside it, a framed photo of me and Nora, and a handful of things she's given me over the years. Aventurine, red jasper, and citrine crystals. A silver necklace with both of our initials. A pocket journal she covered in pressed flowers.

As reluctant as I was to scry again, I've tried every other spell in my books to find things or people, and none of them worked. It's midafternoon, and even with my curtains drawn, it's not dark enough to get the right clarity or reflection in the water. Plus, I can't calm my screaming nerves enough to focus properly. With a groan, I flop onto my back and stare up at the ceiling.

My dad is at work, Henry is napping, and my mom has been on the phone for the past hour, trying to find a therapist who is taking new patients and accepts our health insurance. Judging by the amount of swearing she's doing between calls, it's not going well.

Elliot still hasn't called back. School ends in three minutes, but he usually checks his phone between classes. I'm trying not to panic over why he didn't check it today, especially considering Nora and I never showed up at school. My stomach is in knots, and my head aches from clenching my jaw. I've called Nora ten times and sent her at least as many texts, but she hasn't responded to or even read a single one of them, despite my dad's assurances that she wouldn't make it two hours. I desperately hope that's because she's mad at me for pressuring her to tell someone what's happening, not because she's in danger—or because May started screaming in her head again and made her go find more bodies. I can't stop picturing Nora in one of those long, gray dresses, lying by the water with her eyes blank and dead, with stumps instead of hands.

I try calling Ione again, first on her cell phone and then at Midnight Alchemy. It's strange that nobody is answering the phone at the store. I really, really hope it's a coincidence that Ione suddenly became uncontactable after she tried to help us sever our connection with one of the Hand of Nephthys's victims.

It's the last thing I want to do, but I find Detective Huld's business card in my coat pocket, and I dial the number. It rings and rings, with no voicemail or option to leave a message. Somehow, I'm unsurprised. I wonder how she deleted Nora's private messages and my voicemails, whether she used magic or regular old hacking. Either way, we've vastly underestimated this woman.

My eyes drift to my cello case in the corner. I haven't touched it since that day I couldn't stop, since I felt like May was here listening to me play her song.

If May can still get in Nora's head—and I'm sure she can— she'll know where Nora is.

I open the case and tune the strings. Nervously, I rub rosin onto my bow, then settle in my chair, placing my fingers over the strings. I've bitten several of my nails to the quick, and this is going to hurt.

After playing a few scales to warm up, I ease into May's melody. A few days ago, playing this song was like breathing. Today, it's a long, uphill slog through mud. My body is exhausted, and my bowing arm keeps drooping. It's still a beautiful song, but I feel no connection to it, no humming in my veins, no sense of something beyond myself.

No prickly feeling of someone watching me, either.

I retune my A string and try again.

"Mazzy, could you keep it down?" calls my mom from the living room. "I'm on the phone."

I play the song one more time, my bow barely brushing the strings, but it's just not the same. May isn't here, and I wonder if that's because she has Nora all to herself now and doesn't need me anymore. Everyone always wants Nora instead of me. Petty, irrational jealousy pinches my insides, making me feel like an even more horrible person. For the nine-hundredth time, I check my phone, but there's nothing from Nora or anyone else.

As I'm setting it down, it starts to ring, and I almost drop it.

"Hello?" I say, stabbing at the screen without even seeing who it is.

"Hey." For the first time ever, my heart sinks at the sound of Elliot's voice. "I'm so, so sorry. Ms. Beale caught me checking my phone during first period and took it away for the whole day. What happened? Are you okay?"

As I catch him up on everything, the enormity of it all hits me again, and my heart starts thundering so loud I can barely think.

"Did the police call you or come by the school?" I ask.

"Nope."

I want to punch something. Someone.

"We have to go to the station and show them your photo of the body at Scargo Lake," I say. "Detective Huld isn't working today, so she won't be able to intercept us. Of course, she probably isn't working because she's busy kidnapping Nora, so it's not exactly a great situation."

"Hang on, let me send it to you too," he says.

The line goes silent. The silence stretches out, and my stomach starts to sink.

"Um," says Elliot. "Shit."

"No," I say. "No, no, no. Please tell me you still have it."

"Where is it?" he mutters, but I already know it's gone. Just like Nora's private messages and my voicemails. Disappeared into the ether.

"You're not going to find it," I say. "Every shred of evidence is gone, except for the Polaroids. My voicemails, Nora's messages. Vanished, as if by magic. Probably by magic, honestly. We're on our own."

Elliot swears for a solid thirty seconds. I let him get it out, because he hasn't had all this time to process, to accept what's happening like I have.

"So what the hell are we supposed to do?" he asks.

"We go out and find Nora ourselves," I say.

He starts swearing again, and again I give him some time to process. "Okay, yeah," he says finally. "Of course we have to find her. Where do we start?"

Despite the atrocious mess we're in, I smile. Nora and I have dragged this boy through hell and back, and words can't express how grateful I am that he's still willing to keep crawling through it with me.

"If she didn't go to her dad's, there are two possible scenarios," I say. "One, Nora went to meet Anon09, it turned out to be Detective Huld, and she kidnapped her. Two, Anon09 *wasn't* Detective Huld, and Nora voluntarily ran off with them. What do you think?"

A long pause.

"She's been acting so messed up lately, it wouldn't surprise me if she ran off," he says.

"But did she actually go to her dad's first?" I ask. "Her mom called him, and allegedly he confirmed that she was at his house, but why would she go there?"

"To get away from us because we'd tell her not to go meet some stranger from the internet?" says Elliot, and even though I've been thinking the same thing, it still stings that she'd abandon me on purpose.

"It's not lining up, though," I say. "She barely had enough time to get to her dad's place. Why wasn't he at work? And why wouldn't she have packed any extra clothes? She didn't take her coat, and I'm not even sure she had shoes."

Elliot coughs awkwardly. "She hasn't exactly been acting like the most rational person lately."

Out in the living room, I hear my mom talking to someone, using phrases like *likely PTSD* and *inventing scenarios* and *causing trouble with the police.*

"I, uh, found a meat cleaver at her house," I say, dropping my voice to a near-whisper.

"Isn't that a normal thing to own?" says Elliot. "My parents have one."

"Yeah, but this thing was inside one of her tote bags and hidden at the bottom of a drawer," I say. "The knife is massive, like almost too big for normal cooking. It looks like something a butcher would use."

Sour nausea fills my mouth. Butchery is such a brutal concept in the context of everything we've seen this week.

"Was there blood on it?" Elliot asks.

"No," I say. "So maybe it's nothing."

"Maybe." Elliot trails off, then clears his throat. "Don't you think it's kind of strange that she keeps finding all these bodies, though? The first time could have been an accident, but two more times after that? I keep wondering if she got jealous of that vision you had, so she started pretending she could hear May. Do you honestly believe a voice is telling her where the bodies are? Or do you think something else is going on?"

"Yes and yes," I say. "I had my doubts about her actually hearing May's voice too. But the more I think about it—especially after seeing those DMs—the more I feel like she wasn't lying. Why else would she be so desperate to make it stop that she'd sneak off with a total stranger?"

Elliot shrugs. "You're asking *me* for rational explanations?"

"I also think there's more going on," I continue. "Elliot, you saw an entire hand come out of a mirror last night. Something extremely abnormal is happening. Something way beyond our understanding. And there's a solid chance Nora ran off with someone from the Hand of Nephthys."

"But what was she planning to do with a meat cleaver?" asks Elliot. "Or what did she already do?"

We're both silent. I'm trying not to imagine all the possibilities.

"We need to go to her dad's house tonight and check if she's there," I say. "But I'm borderline grounded, so I'll have to sneak out. Do you think your brother would let you borrow his truck so you can come get me?"

"Probably, if I bribe him," Elliot says. "What time do you want to go?"

"Nine thirty," I say. "That's past my mom's bedtime, and my dad is working a double. Meet me by the woods on Plover Lane, okay?"

"Sounds good," he says. "Should I bring a weapon, just in case?"

"Do you even own a weapon?" I ask.

"Not really," he says. "But I'll see what I can find in Aaron's room."

"I'll bring Nora's cleaver," I say, and dread settles over me like a blanket of cobwebs.

CHAPTER 41

The first thing I notice when we pull up in front of the ranch-style house is the three newspapers in plastic bags strewn across the driveway. Nora and I always used to tease her dad that he was the last person on earth still reading a physical paper, but he would always tell us, "You can't doomscroll on paper." The grass in the front yard is sparse and long, and all the lights in the house are off.

"Doesn't look like they're here," says Elliot.

I climb out of the truck and head up the driveway. The front steps are gritty under my boots. I switch on my flashlight, and there's a fine layer of dirt coating everything. My shoes have made footprints in it, but there are no other prints. After wiping my sweaty hand on my coat, I jab the doorbell, and it dings hollowly inside.

No answer.

I knock, but there's no point. There are no footprints. No one has picked up the newspapers in three days. Swearing, I open Instagram on my phone. Nora's dad doesn't have any social media accounts, but I've met his new wife a few times, and I bet she does.

Traci Hawthorne, I tap into the search bar.

There she is, surrounded by palm trees, wearing a wide-brimmed hat and sipping an electric blue cocktail. Beside her, Nora's sunburned dad holds up a can of beer.

Having a blast in the DR! #blessed #dominicanrepublic #beachvibes #tropicalparadise

The post is from today.

Either Nora's dad lied to her mom on the phone, or it wasn't him she was speaking to. But why would he lie—and if it wasn't him, who could she have spoken to? Who sounds enough like Nora's dad that they could fool his ex-wife? I suppose anything's possible if you use the right spell, and something tells me that wouldn't be difficult for the Hand of Nephthys.

"He's not even in the country," I mutter, screenshotting the image and then showing Elliot my phone.

"Do you think Nora snuck into his house while he's away?"

"Maybe," I say, but the waves of panic are rolling in faster now. We peer into every window of the house, just to be sure, but with each empty room, the certainty in my gut grows stronger. The last window on the back side of the house is Nora's room. Inside, there's no sign of a bag or clothes or even a phone charger plugged into the wall. The comforter and throw pillows on the bed are neatly arranged. In all the years I've known Nora, she's never once made her bed. She likes to let the sheets "air out" during the day.

"She's not here." I stumble back from the window. "She never came here."

Deep down, I didn't think we'd find her here, but that empty room is still a shock. Nora is gone, and I don't know what to do.

The world's worst horror movie keeps playing in my head, of Nora washed up on a beach. Her skin chalk-pale. Her mouth slack and empty. The ocean licking at her hair.

"Hey, hey." Elliot takes my arm and eases me down to sitting, and it's only once I'm on the ground that I realize I'm hyperventilating and that's why everything's gone even darker than it already was.

"Put your head down and try to breathe slower," says Elliot. "I'll count for you, okay? Four counts in, then hold for four, then four counts out."

My chest is so compressed, I think I might be having a heart attack. I can't inhale for four counts without feeling like I'm suffocating. My arms and legs are rigid, I'm covered in cold sweat, and my stomach churns with burning acid.

"Can you inhale for two counts?" Elliot says. "Two is easier, right?"

I nod because I can't get a word out through my hitching breath. Elliot rubs my back and counts to two about twenty times, then three, then four, and slowly the crushing weight in my chest starts to ease. The world comes into focus.

"Thank you," I say once my words are back. "Sorry."

"Don't be sorry." Elliot tucks a strand of my hair behind my ear. "Are you okay now?"

His hand lingers there, his fingers light on my scalp, and I swear every synapse in my brain is firing at once. Our breath is rising and falling, rising and falling in sync. My gaze drifts down to his mouth.

"I'll go to the police with you this time," he says. "We'll show them the Instagram post and make them come here. They'll have to believe us that she's missing."

"They're not going to come here if—" I break off as a car door slams on the other side of the house and an engine revs. Elliot and I jump up and dash through the side yard, stumbling in the long grass.

Taillights glow red in the street as a vehicle speeds off.

"Was someone just here?" Elliot asks.

"I think so." Cringing, I edge closer to the truck, then freeze. There's something tucked under the windshield wiper.

Another Polaroid.

CHAPTER 42

"Get in the truck!" I yell, tugging the photo out from under the wiper.

"What—"

"Just go! I'll show you in a minute." I wrench my door open and launch myself into the truck. I'm still shaking with all the excess adrenaline from my panic attack. We roar off down the road, tires spinning, and I focus on buckling my seat belt, on my breath, so I don't start to spiral again. Once the house is far behind us, I turn on my phone flashlight and peer at the Polaroid.

"It's the third dead woman," I say.

Elliot swears and floors the gas pedal.

"They're not following us," I say, checking my side mirror.

"Let me see the photo," he says, and I hold it up.

The woman faces away from the camera, her gray braid a straight line down her back. Everything around her is murky and dark, but she's walking through an open door in a grassy hill. In her left hand, she holds a long-bladed dagger, pointing toward the ground. In her right, a shorter, wider knife.

"It's the mausoleum," I say. "At Woodside."

"On it." Elliot makes a sharp left and we careen onto the highway.

Someone was at Nora's house, creeping around in the shadows while we looked for her. Someone followed us all the way from Yarmouth, and I'd be willing to bet they know where Nora is right now. I wonder if they watched me having that panic attack. The thought makes me feel exposed and vulnerable and sick.

In the white border underneath the image, someone has written two *I*'s in black ink. Are this woman's initials *I. I.*? And why are there two letters when the other Polaroids only had one? Maybe this is some kind of code.

"Whoever's leaving these photos—are they actually trying to help us?" asks Elliot. "Or is it a trap?"

"Either way, how can we *not* go to the cemetery?" I say. "The police don't believe us about anything, and we don't have any other leads. We're all Nora's got."

"God," mutters Elliot. "Imagine you're in mortal danger and your only hope in the world is *us*?"

I'd laugh if it weren't so depressing. "Are you sure you don't want to drop me off at my house and pretend you never met me? I don't want you getting hurt or killed because of stuff Nora and I started and couldn't stop."

"First of all," says Elliot, "that would suck if I never met you. Second of all, Nora is my friend too, and I want to find her just as much as you do. And even if I wasn't in—" He pauses, clears his throat. "I'd never leave you alone to deal with a psychopathic ghost and a murderous cult that kidnapped Nora."

"Or convinced her to run away with them," I say.

"Either way, it doesn't matter," he says. "You're stuck with me."

~ ~ ~

By the time we reach the cemetery, the clouds have blown away and the waning moon is on the rise. Its light bleaches the gravestones and drenches the ground in shadows. As I push the truck's door open, dread makes all of my limbs heavy. Before I lose my nerve, I loop Nora's tote bag over my shoulder and climb out.

We pass a veiled statue of Mary, her hands pressed together in prayer, and in the dark eeriness, she could almost be real. Everything is so stark, so quiet. Elliot and I cast impossibly long shadows onto the ground, like spindly, fantastical versions of ourselves. My legs look three times as long as the rest of me, and my hair, caught in the wind, writhes and twists like seaweed underwater.

Elliot's shadow reaches for mine, stretching longer and longer until the tip of his finger brushes my shadow's shoulder and trails down my arm. Shivers wash all over me. I'm half expecting our shadow-selves to stop following our movements, to take on a life of their own. I wonder what mine might do.

The mausoleum hill looms ahead, and I stop, fear clawing at my chest. Elliot's shadow drops away from mine, and for a long moment, we both just stand there in black and white, lost for words because everything—everything—is so messed up.

"Do you want to come back in the morning?" he says eventually.

"We can't," I say. "Nobody else is looking for Nora, and if there's even a tiny chance she might be here . . ."

He nods grimly. There's no choice for either of us.

The mausoleum door is cracked open, and my mouth goes dry.

Someone else has a key. As I ease the door open wider, that sweet, ashy scent floods my sinuses and makes me gag. Wiping my sweaty upper lip on my sleeve, I lean in, listening.

"Nora?" I call.

No answer. I shine my flashlight inside. Bare stone floor, closed drawers in the walls, cobwebs and dust. No sign of Nora.

"Hang on." Elliot disappears back around the hill, then returns lugging a bowling-ball-size rock, which he uses to prop the door open. I'd like to add about five more boulders to hold it, but it'll have to do.

My ears start to ring as we tiptoe inside. The ashy scent floods my mouth and trickles down my throat, and my eyes are watering. What could have happened in this place to give me such an awful, visceral reaction?

"How many coffins were here last time?" asks Elliot.

"Six," I say, pressing my hand against the wall because everything is tipping and swaying.

"Do you think it's a coincidence that we've found three bodies and now three coffins are missing?" he asks.

"It's not a coincidence." Someone moved the coffins. Someone stole May's body from the morgue. They also took the bodies from Scargo and Grays. And now they're leading us on a sinister little scavenger hunt with these Polaroids. We're fools for playing their game, but it's not like they gave us any choice.

"She wouldn't have gone down through the trapdoor, right?" I'm sickened by the thought of Nora climbing into that deep black hole.

Elliot nudges the cracked wood panel with his boot. "I really hope not."

Outside, there's a crunch, and then a low creak. Too late, my brain processes the sound.

Too late, we both race for the door.

Too late.

It slams shut.

CHAPTER 43

The heavy door won't budge. The handle won't turn.

"Where's the keyhole?" I fumble in my coat pocket as Elliot sweeps his flashlight across the door.

"There isn't one," he says.

"What do you mean?" I find the key and stab it at the spot under the doorknob where the lock should be, but he's right. There's no keyhole. There's no reason for someone to lock or unlock a mausoleum from the inside. Everyone in here should be dead. My chest is about to explode.

"Do you have any cell service?" I ask Elliot.

He checks his phone, then shakes his head. "You?"

"No," I say. "It must be the hill, or all the concrete."

At the same time, we glance to the back of the room, the trapdoor in the floor.

"God, no," says Elliot. "Anything but that hole."

I shove the door again, twisting the handle as hard as I can, but it doesn't budge. Elliot slams his shoulder into it several times, but it's no use.

"It's the only option," I say, and he groans.

Gulping down the bile in my throat, I head for the trapdoor. There's no dust on it, which makes me think it's been used recently, and as I lift it, a cold breeze wafts out. My nostrils prickle with a smoky, salty, herbal scent, and it takes me a minute to figure out why it's so familiar. It's the smell from my vision of those hooded, dancing figures. It sets off about a million alarm bells in my brain, but I can't spend another second in this claustrophobic, cursed mausoleum. Whatever is down there might be worse, but I'm willing to take the chance. Pulse thundering, ears ringing, I swing my feet onto the metal rungs and climb down.

Muttering about what a terrible idea this is, Elliot follows, and our boots clang as we descend into the dark. Somewhere in the distance, water drips. Eventually, my foot hits a dirt floor, and I step back to let Elliot down and switch my flashlight back on. We're in a small root cellar with a single, rotting door on one side. No coffins, no bodies. Still no phone signal. Faint light glows along the door's cracked-open edge, and incense-scented air streams out. I nudge it gently, and it swings open.

Inside is a square room with mossy walls and a high, stone table in the center. On the table, there's a human skull with a single candle flickering in its eye socket. A thick layer of dust coats everything. Warily, I step into the room. In the back corner, there's a pile of wooden crates. I don't want to think about what might be inside them.

"Nora didn't come through here." I say, my heart sinking. "There aren't any footprints." I point to my own prints in the dust, leading back to where Elliot stands. The rest of the space is undisturbed.

"If nobody's been in here, then how did they light the candle?" he asks.

"I don't know." There's a dangerous, electric energy in this room, lingering like the traces of someone's perfume. In the skull's other eye socket, a second black candle has melted down to a puddle of wax. Nora is capable of a lot of new and disturbing things, but I don't think she can levitate across a floor to avoid making footprints. She was never here. The only thing holding me together right now is the knowledge that the skull is so moldy, it can't possibly be hers.

"This is an altar," I say, taking in the skull and the sigils carved into table's surface. Beside a desiccated bundle of herbs is a small, headless bird. A sparrow. Nausea wells up my throat.

Did May discover the Hand of Nephthys's secret ritual space? Or did this belong to her and her sisters? Given that she had a key, it must have been hers. *If you prove you're worthy, they find you.* That's what the person said on the forum. Did they prove they were worthy, and then the Hand came for them? Maybe the sisters didn't want to join, but they were so powerful, such a threat, that the Hand decided to kill them. That would explain the stalker-esque photos.

Elliot points to the skull. "Is that thing real?"

"Probably," I say. "Do *not* touch anything."

"You couldn't pay me to touch any of that." Elliot shudders and skirts around the altar, heading for the back corner.

"There has to be another way out," he says, peering behind the crates, but I hang back. Something behind the skull is drawing my eye. In a way that Nora would describe as elevated intuition, I can sense that something *wants* me to find it. But I can't bring myself to touch that skull. Standing on tiptoe and twisting my hair back so no part of me even brushes the altar, I lean across diagonally.

And there, behind the skull, is an athame. A ceremonial dagger with a long, glinting blade, just like the one the third sister is holding in the Polaroid.

I should follow my own advice and *not touch anything* on this altar. But my fingers are already curling around the athame's silver handle. I expected it to be cold like the air around us, but it's body temperature, like it's just been in someone else's hand. It buzzes just like the key, the bone cup, the teeth. I can't stand the sensation, so I slide it into Nora's bag, where it clinks against the meat cleaver.

"Do you hear that?" Elliot's standing frozen, eyes wide.

From somewhere overhead, a woman's voice is faintly humming. The song is instantly recognizable, unbearable.

"Over here," Elliot hisses, and I dive behind the stack of crates with him. Something heavy scrapes across the floor above us, raising the hair on my arms and setting my teeth on edge. The humming continues, but it's hard to hear over the pounding bass of my heart. It's not Nora—unless she's taken to speaking with someone else's voice again.

"We have to get out of here," I whisper.

"Give it a minute," says Elliot. "You've got two knives, right?"

I slide my hand into the bag, and the athame fizzes against my fingertips again. "Yeah."

"If we try to go up the ladder and they catch us at the trapdoor, we're screwed," he says. "But if they come down here, we've got the element of surprise and a better chance of overpowering them and getting out."

My throat goes tight at the thought of stabbing anyone. The athame flares hot, like that's all it wants. It takes every ounce of my will to not let go of it.

"Do you, uh, want the meat cleaver or the dagger?" I ask.

Elliot swallows audibly. "Cleaver."

I pass him the huge knife and we wait, breathing hard. My knees ache from squatting, my thighs are cramping up, and heavy things are still sliding around in the mausoleum upstairs. Then the sliding stops, the humming stops. I brace myself, waiting for the sound of feet on metal rungs. The athame is almost too hot to bear, but I tighten my grip on its handle.

"Soon," hisses a voice, sounding impossibly close in the darkness, and I bite my tongue to keep from screaming. Elliot half rises, but I pull him back down.

Footsteps, faint overhead, moving away. A low, moaning creak. The *clack* of a door shutting. Then silence.

Slowly, I count to a hundred. I've never been one for reading people's auras or essences, but it feels like that looming, humming, whispering presence upstairs might be gone. Slowly, I unfold from my crouch, wincing as the blood races back into my legs.

"I think it's safe now," I say.

Elliot chokes on a laugh. "At what point did any of this become safe?"

"Never," I concede. "But I'm pretty sure they're gone."

We creep out to the empty root cellar. Still, it's silent upstairs, and I hope with every last shred of my being that this isn't a trap, that they're not waiting in the dark at the top of this ladder for us.

"Let me go first," says Elliot.

"No," I start to say, because this entire situation is my fault and I should face the consequences first, but he nudges me out of the way.

"I've got six inches and at least fifty pounds on you," he says.

"Plus, my knife is way bigger. If somebody has to fight, it needs to be me."

I absolutely hate his logic, but I let him go. Up we climb, our blades clanking awkwardly against the metal rungs. At the top, Elliot pauses, nudges the trapdoor open a crack, then surges upward. Every nerve inside me twangs like a broken string.

There's a long, nauseating moment of nothing. Then a relieved huff.

"It's okay," Elliot says, and his flashlight beam swings down, momentarily blinding me. "They're gone."

As soon as I pull myself up through the trapdoor, my limbs turn to jelly and I have to sit on the floor, pulling the tangled shreds of my nervous system back together. Elliot swings his flashlight in a jagged arc.

"All the coffins are gone too," he says.

"Awesome," I mutter. "Can't wait to find out who they're for."

"Let's hope we never do." He crosses the space and tries the doorknob again.

To both of our surprise, it clicks and the door swings open.

CHAPTER 44

We run across the sleeping graveyard and out through the gate. The only thing on the road is Elliot's brother's truck.

"What the hell just happened?" I say as we stop to catch our breath.

"Some dickhead locked us in a fucking tomb and then let us back out," says Elliot.

"Was it even the same person, though?" I say. "Someone left us that Polaroid, knowing we'd come straight here. Why would they lure us here and lock us inside, only to let us go less than an hour later?"

Elliot rubs the back of his neck. "I guess it could have been two separate people, and the second person didn't know we were downstairs. But why did they leave the door unlocked when they left?"

"It was unlocked when we got there," I say.

"Either way, I think it's safe to assume that whoever's leaving those Polaroids isn't trying to help us," he says.

Headlights flash on the road ahead, and we move closer to the truck. The lights grow brighter and brighter—the high beams are

242

on—and within seconds, I'm completely blinded. The engine roars, and Elliot nudges me farther off the road.

"Asshole," he mutters as the car slows and then stops beside us. My sight slowly returns, yellow-haloed stars everywhere.

A tinted window slides down. The driver is wearing mirrored sunglasses, which is unsettling in the dark.

"Evening," he says in a low voice.

Neither Elliot nor I respond. We're on a deserted street in the middle of the night, and this man is a stranger.

Wait. I recognize this stranger and the vine tattoo snaking up the side of his neck. Hissing in my breath, I stumble back a step. The man's mouth slides into an oily grin. He knows we're scared. He likes that we're scared.

"Where's your friend?" he asks.

"Go to hell," I say.

The man laughs, a derisive grunt, and then his window slides up. He guns the engine, wheels spinning, and I trip backward over the curb and fall. Already, the SUV is disappearing around the bend. I just sit there on the ground, too stunned to move.

"Did you see his license plate?" I ask.

Elliot shakes his head. "Just that it was Delaware."

"Nora has a photo of the plate number," I say.

"Not that it does us any good now." Elliot pulls me up to standing. My teeth are chattering, even though I'm still hot from running, from panicking.

"Elliot?" I ask.

"Yeah?" He ducks to peer at me in the darkness.

"I'm really fucking scared."

He pulls me into a tight, full-body hug. I press my cheek to his

243

chest, and his heart thuds against my ear. The dark trees rustle and whisper, the shadows loom and slither, but I focus only on Elliot, on his heart steadily pumping blood through his body. On the two of us, alone in the world. He mutters something I can't quite make out, and I think I feel the slightest pressure of his mouth on the top of my head, but it might just be my imagination, and then he pulls back.

"Let's get out of here," he says, unlocking the truck.

As I pull my door open, something that was tucked under the handle falls to the ground. At this point, I'm unsurprised by another Polaroid, but in the amber interior light of the truck, the image takes my breath away.

Two women sit at a metal café table, but they're not at a café—there's snow on the ground, and they're surrounded by trees with bare branches. They're holding paper coffee cups, leaning in toward each other and smiling faintly like they're sharing a secret.

It's May and Detective Huld.

CHAPTER 45

It's one a.m., and once again, I'm sitting on my bedroom floor, spiraling. Earlier, I tried to send the screenshot of Traci's Instagram post to Nora's mom, but it had disappeared from my phone. The post vanished from Instagram too. Neither of those things surprised me, but they did make me want to scream. I called Nora's mom anyway and left a message saying she needs to drive to Falmouth and see that her ex-husband's house is empty, but she hasn't responded. She's probably working another night shift, but I suspect she's also ignoring me because she thinks I'm part of the reason Nora "ran away." I hope if I ever go missing, my mom actually tries to find me and doesn't just blame Nora.

I've also called Ione three more times, even though I can't leave any more messages because her voicemail box is full. It makes no sense that she'd keep ignoring me like this, and after twenty-four hours of silence, I can only assume she's been taken by the Hand of Nephthys too.

But why, why, why am I still here?

Clearly, I'm not unique or powerful enough for the Hand of Nephthys to bother with, even though it was me, not Nora, who had that vision of the ritual. I wonder if they even noticed I exist. I should be used to this sort of thing, but it still hurts. Everybody wants Nora. Nobody sees me. And I know it shouldn't matter, but it does, because I'm not powerful enough to get Nora back. I'm so incompetent that I can't even get the police to investigate. I'm a useless, agnostic fraud, too busy overthinking to believe in anything, too scared to attempt any magic that's not written in a spell book.

My eyeballs are throbbing, and my jaw aches from clenching. I've never been a patient person, and sitting here in my room, with nothing for company except my anxiety, is excruciating. I've asked my tarot cards where Nora is three times, even though you're not supposed to ask the same question more than once. Each time, I pulled the Nine of Swords first. A woman curled up in bed with her hands over her eyes. The card of desperation, anxiety, panic. And then I pulled the Tower. Every single time, no matter how many times I shuffled.

On my quilt, I line up the four Polaroids and let my eyes go blurry, trying to give my subconscious space to make sense of them. My attention keeps getting dragged back to the last one of Detective Huld and May. It's not like the others. The mood is lighter with the daylight and the women facing the camera. In the border underneath are two handwritten *I*'s.

Wait a minute.

My eyes snap back to my tarot deck. Those could be two *I*'s, or they could be a roman numeral two. Detective Huld and May are each holding a cup. If *II* is *two*, this is the Two of Cups.

This photo is a tarot card.

In the first Polaroid, May is standing beside an umbrella stand with five walking sticks in it. If that letter underneath is a *V*, not an *M*, this is the Five of Wands. In the second photo, the blond woman holds a cup made of bone, with an *I* for the Ace of Cups. And in the third image, the gray-haired woman holds two daggers, with two *I*'s for the Two of Swords.

Someone made a tarot deck out of photos of the Hand of Nephthys's victims and, for some reason, Detective Huld. Were they documenting the murders? Were they in league with the detective, or spying on her? The image of May and Huld looks like they were being spied on, so maybe someone was trying to blackmail the detective. But if so, why turn the evidence into tarot cards?

I pull out my tarot book, the one with pages-long explanations for each card, and I read through each description multiple times, trying to figure out how they relate. But I can't make any sense of it, especially the Two of Cups, which is all about love and harmonious relationships. Nothing gives any indication of what happened or is currently happening. Burying my face in a pillow, I scream until my throat is on fire. Then I throw the pillow across the room.

"May," I whisper, wiping my stinging eyes. "I need to find Nora. Please."

The room is silent, the air calm. Just like earlier, I've got no sense of her presence here. She must still be with Nora, or floating around in the ether, or wherever it is she slips away to. I'm going to have to summon her. It's the last thing I want to do, but I'm all out of options. I start toward my bookshelf, then stop. It's time to stop following the rules. I close my eyes and try to clear my mind, let my intuition light like an ember. What would make May happy? What would bring her here? What would Nora do?

Humming May's song quietly, I start gathering ritual ingredients. A labradorite crystal and a dried-up sand dollar. My small, cast-iron cauldron. Four silver candles. Using the skull key, I carve May's name and a sigil into each candle, and then I anoint them with oil and roll them in wormwood. I set the Polaroid of May in the center of the altar and place the skull key on top.

On shaking legs, I climb onto my desk chair and pull the batteries from the smoke detector. I add a charcoal disc to my cauldron, and once it's burning, I sprinkle in some mullein and copal. Tiny curls of smoke trail around my fingers as I light the candles. Then I turn off the lamp. This is my last chance to stop what is certain to be a terrible idea, but I don't stop.

The words come all on their own. My incantation becomes an invitation.

"May," I whisper. "I summon you."

The temperature in my room drops, and all the hair on my arms lifts. A quiet voice in my subconscious keeps whispering *don't, don't, don't*, but I push it away. This type of summoning goes against every magical principle I've ever had, but it has to be done. There's no other way to find Nora.

"May," I say, louder this time. "I know that's not your real name, but I mean *you*."

The candles flicker and waver; the smoke flattens and then curls sideways. I desperately want to turn the lights back on, scatter the things on my altar, and forget this whole ritual. But more than anything, I want Nora back. And to do that, I'll have to go into the darkness, embrace the shadows and the unknown.

I drop the sand dollar into the cauldron and wince as the fragrant smoke turns acrid.

"Please," I say. "I need to find Nora, and you know where she is."

The sand dollar starts to blacken around the edges, and the foul smoke makes me cough. It's getting colder and colder. Every inch of my skin is crawling with nerves, and every instinct is screaming *don't*.

Someone is definitely here now. *Something.* I smell the faintest trace of salt and flowers.

"May, I'll help you if you help me," I say. "Please. I'll do what—"

I choke back the word. I have to draw the line at promising to do whatever she wants.

"I'll help you find the rest of your sisters, if there are more who are missing," I say. "I'll find the bodies for you. But I need Nora back first, okay?"

A gentle puff of air hits the back of my head, like cold breath exhaled, but when I turn around, no one is there.

Don't, don't, don't, says the voice of reason that can't save me anymore. Clenching my fists, I refocus on the candles, the photo and the key, the burning sand dollar.

"Tell me where Nora is," I say.

A tiny zap in the back of my brain. Like a tug on a sleeve.

My teeth are chattering, my fingers numb. It must be thirty degrees in here with the windows closed. The sand dollar snaps and cracks and smokes. Again, a sudden tug in the back of my brain, harder this time, and goose bumps cover my skin. My ears fill with static, then buzzing like insects, then whispering. It's not a language I recognize, and it gets louder and louder until I can't think straight. I press my hands over my ears, but it does nothing to stop the sound. My stomach heaves, my muscles go rigid, my nails dig into my scalp. How could Nora stand this?

"Stop," I gasp. "Please. I can't understand anything."

But the whispering continues, sizzling in my skull until it feels like my teeth are coming loose.

"May," I say, desperately trying to hold it together. "You have to stop. I can't—I can't help you like this."

Abruptly, the whispers cut out. Then everything goes blank.

CHAPTER 46

There's a notepad in my lap, a pencil clutched in my right hand. I'm still sitting beside the altar; I have no memory of getting up and taking them from my desk. *Don't, don't, don't,* says my intuition that's still somehow trying to help, but I set the pencil to the paper.

"Show me," I whisper.

My hand starts moving all on its own. A line, then a curve, then a wide circle, then a back-and-forth scribbling. Faster, so much faster than I thought I was capable of moving. I can't make it stop. My hand is a blur, and I bite my lips together to keep from screaming, because I've never felt so terrifyingly out of control.

Slowly the image comes together. A turned-up nose and round cheeks. Streaky, dark hair. Two wide, scared eyes. I—who can barely manage stick figures—am drawing the most photorealistic portrait of Nora I've ever seen. My fingers start to cramp with the effort of clutching the pencil so hard, but my hand keeps moving, and I'm gasping for breath because it's too much energy coursing through me.

"Stop," I beg. "Make it stop." But my hand keeps going, adding deep shadows under Nora's eyes and wrinkles around her mouth.

A jagged crack runs down her forehead. Black leaks from the corners of her lips. She looks sicker and scarier with every uncontrollable stroke of my pencil.

"No!" I throw every ounce of strength into my right hand, and the pencil tip snaps off against the page. I wrench my arm back and hurl the pencil across the room.

"That's not what I meant by 'show me,' May." Unable to look at this hideous portrait of Nora a second longer, I crumple it up and throw it under my bed. "This isn't a game."

In truth, though, this whole week has felt like one sick game.

"If you're not going to help me, then I'm not going to help you," I say.

The candles snuff out all at once, and I swear under my breath. The temperature drops again, and the caustic scent of burning gets stronger, thicker, making me cough. Then, with a sudden pop and a burst of light, the sand dollar goes up in flames. The fire stretches out of the cauldron, higher and higher, and I reach for the lid in case I need to snuff it out. More than anything, I want to make this stop, but I need May to tell me the truth.

I try to let myself go still, open my mind, but I can't stop coughing.

Mazzy.

Her voice blares in my skull like a speaker accidentally turned up too loud. Pain shoots through my ear canals, and tears spring to my eyes. I can't imagine how Nora tolerated this for days at a time. I should have been more sympathetic to what she was dealing with. I should have realized how hideous this is.

Paper, Mazzy. Show you.

The sound is agonizing, like fingernails clawing at my brain.

Sobbing quietly, I crawl around in the dark until I find the notepad, then grab a pen from my desk. The candles on my altar re-ignite simultaneously.

Good girl.

I want to vomit on the carpet, but I just need to get this over with. As soon as the pen touches the paper, my hand is flying again, so fast it's a blur. It's so violating, so invasive to have someone else in my head like this. My skin burns; my jaw is clenched so tight I think my teeth might break. Tidal waves of anxiety are hitting me so hard and fast that I can barely process what's happening.

My hand draws lines, more lines, parallel and bisecting and veering off. Then a narrow rectangle near the center, shaded in so hard the pen is starting to leak. My breath comes in painful gasps as my hand keeps moving, the lines going off in all directions, and I realize it's a grid—a map—but then I'm back to the rectangle.

M. A., I write beneath the rectangle, tracing the letters over and over until I've torn through the paper and several sheets underneath.

My heart, whispers May.

"Okay," I choke out. "I get it. You can stop."

MY HEART.

I scream as the pen flies out of my hand and hits the wall. May's bitter laugh scrapes at my skull, making my fingers and toes curl.

Then the candles wink out and the overhead light flashes on.

The emptiness is sudden and sharp and cold.

She's gone.

Just in time, I grab the trash can under my desk and am violently sick.

CHAPTER 47

Sitting through first period health class is excruciating, but it has to be done so the school doesn't call my parents to let them know I'm not here. As soon as the bell rings, I dash into the hall, and I spot Elliot by the emergency exit—the broken one without an alarm. My stomach clenches at the sight of him, tall and lean and dressed in all black. I wonder again if he regrets ever coming to the beach with me and Nora that night. But as soon as he sees me, his beautiful face breaks into a grin, and even though my whole world is falling apart, for the smallest fraction of a second, I could almost pretend it isn't.

"How are you?" he asks, and I laugh.

"Horrible. I'll tell you about it in the car."

Once the number of kids in the hall reaches peak swarm, we duck outside and skirt around the back of the building, cutting through the fields to reach my car, which I've left on a side street instead of the school lot.

I move Nora's bag off the passenger seat so Elliot can sit, and I hand him my second drawing from last night—not the picture of Nora, which is still crumpled up under my bed.

"Is this a map?" he asks, and I nod.

"Do you have any idea where it might be?"

He ponders it for a minute. "See that triangle there, with arrows going counterclockwise around it? It could be Main Street, and those are the one-way roads."

"Oh my God, you're right," I say. "And *M. A.* is Midnight Alchemy."

The top of my scalp tingles as I shift into gear, heading for Hyannis. All morning, my brain has felt itchy and tender. To be safe, I'm wearing a smoky quartz pendant and a black tourmaline bracelet, I've got three different protection bags and four more crystals stuffed in my pockets, and I've drawn protection sigils all over my hands and forearms with Sharpie. I can still hear occasional snatches of May's voice, but so far, it's staying muted to a whisper.

"Do you think May is trying to tell us Ione is back at the store?" I say.

"What does that have to do with—" Elliot pauses, and then his voice goes low. "Wait. Where exactly did you get this map?"

"You have to promise not to get mad if I tell you," I say.

He turns in his seat. "Mazzy."

"I, uh, might have accidentally channeled May last night," I say, keeping my eyes carefully on the road. "And she—we?—drew it."

"Are you *kidding* me?" says Elliot. "You never should have done that alone."

"I know, I know," I say. "But I'm pretty sure it wouldn't have worked if you were there."

"You could have at least tried with me there." Elliot's voice rises, his soft baritone gone jagged.

"I'm sorry. I just didn't want to wait any longer."

The map crumples in his hand. "If May gets into your head and you end up like Nora, I don't know what I'll do."

"I'm not going to end up like Nora," I say, but May's laughing inside my head now. I squeeze the pendant around my neck and focus on pushing her away. I *refuse* to end up like Nora.

"You don't know that." Elliot's shoulders are heaving, his face pinched. I haven't seen him this upset in a long time. "Shit, Mazzy," he says. "I can't lose you."

A feeling I don't have words for pierces right through my chest. It's elation over Elliot admitting a thing like that, terror that I might in fact end up like Nora, and sorrow that she's still missing.

"I don't want to lose you either," I say, and the silence stretches out between us, because what can you possibly say after that? There are normal conversation paths, and then there are deeply emotional, unexpected ones that happen when you're on your way to do terrifying things.

"I figured out that those Polaroids are tarot cards," I say finally. "But I still have no idea what they mean or who is leaving them."

"But we're still in agreement that they're not helping, and we're not going to follow them anymore, right?" Elliot says.

"Definitely not," I say. "Oh, and May mentioned something about her heart last night."

Elliot's gray eyes go wary. "What, exactly?"

"Like Nora told us, she doesn't really speak in sentences," I say. "She just said 'my heart' while I was drawing Midnight Alchemy on the map."

"I can't begin to describe how much I hate that," Elliot says.

I couldn't agree more. As the traffic light changes and we turn onto Main Street, there's another sharp tug in the back of my brain.

CHAPTER 48

It's only nine o'clock and Midnight Alchemy doesn't open until ten, but Elliot and I bang on the door anyway. By nine thirty, my mom will be arriving at her store across the street, and this will get a lot more complicated. I try calling Midnight Alchemy's landline, and we can hear it ringing inside, but nobody comes to answer it. When I call Ione's cell phone, I get the same message saying her mailbox is full.

"Ugh," I mutter, hanging up. "She's not even checking her messages, wherever she is. That can't be good."

"Is there a back entrance we can try?" Elliot asks.

"Yeah," I say. "She probably comes in that way. *If* she actually comes to work."

We duck down the narrow alley that cuts between the buildings, and as we emerge onto a small, paved area with trash cans and a couple of empty parking spaces, I spot a familiar silhouette peeking through the back window of the store. Her burgundy hair is piled up in a messy bun.

"Tina!" I call, and she whirls around.

"What are you doing here?" she calls. "And where's Nora?"

"She's missing," I say, blinking back tears, because it's never not going to be a gut punch that she's gone. "You haven't seen her, have you?"

"Oh my gosh, no," says Tina. "Did you call the police?"

A rushing whisper fills my head.

My heart.

"Yeah, we called them," I say, fighting to ignore the whispers. "But we're pretty sure the Hand of Nephthys took Nora, and the cops don't believe us."

Tina hisses in her breath. "Why would they take her?"

My heart.

I can feel May's will almost as strong as my own. She wants us to go into the store. But it's locked, and there's no way I'm breaking in.

"Honestly, it's a long story," I say. "And I was really hoping Ione could help us, but we can't find her either. Have you seen her?"

Tina shakes her head. "I came here to buy some more of that tea she gave me. It really helped with my headaches."

My heart. My. Heart.

Wincing, I try to follow what Tina's saying. My fingers and toes are going numb, and May's whispers are threatening to drown everything out. I force myself to breathe, I repeat my incantation for protection.

"... but this creepy tourist guy was outside asking questions, so I thought I'd try the back door, see if Ione was here yet," Tina says.

My brain snags on the detail. "A creepy tourist?"

"Yeah." Tina shudders. "Some guy from Delaware. I didn't like the look of him."

My skin goes cold. "Where did you see him?"

Tina gestures to the alley. "He was out in front of the store like five minutes ago. You can't miss him. He's got a vine tattooed on his neck."

My hand clamps like a vise around Elliot's wrist, and then we're both racing back down the alley.

MY HEART. MY HEART. MY HEART. May's voice is fingernails raking my brain.

"Stop it." I summon every ounce of strength, I channel my will into a clear, bright halo of light all around me, and I push her away. The sudden clarity feels like diving into cold water.

We round the corner of Midnight Alchemy. There's no sign of a gray SUV. The sidewalk is empty.

"There he is!" yells Elliot, pointing.

The man with the neck tattoo is leaning over the hood of my parked car. He's sliding a Polaroid under the windshield wiper.

CHAPTER 49

I've never seen Elliot get violent once in his life, but he closes the distance between us and the tattooed man in about three strides and wrenches him away from the car.

"What the hell are you doing?" he says, shoving him again. The man is stocky and muscular, but Elliot's taller, and he's also furious. The tattooed man stumbles backward and drops the Polaroid. Before he can pick it up, I grab it.

The photo is shot from the bottom of a tall, sandy cliff that's concave with erosion. At the top sits a crooked old house. Its windows are broken, its roof is caved in on one side, and it looks like it's about to topple right over the edge. In black ink underneath, *XVI*.

The Tower.

Way down inside my brain, May starts to screech, a cascading, violent wave of sound. I clamp my hand around my pendant and push her, hard. The volume of the screaming decreases but doesn't fully go away.

"Where did you get this?" I say to the man.

"I'm sorry, I'm sorry," he says, holding his hands up. "I'm not going to hurt you. I'm just trying to help."

I slide my keys out of my pocket and fit them between my knuckles, blades pointing out. I'm cursing myself for leaving Nora's bag in the car, because I could really use one of those knives right now.

"*Where* did you get this?" I repeat.

"They were my girlfriend's photos," he says. "It's a long story."

"Tell us the abbreviated version," says Elliot.

"My name is Rowan Moore," says the man. "You don't have to tell me your names—I get it that this whole situation is suspicious as hell—but I need you to know that your friend is in serious danger. I've been tracking the Hand of Nephthys, and I think she's with them."

"Thanks for that incredibly useless piece of information, asshole," Elliot says, but I step forward.

"If you've been tracking them, do you know where they are now?" I say. "We really need to find Nora."

Elliot looks startled that I've given this stranger Nora's name, but at this point, I'll take any information I can get.

Rowan drags his hands through his graying, dark hair. "No. I wish I did."

Hideous man, whispers May.

"Why have you been messing with us all week?" Elliot asks.

"If you let me start from the beginning, I think you'll find my story . . . illuminating." Rowan's left eyebrow arches dramatically, but the theatrics are just making me even more uncomfortable. "Like I said, I'm Rowan, I'm a software engineer, and I'm from Bridgeville, Delaware. A couple of years ago, I started dating this woman named Katrin."

May goes completely silent. Something about this story fascinates her.

"She moved in with me after about three months," says Rowan. "I know that seems fast, but her lease was ending and she didn't have any friends or family in the area, so I asked her to live with me."

"What does this have to do with anything?" Elliot's eyes are still blazing.

"Give me a minute and I'll get there," says Rowan. "Katrin said she was from Cape Cod, but she never wanted to talk about it, to the point where I didn't know what town she was from. I didn't even know you guys *had* different towns here."

I groan. Of course it's all one big town named Cape Cod and we all live in lighthouses and ride whales to school.

"She was into witchcraft and spells and stuff," says Rowan. "She put crystals and shells and candles all over the house, and sometimes she'd go off into the woods in the middle of the night if the moon was in a certain phase, but I just figured she was a little ... you know?" He makes a whirling motion with his finger beside his head.

I don't know how I'm supposed to respond to that, so I don't.

"But then last winter, Katrin started getting really paranoid," says Rowan. "She stopped leaving the house, she turned her phone off, and she kept asking me if we could go away for a month or two, like to a different state or country. I told her I was too busy with work and I didn't have the money for it, and she got really upset. I asked her if she was running away from something, but she just shut down and told me if I wasn't going to be part of the solution, I was part of the problem. I told her she was acting crazy." Rowan rubs his bloodshot eyes, but I don't feel too bad for him—I feel much worse for the girlfriend he called "crazy" to her face. "Three days later, she was gone. Just vanished. Didn't take her phone, her computer, not even a suitcase."

I shudder at the similarities between Katrin's disappearance and Nora's.

"So obviously, I called the police," says Rowan. "But when I gave them Katrin's information, they said there was no record of anyone with that name. The only thing she'd taken with her was her wallet, so I couldn't even show them her ID. The police said she must have been lying to me about who she was, and there was nothing they could do."

Rowan sighs heavily, and even though he's awful, I can't help but identify with his frustration. It's such an utterly hopeless feeling when you're following all the rules and procedures that should lead to justice, but no one believes you.

"I went through all her stuff, looking for clues," says Rowan. "I hacked into her computer and searched her browser history, and it turned out she'd spent a ton of time looking up this group called the Hand of Nephthys on Cape Cod. I started to wonder if it had something to do with her past. Every day she'd visit this online forum where people shared all kinds of wild theories about them, but she never posted anything."

Elliot and I exchange a glance. Somebody from the Hand of Nephthys is clearly keeping an eye on those online groups and reaching out to certain people. I don't blame Katrin for never posting.

"Then one day while I was vacuuming, I found a Polaroid under the corner of the bedroom rug," says Rowan.

May hisses like a cat. My entire body goes cold.

"It was a picture of the door to the attic," says Rowan. "I hadn't been up there in years, but when I did, I found a Polaroid camera and a bunch of photos scattered all over the floor." He points to the photo I'm holding. "That was one of them, and you've seen some of the others too. I also found an old driver's license with her picture on it. She was much younger in the photo, and her name was Kaia, not Katrin. Kaia Monroe."

The back of my neck prickles. That's Ione's last name. In the depths of my brain, there's a dizzy sense of suspension, like May is holding her breath.

"Do you have a picture of her?" My voice shakes.

"Hang on." Rowan pulls out his phone and flicks through the screen. As soon as I see the photo, my shoulders relax. This woman has curly, dark hair, olive skin, and looks a decade older than Ione. Now that I think about it, it'd make no sense for them to be the same person. Ione's been here on Cape Cod this entire time. Anyway, Monroe isn't an uncommon last name.

"I don't recognize her," I say, and Elliot shakes his head too.

"I went back to the police and showed them all the stuff I found," says Rowan, "but they said it just proved that Kaia had been lying to me. They implied that she might have a good reason for hiding from me." Rowan's hands ball up into fists. "Like I was a creep. Like I made her feel unsafe."

I edge closer to Elliot.

Liar, whispers May. *Thief.*

"So I got in my car and drove here," says Rowan, as if it's normal to up and drive hundreds of miles on a whim. "I rented a cottage, and I set out trying to find the places in the pictures. I thought they might lead me to her—or to the Hand of Nephthys. But I couldn't make heads or tails of any of them. Nothing is labeled, there are barely any landmarks other than that antique store, and there are so many goddamn beaches that all look the same."

I'd like to tell him they're all very different, but this isn't the time to start an argument.

"Then I heard about that body washing up, and something gave me an inkling that it might be related," says Rowan. "I went to Mayflower Beach, and that's when I saw you and your friend with those teeth. And I thought, 'These kids know something I don't.' I started following you around, leaving the Polaroids for you to find." He laughs, setting my teeth on edge. "You were a lot better at figuring out the clues than I was."

Disgusting. May's rage is just as razor-edged as my own. Elliot looks like he's about to punch Rowan, and I can't say I'm opposed to it.

"So all this time, you knew we were in danger," I say through gritted teeth. "But you didn't just come out and tell us what you knew about the Hand of Nephthys because you were hoping we'd lead you to your girlfriend?"

Rowan's jaw drops open. "I thought you knew all about the Hand of Nephthys. I thought you were trying to join. Why else would you be looking for bodies, hanging out at a witchcraft store, running around in graveyards, all that stuff?"

"Because we didn't know what we were getting into," I say. "We thought we were helping the victims."

"I completely misunderstood the situation." Rowan scrubs his hands over his face. "It's just . . . I really *need* to find Kaia, and when I get stressed out, I don't think clearly."

Beneath the gray vine on his neck, a vein bulges. I feel bad that this man's girlfriend is missing, but that's no excuse to behave like a stalker and follow underage kids around for days. I keep picturing his face last night, when he laughed at us. We were out in the pitch dark, in the middle of nowhere, and he didn't ask if we were okay. Sure, he thought we were trying to join the Hand of Nephthys, but he still knew we were in danger and did nothing to help.

"Are you the one who locked us in the mausoleum?" Elliot asks.

"What?" Horror flashes across Rowan's face, but I can't tell if it's real or feigned. "When did that happen? I saw you go in, and then I saw you on the road later—"

"It doesn't actually matter," I say, because if he did lock us in, he's playing an awfully twisted game right now. "We have to go now, and you need to stop following us."

"I want to make this up to you." Rowan's eyes are red around the edges and gleaming in a feverish way. "I'll help you look for Nora."

Elliot and I both scoff and head for our car.

"Wait." Rowan steps in between me and my door. "There's one other thing I forgot to tell you. I looked up Kaia Monroe online, and I found an obituary with her photo. But it was from eighteen years before I met her."

My blood goes icy.

If that means what I think it does—if Kaia faked her own death, changed her name, and then ran away to Delaware many years later—she wasn't just curious about the Hand of Nephthys or hiding from them.

She was a member.

And she made tarot cards with images of their victims. This is massive.

"How many other Polaroids did you say you found?" I ask.

"Around seventy," says Rowan. "Like I said, some were scattered around the floor, but most were in a pile."

That sounds like a full deck. May's humming and muttering now, though I can't make out any specific words.

"The ones that were on the floor," I say. "Do you remember if they were in any kind of pattern?"

"They were, come to think of it." Rowan pulls out his phone and starts swiping. "Hang on, I took a picture when I found them. I thought the police might actually care about evidence, but no, they were too busy assuming I hurt my girlfriend and she ran off."

It's all I can do to stand there without screaming while he flicks through his photo gallery, but I force myself to stay calm, to breathe, and eventually, Rowan hands me his phone. In the image, about a dozen Polaroids are laid out on a black cloth in what is definitely a tarot spread, though not a traditional one I know. Immediately I recognize the first three photos—May and each of her sisters—in a tight cluster. Above them is a photograph I haven't yet seen. I pinch-zoom in. It's the Three of Swords, a bloody heart on a white dinnerplate with three knives sticking out of the top and a woman's pale hand gripping the center blade. It'd be nice to think that's an animal heart, not a human one, but the chances aren't good. I swallow a mouthful of nausea.

"You kept these mostly in order when you started giving them to us," I say, and Rowan nods.

"As much as I could," he says. "I figured they were like that for a specific reason."

"When did you say she disappeared?" I ask.

"Early March."

May's corpse definitely wasn't nine months dead when we found it, which means that she was still alive when Kaia left Delaware. But we don't know how long ago it was when Kaia took these photos or why she took them in the first place. And why did she turn into a tarot deck?

Elliot leans over with his own phone and snaps pictures of the images as I continue to scroll and zoom. Some are grainy or blurry

267

or both, but I spot the Devil, the Moon, and the Ten of Swords. The whole layout is disturbingly similar to the cards Nora and I pulled from my deck the night we found May.

"Can I see the rest of these Polaroids?" I ask.

"Absolutely," says Rowan. "They're back at my cottage—in Brewster."

Elliot chokes on a laugh. "Do you honestly think we're that stupid? We're not coming to your cottage."

"No. I mean, right, of course not!" Rowan's talking fast now, stumbling over his words. "Why don't you follow me there, and I'll go inside and grab the pictures, and then we can go somewhere public to look at them?"

Liar, hisses May.

Elliot turns so his back is to Rowan. "We're not going anywhere near this guy's place, right?" he says in a low voice.

"No," I say. "But if Detective Huld is in more of the photos, that could finally be enough proof to make the police listen to us about her. Also, I know this is a long shot, but I wonder if I can use this tarot deck myself to find Nora."

"Where in Brewster is your cottage?" Elliot asks Rowan.

"About half a mile off 6A, just before Nickerson State Park," says Rowan.

"Do you know the café near the bookstore on the way there?" I ask, and he nods. "We'll go there and wait, and you can meet us after you get the Polaroids."

My heart, whispers May. *Go back.*

Rowan's forehead creases and he looks like he's about to offer some alternative plan, but I hold up my hand. "If you actually care about helping us, that's your only option."

"Okay, sure," he says. "I just worry about somebody overhearing us in public."

Elliot scoffs. "And yet you're talking to us here?" He gestures at the shops, the handful of people out on the sidewalk, the cars passing by, and I have to agree. Rowan's plans continue to be disturbing as hell, but if we stick to public spaces like coffee shops, I don't see how he can hurt us.

"All right. We can always sit outside." Rowan's cheeks are as pink as his eyes, and something about him makes my tongue sour.

Liar, whispers May.

"So you'll follow me?" he asks, heading for his SUV. "Or do you want me to follow you?"

"We'll see you at the café," I say.

CHAPTER 50

"Let's give him a head start to get to Brewster," I say as we get into the car. "I don't like the idea of him following us."

"Me neither," says Elliot.

Rowan pulls up beside us and lowers his window. Muttering swears, Elliot lowers his.

"We said we'll see you there," he snaps.

"Right, right," says Rowan. "I just wanted to make sure you had the address of the café?"

"We know where it is," says Elliot. "Just go."

Rowan starts to sputter out more clarifications, but Elliot puts his window up and turns away, and eventually the SUV pulls off.

"Can I look at your photos of that tarot spread while we wait?" I ask, and he hands over his phone.

Even though the layout isn't familiar, it seems to be mostly linear, with the cards progressing left to right, starting with May and ending with the Tower. There are a few cards above and below the center line, including the gruesome Three of Swords above May and her sisters, which I'm fairly certain indicates their murders.

Thief, whispers May. *Betrayer.*

Moving right from the photo of May's oldest sister, I see the

Moon, the Devil, the Ten of Swords, the Seven of Swords, the Five of Wands, the Eight of Swords, the Seven of Pentacles with the Ace of Swords overlapping it on top, and, finally, the Tower. The Devil image in particular makes my skin crawl. A robed figure is holding the severed head of a goat with a lolling tongue and wide blue eyes with vertical slits for pupils. The person's own head isn't visible, cut off by the top of the frame.

Strangely, the photo of May and Detective Huld isn't here.

"What do you think it all means?" asks Elliot, and I take a minute to pull all the pieces together.

"The first three are the dead women," I say. "And the Three of Swords indicates something very bad happening to them. I don't know how long ago Kaia took these photos of the victims, but she seems to have predicted their murders in this tarot reading, before she left Rowan."

"Do you think she left to warn them?" asks Elliot.

"No idea, but it clearly didn't work." I return to the image. "After that, there are a lot of dark, shadowy forces at work, deeply evil stuff with harm and control and fear, which I suspect refers to the Hand of Nephthys itself. Then I'm seeing something being stolen or a person being deceived, a big conflict, and someone being trapped or imprisoned." Goose bumps break out on my skin. "I bet that's Nora."

"It has to be," Elliot says, and I'd love to take a minute and gloat over him finally, unquestioningly believing me about all of this witchy stuff, but I don't have the luxury of time right now.

"So if we're assuming that last card is Nora, then we're here in the timeline," I say, pointing. "And here's where it gets a little weird." I shift to the Seven of Pentacles. "Every other card in this reading is super negative, and then there's this one, which is about long-term goals and hard work and hope." I point to the image, which shows seven tarnished gold coins lying in a patch of dirt. "They're metaphorical seeds."

Under the coins lies a rusty shovel. There's a squirmy feeling inside my head, but I can't pinpoint May's exact emotion, other than agitation.

"The next card is the Tower, which means whatever seeds of intention were planted, they're going to cause a massive amount of destruction."

Elliot shudders. "That can't be good."

"And look at this one touching it." I point to the Ace of Swords, in which a wickedly curved crescent blade is stabbed through the palm of someone's hand. Normally, this card indicates a sudden realization or understanding—a *eureka* moment or a breakthrough—which seems at odds with planting seeds and waiting for them to grow.

"I just wish there was more context to understand what will lead to the final catastrophe and what it will ultimately mean," I say. "Is the Hand of Nephthys going to blow up? Will they finally find a way to reverse death and destroy humanity as we know it? Or will they ... hurt Nora?" I can't bring myself to say the word *kill*.

"Nora's going to be okay." Elliot speaks with such firm conviction that I can't help but cling to it. I'll do everything in my power to stop that from happening, and that definitely doesn't involve sitting here in a parked car.

"Let's find her," I say, handing Elliot's phone back and shifting the car into gear.

CHAPTER 51

As soon as we cross the Brewster town line, a silver SUV pulls out of a parking lot and slots into the traffic two cars behind mine.

"That creepy bastard," I mutter.

"He can follow us all he wants," says Elliot. "We're still not going to his cottage."

My heart, whispers May. *My* heart. *Go back.*

I do my best to ignore her, to focus on the road, but it's getting harder and harder. Elliot's phone pings, and he flicks at the screen.

"Is that Nora?" I say, my heart leaping into my throat.

"No, it's a news alert," he says. "I set one up for Mayflower Beach."

The traffic light ahead turns yellow and I floor the gas, zooming through seconds after it turns red. The car behind us stops, blocking Rowan, and I fly off down the road. He already knows where we're going, and I don't need him breathing down my neck the whole way there.

Go back, GO BACK.

"Do you remember if the café is before or after the Natural History Museum?" I ask, but Elliot is absorbed in his screen.

"Hey," I say. "Do you know—"

"Listen to this." He clears his throat and starts to read. "'The police have identified the deceased woman based on tissue samples taken at the scene of the crime. Her name was Rosemary Newcombe, and she lived in Harwich. She died in a car accident nine years ago, at the age of nineteen, and was buried at a local cemetery. When questioned, authorities said they had no explanation for why her body reappeared nearly a decade later on a Dennis beach.'"

The frantic whispers in my brain go silent.

"There's no way the body we found at Mayflower had been dead for nine years," I say, trying to ignore my tingling scalp. "And she looked much older than nineteen."

A manic, frenetic energy is bubbling up inside me. It's not my emotion—it's May's. I need to block her, push her out again, but I can't fully focus on that while I'm driving.

Rose, she croons. *Mary*.

Rosemary Newcombe *didn't* die nine years ago.

Just like Kaia Monroe didn't die eighteen years before Rowan met her.

"May—whose real name is Rosemary—faked her death when she joined the Hand of Nephthys," I say. "And then she died for real last week. That's how her body ended up miles away, looking recently dead and years older."

"Holy shit," says Elliot. "She wasn't one of their victims—she was one of *them*."

My knuckles are white on the steering wheel. How did I miss all the signs? How could I possibly have been this foolish? Rosemary has been tricking us this whole time. Not only did I invite a spirit into my brain, but I invited a cult member with extremely powerful magical abilities and murderous tendencies. And I have no idea how to get her out.

Frenzied laughter echoes in my skull. I close my free hand around my pendant, but its ability to dampen Rosemary's voice is waning. Not only did this monster pass herself off as an innocent victim, but Nora and I continued to fall into every trap she laid, even after we realized something was very wrong. We've been manipulated so perfectly, so thoroughly, it'd be humiliating if it weren't so horrific.

"The other dead women we found were in the Hand of Nephthys too." I fight to keep my thoughts straight. "That's why she called them her sisters."

"Are they killing each other in some messed-up ritual so they can try to come back from the dead?" Elliot asks.

"If that were the case, why would they have cut out their hearts? If all that stuff about weighing the heart against the feather is true, they'd need it for one of the most important parts of the afterlife journey. Not to mention, why would they leave the bodies to wash up on random beaches afterward? I wonder if Kaia had anything to do with the murders."

At the sound of Kaia's name, May—Rosemary—hisses.

"You think she left the group and then went on a revenge-murder spree?" Elliot sounds unconvinced. "Rowan said she was terrified of something before she ran off."

"Either way, she seems to have known they were going to die," I say.

Elliot lapses into silence as we careen around another bend and zoom past a row of empty summer cottages.

"What if there *is* no Kaia?" he says finally.

"Huh?" I check my mirror and make a quick left.

"What if Kaia Monroe doesn't exist?" he says. "What if Rowan's been the murderer this whole time, and he made up a cover story about searching for his ex-girlfriend?"

"I . . . don't know," I say, but goose bumps are lifting on my arms.

"That photo he showed us of her," says Elliot. "That could have been anybody. For all we know, it was a stock image. The guy's been stalking us for days, he has pictures of the murder victims. He shut us in a freaking tomb."

Silver flashes in my rearview mirror, and my heart goes cold.

"And then he conveniently showed up right after Nora disappeared and tried to get us to go back to his cottage to look at more photos," says Elliot. "Don't you think that sounds like serial killer behavior?"

Behind us, the SUV speeds up. Without thinking, I slam on the brake and make a hard right. Elliot clutches the handle over his door as we careen down another quiet street.

"It's possible that Kaia does exist and Rowan is also the murderer," I say. "Those could have been her photos, he's using them to hunt down members of the Hand of Nephthys, and he still needs our help to decipher the images."

I fly through a stop sign and veer left, but the SUV is still behind us.

I want. My heart, growls the voice in my head.

"I don't have time for this right now, Rosemary," I mutter, taking a sharp left just before a garbage truck pulls across, blocking the road.

GO BACK! Rosemary's shriek is so loud, I think my ear canals might be bleeding.

"Oh God," mutters Elliot.

"What?" I say, checking both mirrors. "Is he—"

"Do you think he has Nora?" asks Elliot.

"Wait, what?" My brain is whirling in too many directions to follow what he's saying.

"Rowan could have been Anon09," he says. "Not Detective Huld or somebody in the Hand of Nephthys. And when she ran off, it was Rowan waiting for her."

A white car pulls out behind us, and Rosemary goes utterly, eerily silent. The road curves around a bend, and then we're flying alongside a wide-open marsh, tall grass waving under a blue sky.

"Do you think she's at his cottage right now?" I check the rearview mirror. Still just the white car, no sign of Rowan.

"It's definitely possible."

"We need to go back—" I start to say, but suddenly the white car is so close behind us that I can't even see its license plate. The glare on the windshield makes it impossible to clearly see who's driving, but their face resembles a skull. Their engine roars, and with a loud bang, my car lurches forward.

"Holy shit!" yells Elliot.

The white car swerves into the left lane and then veers toward me again, striking my back fender and sending us spinning. I scream, slamming on the brake and trying to straighten the car, but the wheels lock up and then we're airborne and everything is blue green blue green. With a crashing jolt, we're rolling again, and we're in the marsh. The car crunches to a stop and my vision goes completely white.

The airbag. The airbag is the white.

I'm not dead.

"Mazzy." Elliot's voice is coming from very, very far away. "Mazzy, are you okay?"

My lap is covered in tiny, blue, glinting rocks. No wait, that's glass.

"Hey." Elliot's voice has gone low with terror. "Please answer me."

"I'm okay . . . I think." Nothing hurts, nothing seems broken, but I might be in shock. My neck feels weird, like my head is a balloon attached with a long string. I manage to drag my gaze away from the glass in my lap, and Elliot is still in the car, not far away like I thought. His forehead is bleeding. He's unbuckling his seat belt and trying to shove the airbag out of the way, and I think that means he's not broken either.

"We're in the marsh," I say, as if this is somehow not obvious.

Elliot's laugh is shaky. "Yeah, but we're in the mud instead of the water, which I guess is lucky?"

"As if anything about this were lucky," I say.

"You don't look so great." Elliot still sounds like he's too far away, and my brain is not connecting as fast as it should be.

"I don't feel so great," I say. "Do you still have your phone?"

"It was in my hand a minute ago." Elliot sifts through the rocks—no, glass. It's everywhere: in our laps, scattered over the center console, crunching under my feet. A salty wind blows in through my window, which wasn't open before, so I guess that's where these rocks—glass—came from. Somewhere in the sky, an osprey is screeching. Then there's a rhythmic squelching sound. Footsteps. A shadow falls over me.

Elliot is yelling, but he's miles away again.

A hooded figure blots out the sun. A cold hand slips over my eyes. I want to push it off, but my arms won't budge. A low voice begins speaking words that I slowly recognize as an incantation, but it's too late; shadows are flooding my brain.

The osprey's keening cry is the last thing I hear before I lose consciousness.

CHAPTER 52

I wake on a concrete floor that's gritty with sand. It's freezing, the wind is roaring outside, and everything smells of mildew mixed with the briny tang of seaweed. My throat is parched, and my head is swimming like I've been drugged, but the bitter ache in my teeth tells me it was magic, not drugs, that knocked me out.

That hooded figure in the marsh, that whispered spell. After all the time and energy Nora and I spent trying to find the Hand of Nephthys, it turned out just like everyone said it would—they found us instead. The inevitability of it all is staggering. And terrifying.

As I roll onto my back, there's a slithering clank and a tug on my ankle. I'm chained to something, but my head is whirling too fast to sit up yet. There's no real ceiling—it's just the underside of the floorboards of the room above me, with cracks of light shining through. I must be in a basement, because the walls are also concrete and there are no windows. Outside, the wind howls around the house, which creaks and sways. Waves thunder somewhere in the distance.

Pushing myself up to sit, I swallow hard as the foul aftertaste of magic floods my mouth. When I spit on the concrete, it comes out black. My pockets are empty; my phone is gone. My hair is one big, matted clump, my forehead aches from the crash, and I'm pretty sure I've got a concussion.

There's a loud *thud* overhead. Then something large and heavy is dragged across the floor.

"Elliot?" I shriek. "Are you there? Are you okay?"

No answer. My stomach is full of rocks. He can't be dead. I refuse to consider the possibility. If I'm not dead, there's no reason for him to be.

"Mazzy?" A soft, scratchy voice.

My heart leaps. "Nora?"

Slowly, my eyes focus in the dim light, and there she is in the corner, shivering under a moth-eaten blanket. I don't know why I'm so relieved to find her here, in the clutches of an evil cult rather than locked away in Rowan's cottage, but I am. At least we're together now. That has to count for something.

"I fell asleep waiting for you to wake up." Nora speaks slowly, slurring her words. "It's been hours—I think it's been hours, anyway. I was starting to wonder if maybe you were dead."

I try to stand, but I'm still so dizzy. The chain tangles around my ankle, and I fall hard on my knees. "Oh my God, Nora," I say. The urge to hug her is overwhelming—and painful, because I can't. "I'm so glad I found you."

"Me too." Nora sits up and rubs her eyes. "But I wish you weren't here. I mean, not like that. I missed the crap out of you, but I'd feel a lot better if I hadn't dragged you into this. I tried so hard not to."

I spit onto the floor again. I'd give anything for a sip of water to wash this awful taste out of my mouth. "Are you okay? Did they hurt you?"

"I've been better," she says with a hitching breath.

"Did you actually go to Falmouth?" I ask.

"Falmouth?" Nora shakes her head slowly in confusion. "Why would I go there?"

"Someone pretending to be your dad told everybody you were at his house," I say. "That's why your mom didn't go looking for you."

"She isn't even looking for me?" Nora's voice goes wobbly.

"Elliot and I were," I say. "And I'm sure everyone will start looking soon, once they realize we're missing too."

Nora hisses in her breath. "Was he with you today?"

"Yeah." I peer around, trying to make sense of the shadows. "I guess that means you haven't seen him?"

A pause.

"No."

Dread settles over me, even colder than this dank basement air. He can't be dead. Elliot is *not* dead. They must have hidden him somewhere else in this decrepit old building.

Overhead, a bird's skeleton dangles from a beam—I think it's a seagull, judging from its thick, hooked beak. Without feathers, its wings look thin and insubstantial. Its empty eye sockets take everything in as it slowly spins in the drafts. From one of its feet, a round object dangles on a string. I shuffle closer, then wish I hadn't. It's a rotten apple wrapped in rusty wire and studded with tarnished nails.

"I am so, so sorry, Mazzy," says Nora. "It's just—I couldn't stand having May in my head a second longer. I would have done literally anything to make it stop. I met someone online, and I knew they were probably in the Hand of Nephthys, but they promised they could help."

"Was Anon09 actually Detective Huld?" I ask.

"How do you know about Anon09?" she says.

"I snooped on your laptop, and I'm one hundred percent not sorry."

"And I one hundred percent don't blame you," says Nora.

"But then the whole conversation disappeared, and I assumed it was Huld," I say. "And then when I called the police, she didn't come."

"No, it wasn't her. Anon09 texted me and told me to meet them at the end of my road, and I didn't want you to come too, so I ran away, and obviously that was a terrible idea because it ended up being this creepy woman wearing a mask and she whispered a spell that made me pass out, and I'm such an idiot." Nora starts to cry. "I thought I was protecting you. This is all my fault."

The wind gusts again, the wood above us groans, and I swear the whole building is rocking.

"None of this is your fault," I say. "We've been manipulated ever since we found that body at Mayflower. Probably even before we found it."

"Her name is Rosemary, not May," says Nora. "And she's—she *was* one of them."

"I know," I say. "The police identified her. We saw it in the news just now . . . well, just before they knocked me out. Do you have any idea why they kidnapped us?"

"For some reason, none of them can contact Rosemary," says Nora. "Not through spells or rituals or channeling or anything.

They've been watching us ever since we found her body. Somebody is murdering them, one by one, and those are the bodies we've been finding."

"Rowan," I mutter, but Nora doesn't hear me.

"The Hand still don't know who's doing it," she continues. "So they decided to wait and watch for a few days, make sure it wasn't a trap."

"Elliot and I think the murderer is that guy from Delaware with the neck tattoos," I say. "His name is Rowan, and we finally talked to him today. He's the one who was leaving the Polaroids for us, because he was hoping we'd lead him to more victims."

"So I guess they were right to be paranoid," says Nora.

"Ironically, I think he might be our only hope right now," I say, shuddering at the thought. "He was following my car right before we got kidnapped. Maybe he saw what happened."

"Do you think he'll try to murder us now too?" says Nora.

"He said he wanted to help us," I say. "But that was probably all part of his act. I just hope he wants to murder *them* more than he wants to murder *us*."

We both lapse into worried silence.

"The Hand are extra pissed off now that I can't talk to Rosemary anymore," says Nora.

"What do you mean?" I ask. "She isn't talking to you, or you can't feel her presence?"

"Both. As soon as I got here, she just vanished. Like that." Nora snaps her fingers. "I'm supposed to connect with her, act as her voice so that she can tell them what she needs for a ritual to bring her and her sisters back from death, but I can't. It's like she doesn't exist anymore."

This doesn't make any sense. For days and days, Rosemary has been whispering to us, screaming at us, directing us. Why would she disappear now?

"Hang on." I close my eyes and wait for the tug, but it's not there either.

"Rosemary?" I whisper. "May?"

Still nothing. There must be another layer of magic at work, preventing her from speaking to me. Maybe now that we're with the Hand of Nephthys, whatever was blocking them from communicating with her is also blocking us.

"Why are you—" Nora cuts off as a door creaks open overhead and light spills down a set of narrow stairs. "Oh no," she whispers as a tall figure carrying a lantern descends, their dark robe trailing behind them.

CHAPTER 53

The figure reaches the bottom of the stairs, and as they lift their hooded head, the lantern casts a flickering glow inside. A horseshoe-crab-skull mask covers their face, its spiny tail pointing down from the bottom like some kind of macabre gas mask. The eyes are two black holes, the mouth a set of grinning teeth. I've seen a lot of scary masks in my day, but this one blows them all away.

"It's time for the ritual." Her voice is like gravel. She drops a bundle of clothing beside me, then bends to unlock my chain. "Put everything on. If you even think about running, your boyfriend will die."

At least this means Elliot is still alive. I'm tempted to make a snarky comment that they can't actually know if we're thinking about running away, but it's possible they do know exactly what we're thinking. Sparks of magic are practically sizzling off this woman. She smells like smoke and incense and the ocean, and underneath it all, the copper tang of fresh blood. On her left hand is a ring in the shape of a blue eyeball. At first glance, it looks like a Greek mati charm to ward off the evil eye, but I realize it's more anatomically correct than that. It looks like an actual miniature human eyeball.

"We'll never help you if you kill him." I hate how much my voice shakes.

"You're in no position to negotiate," she says as she unlocks Nora's chain, and maybe there's something familiar about her voice, now that I think about it.

"Detective Huld?" I ask. "Is that you?"

The woman heads for the staircase. "Be ready in three minutes," she says, and then she's gone, leaving the lantern halfway up so we can see a little better.

"You don't actually think *that's* Detective Huld, do you?" says Nora.

"I don't know what to think anymore," I say. "But she was in one of the Polaroids we found after you disappeared. Sitting with May—sorry, Rosemary—at a table in the woods."

"Whoa," says Nora. "I didn't notice an accent, though."

"Maybe the accent was fake." I pick up the bundle of clothing. It's two garments—a hooded cloak and a long, gray dress—and suddenly I'm shaking so hard my fingers don't work. The sleeves are trimmed with lace. This is the same dress all the bodies wore. Now it's going on my own body.

"Two minutes," calls the woman—maybe Detective Huld—from upstairs, and shivers crawl like spiders over my skin. We have to figure out how to escape, but the first step is getting out of this basement. And to do that, we need to follow the instructions.

The dress is scratchy and stiff and smells like institutional detergent. I wonder what kinds of horrible stains they've had to wash out of this fabric.

"What about Ione?" I say. "Any sign of her?"

Nora shakes her head.

"Listen." I drop my voice. "We need to figure out how to get out of here without them killing Elliot. Or at least put off the ritual long enough for Rowan to find us. We've finally done exactly what he wants and led him right to the Hand of Nephthys—if he managed to keep up and saw them take me and Elliot."

The last thing I want to do is leave my fate in that man's hands, but we're out of options.

"One minute," calls the voice, and I tug the dress down over my hips. It's too long, but that's the least of my worries. Wearing her own gray dress, Nora's even paler than usual in the flickering lantern light, and her face is pinched with fear. She looks so much like one of the bodies now, I can barely stand to look at her.

"We'll figure something out," she says, but her voice is shaking worse than mine.

Footsteps creak down the staircase, and I throw the cloak over my shoulders. The damp weight of it makes me want to sink to the floor and sob. But there's no time for crying, because the skull-faced woman is standing in front of me now, and she's carrying two thick lengths of rope.

"Can you please just tell us if you're Det—" I start, but pain explodes in the center of my forehead. With a shriek, I double over. I can't see, I can't think. I can only imagine this is what it feels like to get shot. The agony in my skull blots everything else out.

I'm vaguely aware of Nora yelling, "Stop it!" and I think I'm still screaming.

"Please." I gasp as the pain eases just enough for me to breathe. "Make it stop."

"Then stop asking questions." Even through the blinding pain, I hear the smile in her voice.

"Okay." Tears are pouring down my cheeks, and my mouth tastes like blood. "I promise."

The hooded woman flexes her bony hand, palm out, and the pain lifts, though my jaw still throbs and my pulse is keening in my ears.

"The moon is rising, and I've run out of patience," she says. "Let's go."

Without a word, Nora and I follow her up the stairs.

CHAPTER 54

The stairwell opens onto a dim, empty room with a slanted floor. The walls are covered in symbols. Some are painted, some scrawled in ink and pencil and Sharpie, others carved deep into the plaster. There are Germanic runes, Middle Eastern hamsas, Egyptian ankhs, pentacles, and a whole host of sigils I've never seen before—a jumble of all kinds of magical symbols with no discernable pattern or tradition. Just looking at them makes my eyeballs hurt.

Broken windows look out over a surging ocean under a darkening sky. There's no ground visible anywhere—the building seems to be hanging over the side of a cliff, and I'd be willing to bet this is the house from the last Polaroid, the Tower. The wind heaves, making the timbers creak and groan, and I swear I can feel the foundations tipping, sliding.

My hands are bound in front of me, and as I brush against a doorframe carved with the same disarray of symbols, a familiar, fizzing energy flows through my skin. The same as Rosemary's teeth, the bone cup, the athame. This is the feel of the Hand of Nephthys's magic. It's chaos, borrowed from a hundred different practices with no regard to their traditions or histories. The effect is unsettling and slightly unhinged.

Which reminds me, my head still feels very quiet.

Rosemary, I think, *are you here?*

No answer.

A shorter woman wearing the same robe and horseshoe-crab-skull mask appears in a doorway, and as our captor strides off to speak to her, I shuffle closer to Nora.

"We have to find Elliot."

She tips her head toward the cloaked women in the next room, which is also empty except for a spinning wheel and three large wicker baskets. "How?"

"I don't know." My pulse is racing in a way that makes me dizzy. "I just . . . I need to know if he's still alive."

Nora's eyes hold mine for a long minute, and then her expression softens. "He is. You just have to trust me that I can feel he's around somewhere. His energy is still here."

My eyes are leaking again. I hope she's right, because I can't feel anything except my own surging terror.

"This way." The tall woman's eyeball ring glints as she gestures for us to follow her into the second room and out through a door.

As we pass the spinning wheel, I crane my neck to see what's inside the baskets. The first contains dried seaweed. The second is full of long hanks of human hair. Blond and red and brown and black, all intermingled. The third basket holds what looks like a woven mixture of the hair and the seaweed, and the waves of rotten evil radiating off it make me gag.

The door opens onto a short set of steps that end at the top of a sand cliff. Thirty feet down, out on a wide sandbar, the remaining members of the Hand of Nephthys are hurrying back and forth, their cloaks whipping in the wind. Six lidded coffins are arranged in a star shape, the heads pointed inward. In the center, there's a large statue. Between that and the ocean sits a wide stone altar. Torches flicker at the outer boundaries of the ritual space.

As I stumble down the steps, I cast around, trying to get a sense of where we are, but there are no other buildings in sight, and the narrow road behind the house is covered in sand, with a forest of stunted pines on the other side. Judging by the size of those waves and these cliffs, we're somewhere on the Outer Cape, the Atlantic side, but it's strange to be this isolated in a place with so many summer homes crowding the shores. I've never seen this exact stretch of coastline before.

The shorter woman follows us, lugging a wicker basket that smells like death, and I trip over my skirt trying to get as far away from her as I can.

"This way," says the woman who might be Detective Huld, gesturing for us to follow her onto a path that cuts diagonally down the sand cliff.

It's all happening too fast. Nora and I needed time to plan a ruse, a story, a spell to get us away from this murderous cult. Or at least waste time until *their* murderer shows up. I don't see Elliot anywhere on the beach, and my jagged panic is making it hard to breathe, but hopefully he's locked in a room somewhere, safely away from whatever is about to happen. Not inside one of those coffins.

But the math isn't reassuring. There were nine hooded figures in my vision, the nine members of the Hand of Nephthys. Four are down on the beach, and two are with us, which means three are left—likely the three dead bodies we found. But six coffins lie on that sandbar, which means there are three extra. Nora plus Elliot plus me equals three.

My brain is looping in sickening circles, and I keep stepping on the hem of Nora's cloak. If I'm not careful, I'll send us both tumbling over the side of this cliff. But maybe that wouldn't be so terrible. We're halfway down now, and the sand is soft. We could run away down the beach—but we can't just leave Elliot here. I have no doubt that woman would keep her word and kill him if we ran.

The only way for all three of us to survive is to somehow overpower or outwit them all. But I can't begin to imagine how.

CHAPTER 55

The moon hangs low and whisper-faint over the ocean, and the sun is setting over the land behind us. The sky blazes with bands of orange and gold, layered with wispy pink clouds and gaps of pale blue. *Sky-blue pink* is what my mom used to call it. She told me, and then Henry, that it was the Tooth Fairy's favorite color. My stomach clenches, and I blink back tears. There's a good chance I'll never see my mom again. Or my dad. I can't remember when the last time I hugged Henry was. I need to picture that moment, hold on to it, but my panicked brain can't find it.

Out on the sandbar, a hooded figure picks up a crowbar and pries the lid off one of the coffins. I can't tell if it's already full or they're getting ready to put someone new inside. Someone like me or Nora. As we reach the bottom of the cliff, the wind carries the sweet stench of decay, and I press my hands over my mouth.

The statue in the center of the coffins is about eight feet tall, a curvy woman painted in faded colors, like the salt air has leached them away. Her torso and her feet are bare, and she wears a long skirt and a basket-shaped headdress decorated with stones and crystals. A collar of real shells hangs around her neck, and there are rows of white feathers on her outstretched arms, making them look like wings. She holds an ankh in one hand and a horseshoe crab in the other. With a jolt, I realize the creature is still alive, its ten spindly legs wriggling.

"Keep moving." The shorter woman shoves me with her basket, and I stumble in the deep sand. As we cross the tide pool in front of the sandbar, I let my dress and robe drag in the water. I wish I could let the ocean pull me far, far away from here.

Nora peeks at me over her shoulder, and I can see the whites all around her irises. Rowan isn't here. Nobody is coming to save us. We had no time to make a plan, and we have no way to communicate now.

Up on the altar, I spot the athame and the bone cup beside a human skull. There's something tiny and white on a silver plate that looks like a tooth. Nora's meat cleaver is there too—they must have taken everything from my car after I crashed. The butcher's blade seems strangely out of place with all the other esoteric items.

Two cloaked figures approach the open casket and lean inside. Together, they lift out a body wearing a long, gray dress and lay her on the sand. Her gray hair splays like weeds around her wrinkled face. It's the woman from Grays Beach. They move on to the next coffin, where they pull out the blonde corpse we found at Scargo Lake.

It's no surprise when they lift Rosemary from the third coffin, but something deep inside me still lurches at the sight of her blank eyes, her open mouth, her thin limbs. She looks so powerless, so broken, and it's hard to understand how this is the same person who's been relentlessly tormenting me and Nora. By now, I'm certain I've lost my connection with her spirit. There's no way she could look at her own body and not have a palpable reaction. I wonder what spell is blocking her, and why.

A figure strides past, carrying a large set of brass scales. As they set it on the altar beside a white feather, my blood runs cold. Whose hearts are going on that scale, if none of those dead sisters have hearts in their bodies anymore?

The figure with the crowbar continues around the star of coffins, opening the rest, but no one removes any bodies, and I can only assume that means the empty spaces are waiting for us. But where is Elliot? There are still so many pieces of this ritual—of this entire unhinged week—that make no sense. My eyes keep jumping back to the altar, to the athame and the bone cup, the things we found while following the clues in Kaia's tarot reading. How does it all connect?

The tall woman with the eyeball ring approaches. "Hold still," she warns, holding out her palm and curling her fingers. A sharp snap of pain hits my forehead, and I cringe back, stumbling into a person who's come up behind me. Something heavy falls over my head and shoulders and I drop to my knees, gasping. It's a net made of seaweed and hair, studded with broken shells and barnacles and crab claws. It reeks of marshy decay and rot, and I can't move my arms or legs, not even a twitch. Nora yelps, and I look up just in time to see her fall under the weight of a similar net on the other side of the sandbar.

It's over. Whatever the Hand of Nephthys wants to do now, we cannot resist. Tears sting my eyes, but the wind whips them away before they can fall. If Kaia's tarot reading foretold the fates of three dead women—and ours too—there's no doubt that we've now reached the Eight of Swords, the imprisonment.

"Please," I beg, even though no one is listening. I wish I could crawl closer to Nora so we could at least die together, but it's impossible.

The tall woman strides to the altar and snaps her fingers over the candles. They burst alight, their flames tall and unwavering, despite the wind. The other hooded figures form a semicircle around Nora and me and the coffins. Slowly, they begin to chant. All of the voices are women. All sisters.

The chanting grows louder, stronger. The candles and the torches flicker silver, then blue. Magic zaps through the air, lifting my hair from my scalp like I'm about to get struck by lightning. Across the sandbar, Nora sits, helpless and sobbing, and it's all so cruel and unfair. We were just trying to help Rosemary and her sisters, and now we're going to die for our kindness.

"Bring the boy," says the tall woman, gesturing at one of the open coffins, and my soul nearly leaves my body as two women pull Elliot out. His arms and legs are slack, his eyes closed, and my own vision goes black and starry because this cannot, it *simply cannot* be happening. Acid surges up my throat. I want to scream, I want to rip this net off and murder everyone here with my bare hands. I can't even move a finger.

But as they drag him closer to the altar, he coughs. He's fast asleep, either drugged or spellbound, and I don't know why I'm relieved that he's not dead yet—instead of about to be murdered in front of me—but I am. Somehow, an ember of hope still glows in my chest, even though there's no possible way out of this.

More sisters join them, and together they heft Elliot onto the stone altar. My relief quickly fades as the tall woman reaches into her sleeve and pulls out a crescent blade that looks just like the one in Kaia's Ace of Swords card. If we're following that reading—and I'm sure now that we are—the Tower is next. There's no turning back. The chanting picks up again, morphs into a song, and regret hits me like a sledgehammer as I recognize the tune, as I remember my fingers on the strings of my cello forming this melody. How could I have ever thought it was beautiful?

The tall woman slices a line down the front of Elliot's black sweatshirt, and as it falls open, I squeeze my eyes shut.

"I'm sorry, I'm so, so sorry." My words are broken by sobs. It was so selfish to bring him with me today, knowing how dangerous the situation was. If I hadn't let this stupid crush distract me, I would have known better.

Rosemary's song soars all around me, the voices of the sisters rising to a frenzied pitch, and I can't help it—I open my eyes just in time to see the blade lifted high overhead, flashing in the eerie blue light.

"Stop! *Now.*"

A voice rings through the darkness, and the singing cuts out. The tall woman lowers her dagger and peers at someone behind me. I choke back a shriek, my veins humming with elation, because I recognize that voice.

It's Ione.

CHAPTER 56

"It won't work if you give Rosemary someone else's heart." Ione steps into the torchlight, her red hair wild. Her jeans and sensible wool clogs are soaked, and she clutches a black messenger bag to her chest.

The tall woman steps out from behind the altar. "What do you know about any of this?"

"I knew enough to take their hearts in the first place," says Ione, and every single member of the Hand of Nephthys goes still. "And their hands," she adds, eyes flashing. "To break their magic and sever their connection with you."

I glance at Nora, whose mouth is hanging open. *Ione* is the murderer of those three washed-up bodies? All this time, she's been hunting the Hand of Nephthys, killing them, and hacking them up. How could she have listened to all of our stories about May's spirit without saying a word? How could she have let us believe the Hand of Nephthys killed those three women when it was her all along?

Then again, why would she ever tell us what she was doing? By killing them and taking their hearts, she was trying to protect us all, prevent the Hand of Nephthys from creating some hideous backward path to return from death. She must have been shocked when Rosemary's spirit came back anyway, without her body. That's why she was so rattled, and it must also be why she went missing. She was trying to fix everything without involving us.

Suddenly, I'm thinking that maybe Ione is the Tower. She's here to blow everything up. I almost don't dare hope.

"Let them go." Ione holds up her messenger bag. "And I'll give you back the hearts."

The tall woman tips her head sideways, the eyeholes of her skull mask dark and fathomless. "You know I can't let witnesses go," she says. "Let's not pretend there's an easy fix for this situation."

She whirls back toward the altar, toward Elliot, and I shriek as her long, silver blade swings high. But then I can't hear my own scream, because a roaring blast of sound blots everything out. It happens so fast I don't understand—until the woman tumbles forward, grabbing the altar and falling to the sand. Then I see the gun in Ione's hand, flat-black in the blue torchlight.

"Nobody move," she says, advancing on the altar. The sisters shrink back as she bends low and tears the mask from the woman's face. I gasp.

It's not Detective Huld.

The woman is in her midfifties—surprisingly pretty in a haunted way, with dark hair and sharp cheekbones. She clutches her left shoulder, her full lips twisted in a grimace.

Ione tucks a finger under the woman's chin. "Do you know who I am, Valia?"

The older woman tries to pull away, but hisses in pain. "Should I?"

"You knew my half sister, Kaia," Ione says.

300

"I don't quite see the resemblance." The corner of Valia's mouth twitches. "Especially now. But she's here tonight, right there on the altar. Why don't you say hello?"

My eyes snap to the skull on the altar, and my stomach heaves. Ione grabs the front of Valia's robe and shakes her so hard that her head slams into the ground. The older woman grunts in pain.

"I was sixteen years old when they told me she drowned in a boating accident," Ione says. "They never found her body, but we had a funeral anyway."

"Kaia did what she needed to do," says Valia. "We ask the same of all of our sisters."

"Why would you ask her to devastate her family like that?" says Ione.

Valia shrugs one shoulder, wincing in pain. "Maybe you should ask yourself why your sister was willing to devastate you."

Ione shoves Valia again. "After three years of grief, I finally put most of the pieces of myself back together. I was almost normal again. And then one night, my friend and I went to the beach to look at the stars. There was my sister, sitting at a bonfire with a group of women. It didn't make any sense. She never surfaced after that boat capsized. But there she was, looking thinner and older and more dangerous in a way I couldn't explain.

"I called out to her, and she looked straight at me, and I *know* she recognized me. I saw a flash of pain in her eyes, but then she stood up and walked into the ocean and was gone. I thought I'd seen her ghost."

"She's lucky I didn't hear about that." says Valia.

"Why would it have mattered?" Ione rounds on her, eyes flaming. "You killed her anyway."

"She broke our most important rule," says Valia. "No evidence of our group to the outside world, not the tiniest trace. Kaia made a tarot deck in secret, using photographs of our members and our practice, to amplify the magic and use it for her own personal gain."

"You could have just destroyed the cards," says Ione, but Valia shakes her head, wincing at the movement.

"That deck was concrete evidence of every single one of us performing ritual magic. Of our ceremonial spaces, our secret hiding spots where we left things for each other without having to meet. All of it, laid bare. An outrageous, flagrant display of rule-breaking, a betrayal of every secret principle our group is based on. And then when Kaia disappeared with it, our worst fears were confirmed."

For a speck of an instant, Ione's mask slips, and raw pain glints in her eyes. "Where did she go?"

"We tracked her down to somewhere in Delaware," Valia says. "We were just closing in on her exact location when she appeared in Truro and turned herself in."

To save Rowan. The man is a creep and a coward, but I guess he didn't deserve to die over Kaia's decision to join a group of murderers.

"Imagine our surprise when those photographs started showing up, the same week our dear sister Rosemary washed ashore," says Valia. "We were certain the two things were related, but we decided to keep quiet and watch. And wait."

"But you still couldn't figure it all out, could you?" Ione spits in the sand. "None of you sisters are as smart as you think."

Valia lets out a croaking laugh, and then coughs. Blood trickles from the corner of her mouth, black in the moonlight.

"We're smarter than *you* think, though."

From out of the corner of my eye, I catch a black flash, moving so fast it's almost a blur. A hooded woman flies across the sand and slams into Ione, smashing her head into the side of the stone altar. Ione crumples to the ground, eyelids fluttering and legs twitching, and a swarm of cloaked figures descends on her. Someone snatches the gun. A net just like mine drapes over Ione, and her legs stop twitching.

I'm too stunned to scream or cry—I'm utterly blank from the shock of what's just happened. For a long moment, the sisters are silent, waiting. Then Valia drags herself slowly up to sitting and pulls her mask back on.

CHAPTER 57

"Put her on the altar," Valia says, clutching her shoulder.

Two sisters pick up Ione's limp body, while two others drag Elliot off the stone table. I cringe as they dump him in the sand, his arms and legs bent at awkward angles. But he's still breathing, and for now that has to be enough. My eyes flick to Nora, but she's staring, horror-struck, at the scene unfolding.

Still covered with the net, Ione now lies motionless on the altar.

"Get her arm out." Valia hobbles closer, hissing in pain.

"No," I whisper as she picks up the enormous meat cleaver and hands it to one of her sisters, muttering instructions.

A visible, excited shiver goes through all of the cloaked sisters, and they begin to chant again as the woman lifts the cleaver high with both hands. Then, with a furious, unhinged shriek, she slams it down. Bile surges up my throat as Ione's hand falls off the edge of the table and hits the sand.

An audible blast of energy slams my face and blows my hair out behind me. I want to scream, I want to sob, but I'm frozen, powerless, my legs cramping beneath me because I can't so much as move a toe. And then the roaring wave is gone, and I wait for the sisters to continue their ritual, but they're all just staring at something across the sandbar.

Nora stands with her net in tatters at her feet. Her hair hovers in a full static halo around her head, and her arms stretch out like wings. A faint blue glow illuminates every inch of her.

"The spell is broken," she says in a deep, croaking voice that isn't hers.

Ione wasn't the Tower after all. *This* is.

This is the beginning of the end.

A cautious murmur goes through the cloaked women. My heart is in my throat. Whatever spell Ione did to block Rosemary from reaching her sisters is now undone, and I'm not sure if it's because she lost her hand or her life.

"Don't you recognize me?" Nora laughs, low and broken and bitter, and I wish I could scrub that sound out of my ears.

"Rosemary," I whisper. "Are you in my head too?"

There's a faint . . . something. But this time it's not a tugging; it's more like pushing away. Like she doesn't have time for me right now.

"Welcome, sister." Valia's voice shakes ever so slightly, but she takes Nora's hand and leads her to the altar. The other women gather in a loose circle around them.

"Tell us what to do," says one of the sisters.

Slowly, like she's asleep, Nora's hand floats up to point at Ione. "Get the hearts."

Two sisters pull the net from Ione's limp body and then cut the strap of her messenger bag. There isn't as much blood as I expected, and I desperately hope that doesn't mean she's already dead. Inside the messenger bag are three glass jars, and inside each jar, floating in clear liquid, is a human heart. A soft, keening wail goes through the group.

"Now give them back," says Nora, gesturing to the coffins.

Three women take a jar each and glide toward the bodies of their fallen sisters. The woman in the center unscrews the lid, and I flinch as she reaches inside and takes the heart in her bare hand. The others follow suit, and together they place the hearts over the wounds where they were cut out. A strange, whispering rattle fills the air, and it's only now that I realize the wind has gone completely still.

Nora takes the athame from the altar. She drags it across the sand, drawing a sigil. "Carve this into the palm of your left hand," she says, handing the blade to Valia. "All of you. Deep enough to bleed."

Valia sways on her feet, and I have no idea how she's still standing after getting shot, but she obviously has more powerful magic than anyone I've ever met. Without a word, she drags the blade across her hand. Her blood, still black in the eerie light, spills onto the sand, and she passes the athame to the sister on her left.

Nora takes the bone cup and holds it under each woman's hand, collecting the drips. As she works, she begins to chant, and the sisters join in, growing louder and faster and more frantic with each repetition. Terror flares in my chest as my best friend shrieks words in a language neither of us knows, in a voice that isn't hers, surrounded by bleeding, murderous, masked women. The whispering rattle fills the air again, and I swear I can see the dead sisters' gray lips moving.

"Rosemary," I try again. "Don't. *Please.*"

The last sister finishes carving her palm, and Nora's mouth

stretches into a sinister grin as she collects the last of the blood. Then she takes the tooth from the silver dish and drops it into the cup. Immediately, white flames burst out, missing her face by inches. With a feral roar, she swings the cup in a wide arc, splashing the altar, the bodies, the sand with blood and fire. The sisters all watch, their skull faces expressionless as the flames lick at the hems of their cloaks and the dresses of the corpses.

"Rosemary," I whisper. "Listen to me. You have everything you want. Your sisters, your body, your way back. You don't need Nora anymore. Let go of her."

White flames trail up the front of Nora's robe as she begins to sing that awful, wordless song, and I fight through the waves of terror that are threatening to drown me.

"Rosemary, I'm begging you." My face is soaked with tears now, my body shaking so hard my teeth are clacking. "Let Nora go, or so help me God, we'll haunt the crap out of you after we're dead."

Nora's head swivels in an uncanny, inhuman way, and her eyes lock on mine. She throws her head back and laughs at the moonlit sky.

"So you *are* listening," I say. Nora's gaze snaps away and she turns back to the altar, but it doesn't matter. I know she hears me.

"We're the ones who helped you," I say. "No one else did. It's only fair for you to help us now."

We're almost finished. Rosemary's voice scratches the inside of my skull. *Soon.*

"You'll let go of her soon, or we're going to die soon?" I whisper.

No answer. One of the sisters picks up a bucket and upends it, and horseshoe crabs and water stream out. Instead of heading for the ocean where they'd be free, the crabs crawl toward the altar, their spiky tails dragging in the sand. They form a circle around the chanting sisters and begin to move counterclockwise.

"It's time." Nora is gasping now, in Rosemary's unearthly voice. "Bring . . . the sacrifices."

I watch, horrified, as two sleeping people are lifted from the two remaining coffins. A woman with filthy blond dreadlocks and tattered clothing. And a man I recognize.

Rowan.

He must have seen our accident and pulled over, and they must have taken him too. He was the only person who might have saved us. The only person who knows where we are.

"Bring them . . . to the . . . altar." Nora staggers sideways. Watching her fall apart like this, ravaged by an undead spirit, is tearing me to pieces too.

The sandbar beneath us starts to tremble. Everything's crashing down now, just as Kaia predicted. But still, I can't stop wracking my brain, sifting through all of the cards in her reading, desperate for some shred of hope that there might be something standing between us and our untimely end. The Seven of Pentacles, the card lying under the Ace of Swords, keeps coming back to me, like there's something my intuition knows but my conscious mind can't see.

Those seven gold coins, half buried in the dirt. Seeds planted, seeds tended, seeds that sprout and grow. How do you reverse that process once it's been started? How do you stop a plant from bearing fruit?

And then it hits me, a sudden, powerful Ace of Swords *eureka* moment. The rusty shovel in the card.

You dig it out.

My skin starts to tingle all over. I have my own seed of an idea. Not necessarily a *good* idea. Not necessarily one I can handle. But I'm all out of other options.

"Rosemary," I whisper. "It's too much for Nora. She won't make it through the ritual."

Again, that irritated, pushing, *go away* sensation.

"Listen to me." I swallow hard, focus all of my energy on the vibrating essence that is her spirit, her energy, her aura. "Come to me instead."

"Bring the—" Nora gestures emptily in the direction of the altar. "Bring—" She stumbles again, and this time she falls to her knees. I just want to sob at the horror of everything, but I can't stop now.

"Rosemary." I close my eyes and blot out all the noise, the chaos, the terror. "Use me instead."

Nora coughs and sputters, and I think she might be choking, but I keep my eyes shut and my focus sharp.

"Come here," I whisper.

A jolt like a sudden car crash. A white-hot flash, like being struck by lightning, and then I'm gone.

CHAPTER 58

I'm still in my body—but not exactly. I can feel my freezing fingers and toes, the wet fabric of my dress clinging to my legs, the salty cold on my face, but I'm somehow outside it too, floating like smoke. As my legs straighten and I lurch upright, panic roars through my brain, but it's quickly replaced by an overwhelming sense of numbness, of artificial calm. It reminds me of anesthesia.

"Lay the sacrifices at Nebet-Het's feet." It's not my voice, not my intention, and the words feel like rocks in my mouth.

The sisters all freeze. Their faces aren't visible under those masks, but I can feel their shock, their confusion, their fear. Rosemary feels it too, and she loves it. Her spirit—or whatever this is, latched onto me like a tick—is humming with elation. She's getting stronger by the second.

Nora lies in a crumpled heap, like a marionette with its strings cut, and the panic waves start crashing in again, but just as quickly as before, they're snuffed out and I'm striding across the sand.

"All of them?" asks a masked woman, gesturing to the dreadlocked woman, Rowan, Elliot, Ione, and Nora.

"Yes," I say. "As many as it takes."

That gives me pause. Rosemary doesn't actually know how many people they need to sacrifice for the ritual to work. She's just going to start killing indiscriminately—

The thought flies out of my head.

I'm losing power over my own brain. I try to blink, just to assert some sense of control, but my eyes only make it halfway shut before shooting back open. Mocking laughter fills my skull.

Let go, my sweet.

Never is what I want to say, but my lips don't move, so I think it as hard as I can, but that flies away too, like a feather in the wind.

Yes, a feather.

My body turns and heads for the altar, and everything about it feels so sickeningly wrong. This isn't even how I walk. My gait is long and loping and uneven on one side, and I wonder if Rosemary walked with a limp when she was alive.

Enough.

My hand darts out—I start to pull it back, but Rosemary's will is too strong. I take the white feather from the altar and place it on the scale.

"Nebet-Het will tell us if their hearts are pure," I announce to the sisters, who are arranging the unconscious victims around the statue in a star shape, with their heads pointing inward.

But wait—in the legend, it wasn't up to Nephthys to judge people's hearts. It was Osiris and the divine judges. None of this follows any of the rules of the ancient Egyptian traditions. It makes no sense. Why would Nephthys even want a human sacrifice?

Shut up.

An invisible slap sends me careening into darkness. By the

time I finally claw my way back to reality, to seeing out of my eyes again, everything is ready for the final phase of the ritual. The sisters all kneel in the sand. There's a crescent blade in my hand, and I'm dragging it through the blue flame of a candle. My mouth is forming an invocation, a prayer to Nephthys. I'm summoning the goddess now, demanding that she answer our request. The night air starts to waver and shimmer, and the blue flames of the torches and candles shoot skyward.

No, I think as hard as I can, but Rosemary makes me kneel beside the first victim. Elliot's hair is damp and tangled, and sand coats his sleeping face. He looks so peaceful, so blissfully unaware that I'm holding a razor-sharp blade and my fingers are itching to drive it into his chest.

No, I scream wordlessly, and again, there's that overwhelming slap trying to send me out of myself, but I fight it this time. Furious, desperate, I try over and over to open my hand, to drop the dagger. My thumb twitches, but the rest of my fingers hold tight.

You asked for this, laughs Rosemary. *You begged.*

White-hot rage blasts through me. I may have bargained with Rosemary to save Nora, but I never asked for any of this. Out of the corner of my eye, I spot Ione stirring, but I force myself to ignore it, to empty my brain of all conscious ideas or plans, because Rosemary will hear anything I think. My veins are buzzing with her excitement, her anticipation, her eagerness to kill. I can't stop the giddy emotions, and it's becoming difficult to separate these thoughts from my own.

Let go, she croons inside my head.

Ione's remaining hand inches toward her—

No, I can't look at that. Quickly, I focus all my attention on the blade in my own hand, on Elliot lying in the sand. His dark eyelashes curling against his pale skin. The gentle hushing of his sleep-slow breath. I can't plan how to save him, can't even consider the idea of a plan, because Rosemary is in my thoughts. Instead, I picture the last two tarot cards before the Tower. The Seven of Pentacles and the Ace of Swords. The seeds and the blade.

"Nebet-Het!" Rosemary's voice pours out of my throat. "We offer you this living sacrifice. May it please you, and may it grant us your favor, so that you might help us in return."

I need to let go of any sense of control or will. I need to let Rosemary keep going for now, and I'll know what to do when I need to do it. I'm operating on reflex, on impulse. It's absolutely terrifying to have no control, no plan, no rules, but I have to trust myself. It will all happen as it needs to.

The chanting has become a roar, the sisters' frenzied energy zapping through the night like a lightning storm. I rock back and forth, floating on the tide of their collective bloodlust. My physical self, the one all tangled up with Rosemary, lifts the dagger high, eyes laser-focused on the spot where the tip of its blade will hit, just to one side of Elliot's breastbone. Right between the ribs.

My muscles tense. My jaw clenches. It's time to dig out the seeds.

Rosemary drives the dagger downward.

A millisecond before it pierces Elliot's skin, I yank, as hard as I can possibly imagine, and the blade jerks off its trajectory and plunges into my right thigh. Searing pain blasts down my leg, and Rosemary's scream fills my head.

I am the Tower now.

Gasping, I pull together every shred of focus, of intention, of will, of purpose, of *power* into one massive, crushing wave. I take everything that's hurt me, broken me, controlled me, and I crush it and make it mine.

I wrench the blade out of my leg, and then I explode Rosemary's spirit out of me.

I am the Tower. I am chaos, I am calamity. I am an inescapable, devastating force.

Ione whips something out of her pocket and flips it open. The silver compact mirror flashes blue in the torchlight. Words spring from my mouth as I drop the dagger and my hands flex toward the mirror, and I can see Ione's mouth moving too. Across the sandbar, Nora is yelling, and I'm somehow sure we're all speaking the same incantation. Binding Rosemary to that mirror.

Ione jolts backward at the sudden impact, and the mirror goes flat-black. Quickly, she snaps it shut, then holds it to her mouth, whispering directly into the metal case.

"Watch out!" screams Nora as two cloaked sisters rush at her. Ione rolls over and curls up fetal around the mirror, but more sisters descend on her, and they're ripping and tearing and shrieking. I try to stand, but my bloody leg gives out under me. My dress and robe are sticky and soaked, and the night spins around me.

I lay my cheek on Elliot's chest and listen for his shallow breathing. I need to keep my eyes from slipping shut, but it's a losing battle. It's like sinking underwater, except this isn't the frigid Atlantic Ocean; it's more like a warm bath. The horseshoe crabs are scattered everywhere, their circle broken. One lies on its back, spindly legs wheeling. It lifts its long tail over and over, trying to right itself.

"Mazzy!" A frantic voice in my ear. "Are you okay?"

I stare up at Nora's face, which wavers in and out of focus. "Um . . . no."

She cups my cheek, her eyes soft and sad. "I love you."

And then she's up again, launching herself into the chaos, wrenching people off of Ione like a desperate, doomed action hero. It's the most ridiculous, foolish, beautiful thing I've ever seen . . .

. . . and it takes all of thirty seconds before one of the sisters gets her in choke hold, and Nora is screaming in agony.

I refuse to lie here bleeding out, watching my best friend get killed. Ignoring the blast of pain in my leg, I pick up the crescent blade and stagger to my feet. If I'm going to die—and it's a certainty at this point—I'll gather up every last shred of chaotic, destructive Tower energy that's left in me, and I'll go out swinging.

The knife's handle keeps slipping in my bloody fingers, but it doesn't matter. I launch myself at the sister who's got Nora, and I slash at her mask, her robe. The blade keeps catching on fabric, almost like there's no one inside, but it distracts the woman long enough for Nora to struggle free. Together we shove the woman. She falls and lands hard, and her mask slides back, exposing a pale, freckled neck.

I falter, blade held high. I could channel the last dregs of Rosemary's fury coursing through my veins; I could end this woman in seconds. Stop her from ever hurting another soul. Remove one more murderer from the world. But even though I'm the Tower, I am not a killer. I'm just trying to survive this.

Suddenly, new voices are shouting—male voices—and beams of blinding yellow light are sweeping across the sandbar. Nora and I freeze, gaping as the crisscrossing beams illuminate individual horrors in random order.

A wrinkled old woman, her mask shoved on top of her head, grabbing a fistful of Ione's hair.

Elliot, still and pale as a corpse, lying in the sand.

My black robe, saturated with blood.

A stone Egyptian goddess with arms like wings, staring impassively out to sea.

An overturned horseshoe crab, legs scrambling, tail lifting over and over.

"Police!" calls a deep voice. "Everyone put your hands in the air!"

CHAPTER 59

The water in the tide pool churns as police officers wielding flashlights charge in from the beach.

"Get down on the ground!" yells another officer, a woman, and it takes me a minute to process who she is. Detective Freaking Huld is rushing onto the scene with the others, wearing her black suit and holding a gun.

A shot roars; Nora grabs my arm and we both hunch over Elliot, who is still breathing, still unconscious. There's a scuffle on the sandbar to our left, a woman screams in the water behind us, and then a gun fires again and I bury my face in Elliot's chest. Nora starts to mutter a protective spell, and as I join in, our hands clasped tight, a soft warmth spreads through me. I feel it radiate into Elliot too.

Everything around us is whirling chaos, but we are here. We are safe.

Elliot stirs, mumbles something incoherent, and my heart soars.

"Shh," I whisper, kissing his shoulder. "Everything's fine. Just lie still for a minute, okay?"

A sister falls beside us, thrashing as two officers wrestle handcuffs onto her wrists. Another officer is dragging an unmasked, handcuffed, wild-haired woman through the water toward the beach.

Valia lies motionless in the sand, her blank mask staring up at the waning moon.

Ione is gone.

"Look," whispers Nora, tipping her head toward the ocean. Out past the breaking waves, a figure with short red hair is wading silently into the open water. In seconds, her head disappears beneath the surf.

I don't know what will happen to Ione now. It's out of our hands.

~ ~ ~

Thirty minutes later, I'm sitting on a stretcher at the top of the cliff with Nora beside me and a pressure bandage on my right leg. The paramedics told me I was lucky the dagger missed my artery and the cut was fairly superficial. The bleeding has already slowed, although I'll still need to go to the hospital for stitches.

Elliot's being stretchered up the cliff now, even though he keeps telling the paramedics he's fine and can walk. As soon as I catch sight of my parents and Nora's mom hurrying down the road, bathed in blue and red flashing lights, I burst into ugly, broken sobs. My dad bounds over, wraps his arms tight around me, and mutters into my hair.

"I'm sorry, Mazz. I'm so, so sorry we didn't believe you about everything."

My mom wedges herself into our jumbled hug, also crying. "When the police showed up at the store and said they found your car, I thought you were dead," she says.

"So did I," I say with a rueful laugh. "How did they find my car?"

"That woman over there called the police." My dad points to Tina, who's standing beside a police cruiser with Detective Huld. "She said you and Elliot cut school and were on your way to Brewster, and that a suspicious guy was following you. In the meantime, somebody called in a report of a car in a marsh in that area, and they went to investigate. Do you know that guy over there?" He points to Rowan, who's standing by the cliff's edge, talking to another officer.

I nod. "His name is Rowan Moore. It's a long story, and you might not believe it."

My mom blows out all her breath, abashed. "We'll believe you, Mazzy. I promise."

"How did everybody know to come here, though?" Nora nudges past my parents and perches on the edge of my stretcher. "This is the middle of nowhere."

The road ends at the cliff's edge beside us, broken off by erosion. Surrounded by brambles and beach rose bushes, the decrepit old house is the only structure in sight. On the boarded-up windows that face the street, big red X signs warn that the building is condemned. From this side, you'd never suspect the hideous things that went on inside.

"We were all at the station with Tina," says my mom, gesturing to include Nora's mother. "She convinced them to check Nora's dad's house, and we were waiting to hear back on that when I got an anonymous phone call. The woman's voice sounded familiar. She gave us this address, then hung up."

"She?" I lift my eyebrows at Nora.

"I've been wracking my brain, trying to figure out whose voice it was," says my mom. "And I think it was Ione from Midnight Alchemy."

Nora looks like she just swallowed a mouthful of marbles, and I'm guessing I look the same.

"Oh yeah?" I say carefully.

"How could she have possibly known?" Nora's mom's face darkens. "Is she one of those psychopaths?"

"No!" Nora and I blurt out at the same time.

"Ione warned us about the Hand of Nephthys." I pause, deciding how much of this sordid story I actually want to tell. "She's been trying to . . . uh, stop them for a long time now."

"Hmm." My mom doesn't look convinced of Ione's innocence, and neither does Nora's mom, which is fair. It makes me shiver to think Nora and I have been hanging out with another murderer all this time. Even if she was doing it for good reasons.

"Oh crap," mutters Nora, and I spot Detective Huld heading our way.

"Ladies," she says, nodding to me and Nora. "Mr. and Ms. Carlin. Ms. Hawthorne."

We all wait in awkward silence for her to say anything else, but she just stands there with her hands in her pockets and a patiently expectant look on her face. Despite the roaring wind, not a strand of her hair is out of place.

"Sorry we didn't call you back," says Nora, and it's so pathetically inadequate that we both start to laugh.

Detective Huld purses her lips. "You might have saved yourselves a lot of trouble if you had."

"It's just, you were acting kind of suspicious," I say. "And then you disappeared right when Nora did, so we assumed the two things were related."

"I was acting *suspicious*"—Detective Huld's nose wrinkles at the word—"because I've been quietly investigating the Hand of Nephthys for years, and I didn't want to compromise the investigation."

"That explains the Polaroid of her and Rosemary," I whisper to Nora, who nods.

"And I disappeared yesterday because my mother had a stroke," says Detective Huld.

"Oh, I'm so sorry," murmurs my mom, but the detective waves her hand dismissively.

"She's going to be all right, but there were a lot of logistics to manage, so I took a couple of days off. It was . . . very unfortunate timing." She grimaces.

I wonder if the timing was more intentional than unfortunate, and I suspect Detective Huld agrees, but it's not like she can prove to anyone that a mystical cult caused her mother to have a stroke.

"Girls!" Tina comes running over and crushes me and Nora into a hug. "Jeez Louise, I'm so glad you're both alive."

"Us too," I say. "Thanks for calling the police. I didn't realize you heard that conversation we had with Rowan."

Tina taps her ear and grins. "Every word of it. I didn't trust that guy as far as I could throw him, but I'm glad he didn't get chopped up in some weird-ass Egyptian ritual tonight."

Nora and I laugh, my parents look confused, and Detective Huld just stands there, expressionless as usual.

"Um, Detective?" says Nora. "Can I ask what's on your necklace?"

Detective Huld looks confused for a second, then pulls the chain out from beneath her collar. "This? It's an Icelandic sigil called a galdrastafir. My friend gave it to me before I moved away."

I can tell by the gleam in Nora's eyes that she's got all kinds of questions and theories, but I am utterly magicked out for the day. For the week. Probably for the rest of the year, if I'm being honest.

"We should check on Elliot," I say.

"Oh yeah," says Tina. "Where *is* your fella?"

My face twitches, because Elliot isn't exactly my "fella," but I point to one of the flashing ambulances. Elliot's sitting up, and as his gray eyes lock on mine, a hot flush washes over me. I'm certain now that I love this boy. I'm going to tell him soon, no matter how it ends up changing our friendship.

The paramedic checks his pupils and reflexes, then asks him a few questions. They must be satisfied with his responses because they unstrap him from the stretcher and let him get up. Nora waves him over as our parents, Detective Huld, and Tina head to one of the cruisers to fill out paperwork.

"Hey, nice outfits." Elliot moves gingerly, but he's still smiling, and I'd like to jump off this gurney and wrap all my limbs around him. "How come I didn't get one?"

"Be glad you didn't," I say. "I can't wait to take this thing off."

His cheeks redden at that, and I'm sure mine do too, but Nora pulls him into a group hug before he can respond. As I inhale the warm, clay-dust scent of him, the aching tension in my shoulders finally eases. I still have Nora and Elliot. We made it out alive. We are here. We are together.

We stand there for a long time, holding each other as people dash around and various members of the Hand of Nephthys get loaded into ambulances or ushered into the back seats of police cars. The final stretcher to come up the cliff holds a body with its face covered by a sheet. A limp hand dangles out one side, and I spot Valia's blue eyeball ring.

"Good riddance," mutters Nora.

"I hope the whole hideous legacy of the Hand of Nephthys dies with her," I say.

"Just one member left." Nora shoves her hand down the front of her dress and starts rummaging around in her bra. Before I have time to ask what the heck she's doing, she pulls out a round silver compact with a triumphant flourish.

"Is that Ione's?" I ask, dumbfounded.

"Yep." Nora laughs as I lean far away from the accursed mirror with Rosemary's soul trapped inside. "I grabbed it in the scuffle. Once we get out of here and you get all stitched up, we're going to have a little going away party for her."

"Are you sure we can actually manage it this time?" I say.

"Mazzy." Nora levels her gaze at me. "We just decimated the entire Hand of Nephthys. We can do literally anything we choose to."

I feel it deep in my bones. She's right.

CHAPTER 60

Five days later, I'm sitting on my bed, trying not to scratch my stitches, which have been getting progressively itchier as the wound heals. Nora lies beside me, her eyes shut, and as a smile drifts across her face, hope flutters in my chest.

"This is so incredibly good, Mazzy," she says, adjusting her left earbud.

I wrap my arms around my knees, hugging them tight as I watch her listen to my music. In the days following our rescue, while I was stuck home recovering, these random, beautiful melodies came spilling out of me. I started playing my cello every morning for hours, mainly to take my mind off everything that happened, but also because the songs simply refused to go away. But not in a creepy, haunting way like May's music. It was more of an insistent, lovely *eureka* kind of thing.

When Nora finishes the seventh and final track, she sits up, pulls out her earbuds, and takes both of my hands in hers.

"You better save me front-row seats at all of your concerts when you're famous," she says, and I burst out laughing.

"I'm not kidding," she says. "I always thought you were amazing, but that was"—she searches for the right word—"transcendental."

"Wow," I say. "No one's ever said that about anything I've done before."

"Get used to it, because everyone's going to be using that word," she says. "I'm not saying all the stuff we went through was worth it, but it changed something massive for you creatively, didn't it?" A dreamy look floats over Nora's face. "It's like your mind has opened another dimension, or your aura has changed color or something."

"I thought you said auras were for basic bitches." I poke her in the ribs, and she squeals and almost falls off the bed.

In the five days since we saw Ione slip away into the water, Midnight Alchemy has remained closed. There's no sign on the door saying when it'll reopen, no message on the website or the store's voicemail. Ione has simply vanished. They never found her hand.

For some inexplicable reason, one of the sisters—a woman named Jasmine Weaver—is claiming she shot Valia. I don't understand why she'd take the fall for that, why she'd protect Ione. But so far, all of the hype surrounding the story has been less about Valia's murder and more about the fact that every single one of the women they arrested had faked her own death, ranging from a couple of years ago to thirty-three years, in Valia's case. Families and friends and whole towns around the country are reeling. They swear they buried those women, or cremated them. But somehow, impossibly, they didn't.

It's all over the international news, with headlines like *Murder Coven Exposed on Cape Cod*. Valia was the only sister to die, and four more were arrested. One escaped. Based on the mug shots we've seen in the articles, it was the old woman I saw trying to rip Ione's hair from her scalp. I wonder if Ione is hunting her as we speak. I wonder if Detective Huld is too.

That same sister, Jasmine, is allegedly cooperating with the authorities, despite lying about the shooting. She told them the Hand of Nephthys has killed at least a hundred people over the years, which is an absolutely unholy number when you think of all the bodies left to find, the grisly brutality of that discovery. Most of them are sunk deep in the ocean, so there's not much chance they'll wash ashore, but a handful are buried around the Cape, and the sister says she's willing to share the locations, probably in exchange for a lighter sentence. We'll see what gets unearthed. I'm not sure I want to know the details.

In better news, my dad hasn't started drinking again, even though I almost died. That has to be one of the most stressful things a father could experience, and I figure if he can make it through that, he has a fighting chance of kicking this addiction. I'm also working on not holding myself responsible for his choices. It's a process, as my new therapist says. She's been surprisingly accepting of every wild story I've told her so far.

"Still no sign of Rosemary escaping from the mirror?" I ask Nora.

She shakes her head. "I haven't heard a whisper from her since that night. I even downloaded one of those apps that checks if you're snoring at night, just to see if I'm talking in my sleep."

"Or singing," I add.

Nora shudders. "Or that. But no, no talking or singing."

"Me neither," I say. "And Henry says he hasn't seen or spoken to her since that day you ran away."

"We're going to have to keep an eye on that kid," says Nora. "He's clearly very receptive to spirits."

I cringe, thinking of all the possibilities. "We'll teach him everything we know about protection, whether my mom likes it or not."

"Absolutely. But it *is* pretty cool, you have to admit."

"It's probably cooler if he isn't your brother," I say. "Anyway, I don't think we should push our luck much longer with Rosemary. Let's do the banishment tonight."

"Are you sure?" Nora squints at my leg.

"Yes," I say. "The doctor said it's healing well, and I've got some ideas for the ritual."

Nora laughs. "You're not going to look up how to do it in twelve different books first?"

"Nope." I pause. "Okay, maybe one or two, just to make sure we're going in the right direction. But for the most part, I think we need to go on intuition, don't you? We tried using books, we tried Ione's spell, but we never put enough of ourselves into it. We're the ones who know Rosemary best. That makes us the best ones to break the bond."

"Absolutely." Nora plants a kiss on my cheek, then hops off the bed and starts rummaging through my crystal collection. "I've got a few ideas too. Can you text Elliot and ask if he can come to Mayflower tonight?"

CHAPTER 61

My car is still in the shop after crashing into the marsh, so the three of us squeeze into Elliot's brother's pickup truck. I'm sitting in the middle, trying to concentrate on the words we need to say tonight, the steps we need to follow, but every time Elliot shifts gears, his hand grazes my knee and I lose all my focus. I've only seen him twice outside of school this week, and both times Nora was there too. I've written and deleted hundreds of text messages to him.

But after the ritual tonight, I'm going to tell him how I feel. I don't care if it changes our friendship. If he doesn't like me back, I'll deal with the awkwardness and rejection. The last two weeks have completely shifted my perspective on what's important. As terrified as I am to let this all out, I owe it to myself to try.

We park on the same quiet road near Mayflower Beach and steal across the empty parking lot. Nora's pentacle bag bumps rhythmically against her hip, the ingredients inside clanking. The wind is calm, but the air is frigid. It almost smells like snow.

Tonight, we reverse everything from the spell that led us to May.

Nora lays out all the same items, upside down and in backward order. We light a black candle instead of a white one. I'd like to burn the Polaroids, but they're gone, collected as evidence by the police along with everything else from the crime scene. In their place, Nora and I set Henry's drawings on a black ceramic plate that Elliot made.

This time, Elliot sits with us at the makeshift altar in the sand. He says he's not going to actively participate in the ritual, but having him as the third point in our triangle makes everything more balanced. Plus, he still ended up just as tangled with Rosemary and the Hand of Nephthys as we did, so he needs to be part of this in some way.

The clouds drift away from the silvery half-moon as Nora and I speak our incantation. Some of it is planned and some is made up on the spot, and sometimes we stumble over the words or speak over each other, but it doesn't matter. I feel a growing sense of rightness, of correction, of stabilization as my words make clouds in the dark.

We burn Henry's drawings, and then Nora pulls out the silver compact and sets it on a flat stone. As we sprinkle the ashes of the drawing over the mirror, Elliot picks up a large rock and holds it at the ready, just in case we need to smash it.

"Rosemary Newcombe, we release you," I say, unsnapping the latch.

The lid flips open and the mirror sends a beam of reflected moonlight shooting upward.

Nora and I speak our words of banishment, our voices firm and certain, and in the darkness, I see Elliot's lips moving along too. I feel traces of Rosemary, hear broken whispers and snatches of her voice, but she's weak, worn down. A threadbare version of her old self. None of her plans worked, her sisters can't help her now, and Nora and I refuse to let her in ever again.

"It's time to go," I say, and sorrow swirls like smoke around us.

I push Rosemary away with my heart and my mind and my will. We are the ones in control now. This whole, sordid ordeal has made us infinitely stronger, even without Rosemary's presence in our heads anymore, and now she's fading, dissolving, disappearing. It's like she's floating into outer space, tumbling away to whatever else, whoever else might be out there.

Then, in the air around us, there's something I can only describe as a tiny snap, a sudden emptiness. Nora smiles. I know she felt it too.

The mirror goes dark.

Our words fade away into the night sky.

Rosemary is gone.

The three of us sit silently for a long while. Gauzy clouds shroud the moon, and the waves whisper and kiss the sand. Already, the horrors of the past two weeks are turning into memories, no longer a terrifying reality we have to constantly react to. Things are returning to their proper place. As impossible as it seems, our lives will return to normal again too.

Well, as normal as we ever get.

CHAPTER 62

Elliot drops Nora off first. I'd been hoping he would, but also dreading it because now that we're alone, I have to tell him. I still don't know what exactly the words will be, but I have to trust that they'll come to me when they need to.

As we near the turnoff to my neighborhood, Elliot slows.

"Do you mind if we stop somewhere first?" he asks.

I check the time—there's still an hour left before my curfew. It seemed odd that Nora wanted to go home so early, but I assumed she was tired after the ritual. After everything. Plus, she has to move in three days. I'm going over tomorrow to help her pack.

"Sure," I say. "Where?"

"Can't tell you—it's a surprise." He sounds oddly anxious, which makes me anxious too. But in a good way, I think. I can't imagine where Elliot's taking me at ten o'clock on a Wednesday night in November. Everything is closed. Either way, I decide I'll wait until we get wherever we're going to tell him how I feel. It lowers my stress levels to know I've got a few more minutes, at least.

We're both so quiet now, I want to plug my phone into his aux cable and play some music. But it feels like we're so close to something, and I'm afraid that whatever song I choose, it might affect the mood. I don't want to ruin anything. So we drive in silence, the road bathed in the headlights' yellow glow. Then we're turning into Elliot's neighborhood, and as we coast down the dirt road that leads to his house, I squint out the window.

"The surprise is your house?"

"Not exactly." He stops by the woods at the far corner of his property and shifts into park. I swear his hands are shaking.

"Are you okay?" I ask. "Why are we stopping here?"

"I'm fine," he says. "Do you mind waiting here for like five minutes? I'll be right back."

I crane my neck to look at his house. Most of the lights are on. "Do you not want your parents to know we're here?"

Maybe we're sneaking into his room. The thought gives me all kinds of flutters in all kinds of places.

Elliot's mouth cracks into a tiny smile. "Just give me five minutes, okay?"

"Okay." I pull out my phone as he gets out. But instead of heading for his house, Elliot circles around to the bed of the truck and takes out a duffel bag. Still looking vaguely nauseous, he gives me a quick wave and then heads down a narrow path that leads into the woods.

"What are you doing?" I mutter.

My phone pings.

> Nora: Did he???
>
> Me: Did he what
>
> Nora: Nothing

Elliot has disappeared into the woods. Maybe he's taking a shortcut around to the back of his house, but that makes no sense. I chew my lip, wondering what on earth he's up to. And what Nora knows that I don't.

Me: Seriously what are you talking about

Nora: I meant to send that to someone else sorry

Me: Nora

No answer.

Me: NORA

She leaves me on read for a full five minutes, and I'm about to video call her and force a confession when I spot Elliot heading back through the trees. A tiny light flickers in his hands, and he crouches to set it on the path. Then he comes around to my side of the truck and opens the door.

"Can I show you something?" he asks, and there's something so delicate and hopeful in his expression that I climb out of the truck without a word.

Little ceramic lanterns flicker all along the path, leading into the forest. My breath catches. It's like something out of a fairy tale.

"Did you make these?" I say.

"Yeah." Elliot's warm fingers thread through mine, and my heart is thrumming, racing with possibility. The glow of the lanterns stops at the edges of the path—the woods around us are cold and black—but I've never felt safer in my life. The trail rounds a corner, and I have to stop to take it all in.

In the center of a clearing stands a massive weeping beech tree.

Its trailing branches cascade to the ground like a huge, open umbrella, with even more flickering lanterns tucked among the boughs. There's a narrow gap that leads inside the space under the branches, which glows even brighter with candlelight.

Reality starts to bend as I let go of Elliot's hand and step inside. Any words I'd been thinking of saying disappear as I take in the sweeping boughs, the tiny, glazed lanterns, each a different shape and color. All I can do is absorb the luminous beauty of this night, this radiant space that Elliot made for me.

He follows me inside, and as I turn to face him, his eyes lock on mine. He's golden and beautiful and nervous in the candlelight.

"What do you think?" he asks.

"I . . . love it."

What I mean to say is that I love more than just his lanterns and this tree.

Elliot takes a deep breath.

"It's been *you* for years, Mazzy," he says. "Not Nora. I didn't think you wanted to hear that, though. Especially after the, uh, dog-kissing incident."

I laugh. My chest feels like it's full of fireflies.

"But that night at Evie's, it felt like something was changing," he says. "And when we went to Mayflower, I decided I was finally going to tell you how I felt, but then a dead body washed up. And then it happened *again* the second time I tried." He laughs ruefully. "I started to think we were cursed."

"I know," I say, stepping closer. "But we're not cursed. We made it through. We're here now."

"I'm sorry if this makes everything awkward forever," says Elliot. "I don't want to wreck our friendship. But I can't stop thinking about you—sometimes even when I'm sleeping, Mazzy—and after everything that's happened, I couldn't *not* tell you."

"I can't stop thinking about you either," I say. "I wish I had a time machine so I could go back and kiss you instead of that dog."

All the worry and doubt in his face melts away, and I still can't believe this is finally happening. My heart is rocketing, and I want to laugh or scream or maybe both. Slowly, carefully, I cup his jaw with both hands and pull him down to me. His face is so close, our noses almost touching. He smiles, his breath warm on my face.

This is happening.

His lips brush mine, so faintly it makes me ache.

Then I'm pulling him to me and Elliot and I are finally, fully kissing, and it's somehow inevitable, unquestionable. We're both shaking a little as I wrap my arms around his broad shoulders, wishing I could melt into him. He deepens the kiss, and then my back is pressed against the tree's trunk, and I can feel all the glowing, soft energy of its bark, its roots, its illuminated branches, all melding into this. I've imagined this moment with Elliot so many times, wondered what it would feel like, what it would taste like, whether it would ever actually happen. And now it's blowing all of my expectations away.

Eventually, he pulls back, his eyes dazed and glittering.

"I'm so glad that finally happened," he says.

"Me too." I tuck a loose strand of his dark hair behind his ear. "Nora's going to have a heart attack when she finds out, though."

Elliot laughs. "She already knows. Why do you think she wanted to go home early?"

I slap my forehead. "Oh God, that message!"

"She said it was about time I did something, because she was sick of the two of us 'silently pining with tragic auras.'" Elliot makes air quotes around the words. "I wasn't sure I could trust her aura-reading, but I hoped she was right about you."

"Damn, I thought I was hiding it so well," I mutter.

"Me too." Elliot grins. "Guess we can't hide anything from Nora." As if on cue, my phone pings.

> Nora: Sorry I just saw this
>
> Me: No you didn't
>
> Nora: Where are you now
>
> Me: Under a beech tree with Elliot
>
> Nora: yessss

I send her a heart emoji and pocket my phone. Then I wrap my arms around Elliot and kiss him again.

CHAPTER 63

Two weeks later, I'm tucked in bed with Nora, in her new apartment in Dennis Port. The place is tiny, but her mom has done a solid job of making it feel homey, and since the landlord said it was okay to paint the walls, she let Nora and me take charge of that. The living room is now a positively metaphysical shade of purple, and Nora's bedroom is deep-ocean blue. She says she feels tranquil and cerulean these days, so we went to the paint store and picked through the swatches until we matched her not-tragically-pining aura.

Nora's fast asleep now, and I'm trying to do the same, but ever since that night when we almost died, I've been struggling with insomnia. It's not that I'm worried about the Hand of Nephthys coming back. They're all facing serious jail time, and that one woman who escaped is probably too old to be much of a threat—if Ione hasn't already gotten to her. Even still, whenever I get to that weightless, letting-go moment right before sleep, my body fights it. I can't quite let myself go.

My therapist says this is okay and normal, and I just have to give myself time to heal and probably take some melatonin. I believe her, but it doesn't make the nights any shorter or less lonely. I texted Elliot ten minutes ago, but he didn't answer and must be sleeping, so I've just been flicking randomly through the internet.

Nora stirs and rolls over, and I switch off my phone so the light won't wake her, but it's too late.

"Mazzy?" she mumbles. "Are you still up?"

"Yeah," I say. "It's okay. Go back to sleep."

She props herself up on her elbow. "Is something bothering you?"

"Other than the fact that I can't sleep, not really."

"Do you want me to sing you a lullaby?" she asks.

"I don't think that'll help."

"Let's try anyway," she says, pulling the blankets higher over us. "Close your eyes."

With a reluctant sigh, I lie flat on my back and shut my eyes, and she begins to hum. The melody starts out formless and random but slowly becomes familiar.

"Nora, no," I whisper, but she keeps on humming until the song is finished. Goose bumps lift all over my skin.

"Just let it sink in," she says. "Let it exist. What happened to us happened, and we can't change anything. We have to make our peace. We have to own it."

She starts from the beginning again, and maybe she's right, because I'm hearing the beauty in Rosemary's song and my muscles are slowly letting go. I'm drifting in the darkness, letting it all exist. Letting it settle. Letting it be.

I start to hum too, my voice joining with Nora's. It's a good thing her mom's working the night shift, because this is extremely weird and maybe not the best idea, but somehow it's exactly what I need. The two of us finish the song, and the silence folds around us.

"Sing me one of yours now." Nora curls up, knees resting against my hip.

And so, I do. Like Rosemary's song, this one has no words. It doesn't need them. I hum the melody, and on the second repetition, Nora joins in. She's always had a quick ear and perfect pitch, and I'm amazed by how lovely my creation sounds in her voice.

And then it's done. Nora's breathing slows, and so does mine. I'm floating. I'm fading. I'm letting go. Rosemary is gone, and her voice has no power over us anymore. We're singing our own songs now.

AUTHOR'S NOTE

This book is set in the mid-Cape area, where I grew up. Most of the places in it are real, but I've taken some liberties with exact locations and details, and some of the places probably don't exist in quite the same way as they do in my memories. For example, Woodside Cemetery is real, but the mausoleum as described in the book is not. Some of the businesses Mazzy and her friends visit don't actually exist. And the boardwalk on the Grays Beach trail isn't quite the right height for the things that transpire in the story to happen. Hopefully, those of you who are familiar with the places will forgive my artistic license!

The following books were helpful in the writing of this story:

> *The Witch's Mirror* by Mickie Mueller
>
> *The Green Witch* by Arin Murphy-Hiscock
>
> *The Book of Spells* by Ella Harrison
>
> *Cunningham's Encyclopedia of Magical Herbs*
> by Scott Cunningham

And for anyone interested in learning more about tarot, I highly recommend Brigit Esselmont's website, Biddy Tarot, as well as her book *The Ultimate Guide to Tarot Card Meanings*.

ACKNOWLEDGMENTS

First and foremost, I want to thank my editor, Gretchen Durning. The initial outline of this book was a loose collection of vibes and vaguely plot-like ideas held together with string and duct tape. Using your own magical powers, you helped me shape it into a proper story with twists and subplots and character arcs. Thank you for your guidance and astute observations and for making me laugh with your comments on the manuscript! I can't think of a better partner to work with on my books.

Thank you to my agent, Kathleen Rushall, for seeing the initial spark in this project and encouraging me to continue working on it. I'm so grateful for your insight and patience, especially after a year of me sending you various plot ideas and snippets of manuscripts, and for helping me narrow things down and get this one published.

Thank you to everyone who had a "hand" (pun intended) in the making of the book. Krista Ahlberg, Sola Akinlana, Marinda Valenti, Purvi Gadia, and Tricia Lawrence, thank you for combing through these pages and making sure everything was in great shape, from the plot all the way down to the punctuation. Thank you also to Amanda Cranney and Natalie Vielkind for managing the process. Thank you to Liz Montoya Vaughan in publicity, Christina Colangelo and Bri Lockhart in marketing, and Felicity Vallence and Shannon Spann in digital marketing.

A gigantic thank-you to Kristin Boyle for designing this book's cover, and to Cocorrina for the spellbinding illustrations. It's the perfect blend of witchy and Cape Coddy (which is definitely a real word) and is everything I could have hoped for.

To my writer friends, I don't know what I'd do without you. Margot Harrison, Jesse Sutanto, Marley Teter, Grace Shim, Shanna Miles, and Anne-Sophie Jouhanneau, you are absolute rock stars and creative geniuses. To everyone in the Bridging the Gap group, I'm still floored by the wealth of knowledge and kindness you all bring.

Paul, Casey, Megan, Leigh, and all of the booksellers at the Silver Unicorn Bookstore, I can't thank you enough for your support, and I'm so grateful for the vibrant book community you've created.

To my high school crew (Keely, Shannon, Liz, Jodie, Michelle, Anya, Mike, Chris, TJ, and many others), thank you for being such a fabulous bunch of weirdos. I'll never forget our nights spent skulking around beaches and graveyards, among other places, and this story wouldn't exist without you.

Mom, your unwavering belief in me and my writing has made such a difference, and I never could have done this without you. Alissa, I'm so glad you're my sister—writing this book brought back so many memories of us dabbling in tarot and various esoteric things as teens. Ciaran, thank you for all of your support, and especially for putting up with my melodrama and endless monologues about publishing. Isla and Neil, you are both wonderful human beings, no one makes me laugh the way you do, and I love you to the moon and back.

Finally, thank you to you, my readers! I hope you enjoyed this book.